BRASS MONKEY

A James Acton Thriller

By J. Robert Kennedy

James Acton Thrillers

The Protocol	*Pompeii's Ghosts*
Brass Monkey	*Amazon Burning*
Broken Dove	*The Riddle*
The Templar's Relic	*Blood Relics*
Flags of Sin	*Sins of the Titanic*
The Arab Fall	*Saint Peter's Soldiers*
The Circle of Eight	*The Thirteenth Legion*
The Venice Code	*Raging Sun*

Wages of Sin

Special Agent Dylan Kane Thrillers

Rogue Operator
Containment Failure
Cold Warriors
Death to America
Black Widow

Delta Force Unleashed Thrillers

Payback
Infidels
The Lazarus Moment
Kill Chain

Detective Shakespeare Mysteries

Depraved Difference
Tick Tock
The Redeemer

Zander Varga, Vampire Detective

The Turned

BRASS
MONKEY

A James Acton Thriller

J. ROBERT KENNEDY

ISBN: 1466218150
ISBN-13: 978-1466218154

Third Edition

10 9 8 7 6 5 4 3

For my dad, who tirelessly scoured the web and harassed his contacts, in search of answers to hundreds of questions posed, with no hint of the context in which they were asked, and for no reward other than the love of a grateful son.

BRASS MONKEY

A James Acton Thriller

DEFINITIONS

Peacetime definition of Brass Monkey:

The Brass Monkey recall procedure is to prevent violations of the neutral airspaces of Austria and Switzerland by allied aircraft. Brass Monkey is a peacetime procedure initiated by the units of the Tactical Air Command and Control Service, and is applicable to all allied aircraft in German airspace.

Cold War definition of Brass Monkey:

A Brass Monkey recall indicated a NATO aircraft had violated Warsaw Pact airspace. When this occurred, a Brass Monkey was broadcast and all combat aircraft operating in the vicinity of the eastern borders were to immediately reverse course and return to base, regardless of whether they thought they were in the correct location. During the Cold War, Brass Monkey recalls were never publicized. To this day, NATO has never acknowledged they occurred, and deny any aircraft were shot down violating Warsaw Pact airspace.

Definition of Nap-of-the-Earth (NOE) flight:

A very low-level type of flight designed to avoid detection by the enemy. During the Cold War, NATO air forces would routinely practice NOE flying, rushing the Warsaw Pact borders then suddenly turning back at the last minute. Typically, these flights were armed with conventional weapons, and on occasion, fully armed tactical nuclear weapons. NATO has never admitted to these flights, and denies any were lost.

"In Germany they first came for the Communists, and I didn't speak up because I wasn't a Communist. Then they came for the Jews, and I didn't speak up because I wasn't a Jew. Then they came for the trade unionists, and I didn't speak up because I wasn't a trade unionist. Then they came for the Catholics, and I didn't speak up because I was a Protestant. Then they came for me—and by that time no one was left to speak up."

Reverend Martin Niemoller

West German Airspace
July 23, 1985

Major Simon Donavan, call sign Juggernaut, yawned. He had done this run a hundred times before, and he'd do it a hundred times again. This time was different, what with the nuke he had loaded in the bomb bay and the fact his wingman had returned to base with an equipment malfunction. Everything else about this nap-of-the-earth flight was routine. They hugged the deck as the mighty engines of the FB-111F fighter-bomber, unofficially but affectionately nicknamed the Aardvark, strained, eager to reach the battlefield its crew hoped they would never see.

He pulled up on the stick slightly as a thatch of tall trees neared, his fun meter momentarily pegged as he recalled the report of the Canadian F-104 Starfighter pilot that flew his single-engine jet home last month after a bird strike. Unfortunately, the bird was in its nest and the pilot had the branch in his intake to prove it. Pilots across NATO had assigned him a new call sign—Treehugger. He wasn't amused.

"If only the peaceniks knew what we were doing!"

Juggernaut smiled at his Weapons Systems Officer. Captain Mike "Minkey" Trotter had been his WSO for the past two years, and like him, knew the routine like the back of his hand. This was one of their assigned runs, the actual one decided when hostilities broke out. And if it *were* this run, this was the exact route they'd take. No exceptions, no deviations. Rush the border at treetop level, cross into enemy territory, and deliver your nukes. This was NATO's answer to the Warsaw Pact's overwhelming numbers. If the enemy reaches the Rhine, we go nuclear—Europe would not be lost.

"I'm hugging the deck so hard if this plane had balls, they'd be shaved. If those pinkos knew, they'd probably try to shoot us down themselves!"

1

"Yeah, the morons. Don't they realize nukes are the only things keeping those damned *Rooskies* out of their backyard?"

"Yeah, and Ivan would love a little payback on the Germans."

Minkey snorted, summoning his best Russian accent. "Allo, Siegfried, my name Ivan. Payback is ah beetch!"

Juggernaut's laugh was cut off as he entered heavy low-lying clouds. His TACAN indicated he was twenty nautical miles from the border but it didn't jive with his knowledge of the terrain. "Hey, Mike, check our position, will ya?"

"Roger." Minkey examined the readings. "TAC says we're sixteen miles but Inertial says one. That can't be right. We'd be in the Buffer Zone."

"Inertial's been off before. Contact GCI just to make sure."

Before Minkey could make contact with Ground Control Intercept, their comm squawked.

"Brass Monkey! Brass Monkey! Brass Monkey!"

Juggernaut's heart leaped.

"Is that us?" yelled Minkey.

"I don't know, but let's get the hell out of here." Juggernaut jerked his stick to the left, banking the lumbering Aardvark in a one-eighty he had done innumerable times before, though never in a Brass Monkey situation where he was this close to the East German border. A flashing indicator on his cockpit followed by an alarm momentarily distracted him.

"We've got a threat alarm!" exclaimed Minkey. "I'm showing a SAM launch!"

"Castle-Rock, this is Foxtrot two-ten. We are under attack, say again, we are under attack. TAC shows us in friendly airspace, am deploying flares." Minkey was already launching flares and chaff to try and confuse the missile. Juggernaut knew if they had indeed strayed into enemy airspace, it was probably due to the Soviets spoofing their TACAN.

"Foxtrot two-ten, this is Castle-Rock. We show you two nautical miles outside the green zone, over."

2

"Damn!" Juggernaut had the engines maxed but this beast wouldn't make two miles before the SAM hit. "Status on inbound!"

"Flares had no effect, still on target. Estimate impact in ten seconds. We've got to eject!"

"Not with this goddamned cargo!"

If he could get them back across the border, they might have to jettison the missile on bailout, but at least it would be in friendly hands. He pushed the engines even harder as he flattened from his turn and glanced out his canopy at the contrail rapidly approaching. In a last ditch effort, he pushed the stick hard forward, sending the aircraft into a rapid dive. He thought of his wife and son as the plane's tail jerked from the missile contact.

Mobile SAM Site
East Germany

Major Grigori Andreievich Trubitsin stared through his binoculars, his face revealing none of the elation he felt inside. For years, he had spoofed the NATO TACAN with no success, using a hobbled together system based upon plans obtained from a French contact. He always laughed at the fact NATO continued to let France sit at the same table when they refused to commit to the organization, and was happy to take advantage of NATO's naiveté.

Capitalist pigs. Your arrogance will be your undoing.

He watched as the SA-8b Surface to Air Missile he had ordered launched moments before, sped toward its prey. In less than a minute it was all over. A cacophony of shrapnel from the airframe, burning jet fuel and exploding ordnance was all that was left of the FB-111F that had strayed illegally into their airspace.

Of course, the Motherland would never admit to the fact the plane was tricked and had innocently crossed into East German airspace. That was irrelevant. All that was relevant was that he, Major Grigori Trubitsin, highly decorated member of the Russian Armed Forces, hero of Kabul, Order of Lenin recipient, had brought down a NATO aircraft. And now he would claim credit for whatever technology they retrieved from it.

He and his squad of five men climbed into two UAZ-469 light utility vehicles and raced for the smoldering wreckage in the nearby hills. Within minutes they arrived, covering the final few feet on foot. As they neared the crash site, Trubitsin saw larger and larger pieces of debris, debris that might yield valuable secrets for Mother Russia.

Ordering his men to fan out, they moved forward in a straight line, searching for the cockpit. It didn't take long to find it lying on its side, its canopy glass shattered, severed from the plane's rear half. Trubitsin bent over and peered inside, finding the two crewmembers still strapped in their seats. Drawing his weapon, he slapped the pilot. The man stirred slightly.

Good, prisoners for interrogation!

Leaning over the pilot, he reached out with his left hand to see if the weapons officer was alive. Before he could check, the man's eyes opened. Startled, Trubitsin accidentally squeezed the trigger, shooting him through the neck.

This brought his squad running toward his position, his second-in-command jumping onto the nose cone from the other side. "Comrade Major, are you okay?"

"Yes, Lieutenant." He pointed at the pilot. "This one is alive. Get him out and tend to his wounds. Don't let him die, the KGB will want to interrogate him."

"Yes, Comrade Major." Trubitsin swore the young man's boot heels clicked, which should be impossible since he was sprawled across the front of the aircraft. He was a good soldier of the empire. Followed orders, impeccably neat, fiercely loyal. Exactly what you wanted in a second-in-command. Someone who would back your orders without question, who the men could respect.

He explored more of the fuselage as several of his men extricated the now moaning pilot. From outside an excited corporal yelled. "Comrade Major, come! You must see this!" Trubitsin frowned. The man should have gone to his Sergeant first.

Follow the chain of command!

He ignored him.

"Comrade Lieutenant, you and the Major must see this!" This time it was his Sergeant, Boris Yakovski, a career military man who had seen action in more conflicts than the empire admitted to being in. Trubitsin wasn't sure he had ever heard him excited about anything in the two years Yakovski had served under him.

Trubitsin climbed down from the cockpit and rounded to where the rest of his squad was now staring. A bomb bay door at the bottom of the fuselage was torn away, revealing a missile inside.

A tactical nuclear missile.

This time, Trubitsin smiled outwardly.

Alamut, Persia
November 18, 1256 AD

Exhausted, Faisal slowly shoveled the food into his mouth. Every muscle in his body ached. Covered in cuts and bruises, some new, some days or weeks old, he ignored them, the pain no longer registering but the fatigue inescapable. The training he had undergone was beyond anything he had ever endured, and in training for most of his life, that was saying something. Both his father and eldest brother were members of the Hassassins, the name given to the Order of the Assassins, whispered in reverence by their supporters, and in fear by their enemies. His father had reached the rank of Greater Propagandist before dying in battle against the Saracens a year ago, and his brother was now a Propagandist. They had prepared him for the better part of ten years to join with them in their quest to maintain balance between Islam and the infidel Christians, a task handed down by the great Sabah, the Order's founder.

But now he was on his own. His brother and father could no longer help him—he had been handed over to the Order. He was shocked at first by some of the rituals. His kin had hinted at them but never filled him in on any, begging off his questions by citing the oath they had taken when accepted into the fraternity of the Order. And as a good son, a good brother, and a good Muslim, he hadn't pressed. They had their reasons and it made him all the more determined to join the Order and learn its secrets.

His entire squad had trained for four straight hours with the sword and bow on foot and on horseback, followed by sessions studying the Koran with the Imam, and finally another four hours of unarmed hand-to-hand combat, all with no food and little water. The sun had now set, this meal and fresh water their reward, a reward that would last for mere minutes before evening prayers and study, then bed.

The double-clap of a pair of hands raised the drooping heads in the mess hall, all eyes now on the Lasiq who had just entered. He scanned the room and pointed at a student at a nearby table. "You, report to the corral!"

The young man rose from the table and dutifully hurried to the exit. Everyone in the hall lowered their heads, avoiding eye contact—no one wanted to report for corral duty. Faisal hid behind the piece of bread he had taken a bite of.

The Lasiq pointed at him. "You!" He jerked his thumb over his shoulder, indicating Faisal should follow his companion.

Faisal's heart sank.

I hate corral duty.

He rose from the table and headed through the tall stone archway of the mess, glancing back to see who else would receive the duty usually reserved for new recruits, not those who had trained for almost a year. He smiled when his friend Jamar was selected, and outright grinned when the son of a camel's behind, Momar, was also chosen, the look of shock at being selected for such a task worth whatever amount of dung that required shoveling tonight.

The four were brought into the corral, one side the high southern wall of Alamut, the massive mountain-top fortress that had served as the Hassassin stronghold for over a century, the other three of piled stones about chest high, the horses normally held there nowhere in sight.

But their manure was. Faisal flashed back on his first weeks, thankful they were over—nothing was worse than cleaning up horse droppings in the baking Persian sun. And thankfully, it appeared that was not to be their task tonight as their instructor stood in the center of the corral, beckoning them to hurry. The four students lined up in front of him and bowed.

Master Hasni bin Saeed Al-Maktoum, who held the rank of Greater Propagandist within the Order, stared at them gravely. "You have all been taught in the ways of killing. Your mastery of these techniques, I have no doubt in. You have also been trained in how to incapacitate your opponent without killing him. Interrogation can be critical. Before a great battle, you may be sent by your commander to capture an enemy patrol in order to gain valuable information that might mean the difference between victory and defeat. But in the heat of the moment, the skirmish between you and your potential fountain of information could turn into a fight to the death. You must overcome that temptation, the temptation to slay your opponent who is so determined to slay you. And this makes your task all the more difficult, for he is only trying to survive and he cares not if he kills you or merely maims you enough to escape. You, however, *must* care. Your task of gathering information is more important than your life. Succeeding in your mission could save hundreds or even thousands of your brothers."

Hasni slowly stared down each of them as he spoke, making sure his words sank in. "And that is why, tonight, you practice on each other, your own brothers, your friends. Your mission is to incapacitate your opponents." Faisal glanced to his left where his three comrades stood. They had trained together for almost a year. Two he considered good friends. They, like him, had worried expressions on their faces. None wanted to hurt the others, except maybe Momar. "But!" snapped Hasni, his voice piercing, all four whipping their attention back to him. "If any of you kills one of the others, you will be joining them by my own hand!" Faisal gulped. Hasni clapped his hands together. "Prepare yourselves!" The four recruits stared at each other in confusion. "Begin!"

Faisal tensed as he and the other three slowly backed away from each other, none wanting to strike their friend first. Faisal faced Jamar, one of the more gifted students at the academy. In fact, if Faisal thought about it, all four were the top of their class.

I wonder if—

Jamar lunged at him, cutting off the thought. Faisal clasped Jamar's leading hand and pulled it toward him, causing Jamar to lose his balance slightly. Faisal whipped Jamar's feet out from under him and threw him unceremoniously to the ground. Jamar leaped back to his feet and approached again, this time more warily.

From the corner of his eye, Faisal caught a glimpse of the other two students, Momar and Eid, locked in combat. Unlike Jamar and himself, these two were not friends. In fact, they were competitors since the beginning, Momar unable to make friends or peace with the fact he was now one of many gifted warriors. In his clan, he was praised as a future great warrior, and sent to train with the best, the Hassassins. But upon arriving, he was treated like everyone else, no better, no worse, but the same, and he no longer stood out. Yes, he was gifted, one of the best there, but just one of. Not *the* one. And this irritated him to no end.

Jamar lunged again and this time gripped Faisal's robe, jerking him forward and kneeing him in the stomach. Faisal gasped as the wind was knocked out of him. Jamar whispered an apology as he was tossed to the ground. This continued for almost five minutes before Eid cried out. Faisal, who had Jamar in a particularly painful hold, looked up to see what had happened. Momar released Eid from a headlock and threw his crumpled body to the ground, his neck in an unnatural position, a look of shock frozen in place.

He was dead.

That much was obvious. Momar had a satisfied expression until Hasni screamed at him. "What have you done?" He raced from the side of the corral where he was watching with several other instructors.

"I—" was all Momar said before Hasni drew his scimitar and spun clockwise, his arm fully extended, the blade swinging in a clean arc. It made contact with the still speaking Momar's neck, slicing clean through. Momar remained standing for a few seconds, an expression of confusion on his face. Finally, slowly, his knees gave way and his head slipped off the neck that once held it. His body collapsed to the ground in a heap, his head landing beside it with a thud, rolling several paces away.

Faisal and Jamar stared in disbelief. Hasni turned on them. "Continue!"

They didn't budge.

Hasni raised his sword, still dripping with Momar's blood. "Now! In the heat of battle your brothers will die by your side. Will you stop and stare while the enemy runs you through, or will you continue to fight and avenge your brother's death? Continue!"

Faisal spun at Jamar, grabbed him around the neck and twisted him into a sleeper hold. Within less than a minute Jamar was out cold.

Hasni came over and congratulated him. "Well done, my brother. I knew you had it in you." Faisal's stomach churned. He couldn't stop eying the body of his friend and the severed head of Momar. Hasni glanced at the bodies then back at Faisal. "This is the first time you have looked upon death?"

Faisal nodded.

"Then look at it. Gaze upon it in all its sickness and glory. Learn to hate it and learn to love it. Despair in that you have lost a friend. Rejoice in that you have lost an enemy. But most of all, remember the lesson learned here tonight. Obey your orders or you may die not by your enemy's hand, but by that of your brother." Hasni placed his hand on Faisal's shoulder and lowered his voice. "I know he was your friend. Honor him tonight in your prayers, and tomorrow we will feast to his sacrifice." He gave Faisal's shoulder a squeeze then swatted him on the back. "Off to bed with you, we will see you in the morning."

Faisal bowed and headed to his bedchambers. As he lay exhausted, he couldn't help but think of what had happened in the corral. Two students dead. He tried to shake the image of Eid's face staring up at him, but he couldn't. It wasn't until the sweet release of sleep mercifully overtook him that he was rid of the evening's horror.

But not for long.

As he was about to drift off, the door to his room was kicked open and three men stormed in, brandishing shamshirs he recognized as Mongol, bitter enemies to the Hassassin. He flipped over the side of his bed, avoiding a blow that split the frame in half. Reaching for his sword, the other two men leaped at him, and before he could stop them, seized him by the arms. As he struggled against his captors, the third who had struck the initial blow approached him, his menacing grin revealing a mouthful of rotting teeth. But rather than run him through, he held a cloth over Faisal's mouth. A pungent odor filled his nostrils and he felt drowsy. One of his captors let him go and he watched in a daze as the man raised his sword high over his head. As he brought it down, Faisal passed out, praying he had led a good enough life to reach paradise.

Sixth Round of New START Negotiations
Geneva, Switzerland
September 24, 2009

"Gentlemen, it is now time to turn our attention to the problem of Broken Arrows."

The silence in the room defined uncomfortable. Justin Lee, chief negotiator for the United States in the Strategic Arms Reduction Treaty talks, stared across the table at his Russian counterpart. He leaned toward his official translator who whispered in his ear.

As if you didn't understand what I just said.

Lee knew the "translator" was the puppet master's representative in the room, and that Lee's honored counterpart, Aleksandr Petrenko, was merely a marionette on the international stage, with strings extending all the way back to the office of the man who truly controlled Mother Russia, the Prime Minister.

Petrenko grunted and said something in Russian to the room. His delegates nodded and then the translator spoke.

"Mr. Lee, Mr. Petrenko repeats our previous position on this, that Russia has had no Broken Arrow incidents, as you call them, no lost nuclear missiles, therefore does not see the need to discuss this."

Lee nodded. "That's interesting." He held his right hand up over his shoulder and his aide, standing behind him near the wall, stepped forward and placed a file in it. Lee opened it and read from the text on the single page.

"Item: One Soviet 15F42 1.2 Megaton warhead, recovered from a failed SS-11 launch, September 14th, 1962." Lee stared at Petrenko.

That's a new shade of red.

"Item: One Soviet VA-111 Shkval torpedo, armed with a twenty kiloton nuclear warhead, recovered January 12th, North Sea, 1989." He paused again as he surveyed the Russian delegation. "Need I go on?"

Petrenko held up his hand and shook his head. "There is no need, Mr. Lee."

"Very well," said Lee, leaning forward. "We are willing to return all *six* of the Broken Arrows listed in this file." He pushed it across the table. Petrenko took it but didn't look at it.

"And what is it you want in return?"

Lee leaned back in his chair. "We want our *one* Broken Arrow."

Geneva Suite, Grand Hotel Kempinski
Geneva, Switzerland

"And you're certain we have no American warheads in our possession?"

"Sir, I've done a thorough search of all our computerized files, I've even interviewed every man we have who was on staff in 1985, and none are aware of this."

"Dymovsky, I find it impossible to believe that the Americans would offer to return *six* of our warheads in return for *one* that does not exist!"

"I agree, sir, it's most puzzling."

"Puzzling?" Petrenko leaned back on the leather couch, glaring at the speakerphone, the rest of the room not daring to say a word, all eyes on him to see how they should react. "Puzzling? That's a word for it. Or as *they* might say, it's bullshit!"

There was silence on the other end.

"Dymovsky, you now have one duty. You must find me that missile at all costs."

"Yes, sir."

Petrenko mashed the button with his fist, disconnecting the call. He motioned to his aide. "Vodka."

His glorious leader's "eyes and ears", sitting across from him, looked up from the file the Americans had delivered. "What do we tell the Americans?"

Petrenko sighed, waiting for his vodka. His aide handed him a filled glass then wisely placed the bottle of Stolichnaya on the table in front of him. Petrenko downed the drink then leaned forward, pouring another. He sipped this one, considering the man sitting across from him, the liquid courage surging through his veins, numbing his limbs and loosening his tongue ever so slightly. "We tell them the truth."

Bulgakov Hotel
Moscow, Russian Federation
July 8, 2010

"Here they come."

Colonel Grigori Trubitsin, "retired", ignored his former Sergeant's unnecessary commentary as they sat in a hotel room, an old television tuned to the international edition of CNN, waiting for the American plane to touch down in Vienna, signaling the beginning of the end of a plan twenty-five years in the making. He hadn't taken his eyes off the screen since the exchange coverage had begun. The camera zoomed in on a man standing on the walkway in front of the Russian jet. He was a nobody. They would never let the throng of press see a *somebody*. Another camera showed the American plane landing then taxiing to a closed off area of the airport, coming to a halt near the Russians.

Yakovski grunted. "A little more public than we wanted."

"Da," agreed Trubitsin. These types of exchanges happened far more often than the public was aware, but this case was so high-profile, there was no hiding it. "Here they come." He pointed at the screen as four men, appearing tired but excited, emerged from the dark entrance of the plane, then one by one descended the stairs to the tarmac below where officials directed them toward the waiting American jet. At the same time, ten people exited the American plane and made their way on board the Russian jet.

Trubitsin's heart pounded as he saw her.

My God, she's beautiful.

"There she is!" Yakovski slapped Trubitsin on the back and downed a shot of vodka he had poured. The group climbed the stairs, showing no emotion. He knew they were relieved to be free, but he was sure they weren't happy to be forced to live the rest of their lives in Russia, a shithole if there ever was one. Trubitsin loved his country, rather, he loved what his country once was, but now criminals and whores had taken it over, and he spent as little time here as he could.

Don't worry, Anya, I'll have you out of here in no time.

As soon as he saw her board the Russian plane, he turned off the television and turned to Yakovski. "She'll be under close supervision for months. We've waited twenty-five years, what's a little longer?"

"Da. Let's hope she has the code."

"We know she has it, why else would the Americans have arrested them? They know she has it, but they couldn't prove it, and they couldn't arrest only her otherwise it would tip their hand as to why she was being picked up." Trubitsin leaned back in the threadbare hotel chair and sipped his vodka. "No, she has it. The question is, how did she smuggle it out?"

National Security Agency Headquarters
Fort Meade, Maryland
Present Day

TRANSCRIPT OF ECHELON INTERCEPT
SECURE BBS IDENT: THE EXCHANGE
BBS INTEL: THE EXCHANGE - WEAPONS TRADING
SECURE ELECTRONIC BULLETIN BOARD SYSTEM
UTILIZED BY ARMS DEALERS/CUSTOMERS
DECODE PROTOCOL DELTA 5-6 BRAVO

XXXXXX

INITIATOR: UNDERSTAND YOU HAVE SPECIAL ITEM
FOR SALE.

RESPONDER: PERHAPS

INIT: AM INTERESTED IN PURCHASING

RESP: FOR WHAT PURPOSE?

INIT: DOES THAT MATTER?

RESP: YES

INIT: I CAN'T TELL YOU SPECIFICALLY

RESP: DO YOU INTEND TO USE IT?

INIT: YES

RESP: WHAT IS THE TARGET?

INIT: WHY?

RESP: BECAUSE I DO NOT WANT TO BE THERE WHEN YOU USE IT.

INIT: UNDERSTOOD. THE TARGET IS XXXXXXX

TRANSCRIPT INCOMPLETE OR CORRUPTED

Unknown Location
November 19, 1256 AD

Faisal slowly became aware of his surroundings. A rush of sound filled his ears, soon accompanied by a splitting pain, the din and throbbing sensation too much. He focused on the pain, as he was taught to, and pushed it aside. Within minutes the roar in his ears had subsided, replaced with curious sounds coming from all directions. The shuffling of padded feet, water splashing in a fountain. And giggling.

Giggling?

Faisal opened his eyes then squeezed them shut, blocking out the blinding light surrounding him. He slowly opened them again, just a sliver. This time, it was more bearable. It took a few moments before he could open them enough to make out anything. A shape moved in front of him, toward him.

He scrambled backward, remembering what had happened in his bedchambers. The shape came closer, filling his entire field of vision, for what it was worth, everything still a blur. A cool, gentle hand touched his outstretched arm as he grasped the empty space beside him, his sword nowhere to be found.

"Be at peace, everything will be fine." The voice was soft. A woman's voice. His racing heart calmed slightly. If a woman was nearby, he must be out of immediate danger. He blinked several more times and the shape in front of him slowly became clear.

He gasped.

She was beautiful. Unlike any woman he had ever seen. And *more* of any woman than he had ever seen. He quickly averted his eyes and held his hand up to block her from his sight. A giggle sounded behind him. He looked and another woman, as scantily clad as that in front of him, smiled. In fact, there were several behind him.

The hand on his arm gently squeezed. "There is nothing to fear."

He turned to face the woman and found, this time, he couldn't tear his eyes away. Her dark brown hair flowed like tiny streams of water down past her shoulders, a few stray rivulets dangling over her forehead as her deep brown eyes stared at him like two gems sparkling in a pond. Her light brown skin, unmarred by hard labor, was partially hidden behind a nearly translucent, pink veil. He could see her smile through it, a smile that set him at ease.

Her fingers slid down his arm then grasped his hand. "Come, rise and behold your reward." She pulled at his hand and he climbed to his feet, all the while staring at her. Her silk covering barely hid her large breasts, one shoulder bare, the opposing side of her exposed midriff revealing a belly button filled by a large ruby, the sash she wore wrapped and tied about her waist, left her legs bare above the knees. It was more skin than he had seen in his life.

A stirring in his loins shamed him, and he looked away again. The woman smiled. "Behold all that is your reward for your loyal service to Allah."

Faisal followed her outstretched arm and gasped. He was in a large chamber, flickering candles and several cooking fires providing the illumination. A large fountain occupied the center, and set into the surrounding walls were bedchambers open to the spacious room.

And there were women.

Dozens of women. Everywhere he turned, he found the most beautiful women he could have imagined. And they were all staring at him, smiling.

"What is this place?"

The woman, still holding his hand, smiled. "Do you not recognize it?"

He almost dared not answer. "Jannah?"

"Yes."

"And you? You all are…"

"Your vestal virgins, for you to enjoy for eternity, your reward for a life of service to Allah."

He gulped. "Then I am…"

"Dead?"

He nodded.

"Yes, yes you are. But be not sad, for now you will have eternal joy." She leaned forward and kissed him on his cheek. "With us."

He blushed. It was his first kiss.

"Come!" she announced, waving to several girls. "Let us bathe you!"

Faisal blushed an even deeper red.

And smiled.

Andes Mountains, Peru
Present Day

Professor James Acton glanced over his shoulder as the distinctive laughter of the woman he loved fluttered over the dig site. He smiled as she tossed her head back, her auburn hair dangling over her shoulders and back, slightly blowing in the breeze.

I'm a lucky man.

He had met University College London Archaeology Professor and British Museum Archeology Head, Laura Palmer, in London only a year before while getting mixed up in a feud between warring factions of an ancient Roman organization called the Triarii. The bond created by those terrifying events had yet to break, and with it having been so long, he was certain they wouldn't. He had never been serious with a woman before, his two decades of gallivanting across the globe, preventing it, but now he had a kindred spirit to share in his life, a fellow archaeologist. If someone had told him a year ago he'd now be madly in love with a millionaire archaeologist, he'd have called them "daft", as Laura might say, her quirky British sayings slowly mixing in with his vernacular, as his were with hers.

The honking of a horn brought work to a halt, students and professors alike, as the supply truck rounded the final bend into their now fairly large dig site, ancient Incan ruins giving up their secrets readily since the massacre last year.

Acton rounded the brass memorial to those who had died, donated by the new students on the dig, and held out his hand to Laura who grasped it and squeezed.

"I hope there's news!"

"Leo isn't exactly FedEx, babe, but you never know." He gave her hand a squeeze, knowing how eager she was to get the package she was waiting for—government documents granting permission for a new dig

24

in Egypt. The approvals had apparently come through, only her signature needed for the new dig to be a go.

Acton was of mixed feelings. He was delighted that a dig his partner had been working toward for years might finally come through, but it also meant they would be apart for the first time in months.

Leo, their new supply driver—their previous driver refusing to return to work after the murders—brought the truck to a skidding halt, a cloud of dust momentarily obscuring it as he jumped from the cab.

"Professor Palmer, I have your mail!" Leo waved a sheaf of envelopes over his head as he rushed toward them, fishing out one large envelope from the bunch. "Look here, from your college!"

Laura reached out and eagerly grabbed the large manila envelope, Acton taking the rest of the mail and handing it to one of the students to sort. He looked over Laura's shoulder as she pulled out the pages.

"This is it!" She smiled and planted a kiss on his cheek.

Acton felt a tightening in his chest. "When do you leave?"

Laura scanned the pages.

"October."

Oak Grove, Kentucky
Four Miles outside Fort Campbell

Edison Cole stood near the cargo area of a black Humvee, his sunglasses revealing nothing to the two men who stood before him. His face was devoid of emotion, his hands clasped in front of him, his dark, tailored business suit neatly hid the shoulder holster containing a Glock 31 .357 SIG, as well as the Ruger LC9 9mm tucked into his belt behind his back. Two of his men unlatched the rear hatch after patting down the duo he now stared at.

Pieces of shit.

Inside he was sneering at the ragheads standing before him. He fought the desire to beat the living shit out of them then introduce two bullets to the back of their heads. His finger twitched, as if it had a mind of its own, as if it wanted to reach for his Glock and send these idiots to their seventy-two virgins.

Sorry, Mohammad, I'm going to send so many of these bastards up there, you'll run out.

His men hauled two large wooden crates, painted in standard-issue army green, halfway out of the truck. One pried open the cases, revealing dozens of M16A2 assault rifles and hundreds of thirty round magazines. The two men, who Cole knew damned well were al Qaeda, inched toward the truck.

"Hurry up, we haven't got all day!" yelled Gabriel Atkins, one of the more recent recruits to New Slate. Cole turned his head slightly, all the man needed to soften his tone. "These are fine M16A2s, taken straight off Fort Campbell." Atkins pulled one from the case, loaded a magazine, and tossed it to the nearest man. The buyer caught it easily, flipped the safety off then spun around, squeezing the trigger and chewing up a nearby concrete wall. The magazine lasted less than ten seconds, the fully automatic weapon leaving deep scars in the concrete. He ejected the mag and tossed the weapon back.

"We will take them."

He snapped his fingers at his partner carrying a black briefcase. The man stepped toward Cole. Cole shook his head slightly, stopping the man in his tracks, unsure where to go.

"Over here, Mow-haw-mad." Atkins' southern drawl massacred their sacred prophet's name.

What do you expect when you name all of your sons after the same guy? You don't see a whole lot of guys named Jesus walking around America, do you?

Cole pointed at Atkins. "Show *him* the money."

The man winced and turned to his partner who glared at Atkins, but motioned for the bagman to proceed. He placed the case on top of the crates, unlocked it, then flipped open the lid.

Atkins whistled at the stacks of neatly bundled twenty-dollar bills. Cole watched as several bundles were inspected and a quick count performed. Atkins nodded at Cole and snapped the lid shut, taking the briefcase and walking it over to him. Cole took the case then his men resealed the crates and removed them from the truck.

"Pleasure doing business with you," said Atkins with a sneer.

Remind me not to take him along on one of these missions again.

Cole snapped his head, indicating the others should get in the vehicle, then stepped toward the man clearly in charge.

"We can get anything you may need. You have my number."

"You can expect to hear from us soon," said the man in perfect English, a hint of a Limey accent suggesting he may have been educated, or hell, born, in England.

Cole took the plunge. "How's your financing?"

This caught the man off guard, this a question you never asked, at least not on the first date.

There was a pause before he replied. "Why?"

This is it!

"I can get you something *very* special, for the right price."

The man's eyebrows furled toward his nose. "How special?"

"Russian. That makes things glow in the dark."

"Sounds expensive."

27

"It is."

Now for the money shot.

"Fifty million, firm, half upfront, half on delivery, includes weapon and arming codes."

The fact the man's facial expression didn't change at all confirmed Cole's suspicion. Definitely al Qaeda, well-funded, probably from Saudis rich off our appetite for cheap oil.

Hey morons, if you turn us into an Islamic state trapped in the twelfth century, who's going to buy your oil then?

"We will need proof."

Cole reached into his pocket. The man's partner stepped in front of his boss when the butt of Cole's gun was revealed, but relaxed when his hand withdrew, holding an envelope. Cole held it out to the boss who motioned to his subordinate to take it. A shaky hand snatched the envelope from Cole then opened it, revealing half a dozen photographs. He handed them to his boss, who flipped through them.

"This is American."

"You know your ordnance," smiled Cole. "Yes, lost during the Cold War in Soviet airspace and recovered by a Russian soldier with not only a capitalist leaning, but an abundance of patience."

The man tucked the pictures into his jacket pocket.

"We will be in touch."

Inebolu Sokak Street, Istanbul, Turkey

"It is essential that we possess this weapon before anyone else."

There were nods of agreement from the men sitting at the round table.

"Can we trust this report?"

Abdullah bin Saqr turned to the man at his left, someone he trusted with his life, as he did with every man in the room. "Absolutely. It comes from one of our agents implanted deep within the CIA."

"But he's a convert!" exclaimed another.

"My brothers, not all of us are blessed to have come to Islam at birth. Islam is a religion of peace, and we must trust our brothers, whether they were born of the Prophet, peace be upon him, or discovered his teachings later in life."

Grunts of agreement rounded the room, but Abdullah knew they weren't all convinced—nobody would look him in the eye.

"You may not all trust in the source, but you must all agree that we cannot risk ignoring it."

More grunts of agreement, this time the heads rising, making eye contact.

"If indeed there is a nuclear weapon on the black market, then we must be successful in purchasing it before any of the enemies of Islam can use it to further their goals of corrupting the teachings of the Prophet, peace be upon him. Should we fail in the task before us, I fear the consequences of the calamity we may all face, Muslim and Christian."

Bulgakov Hotel
Moscow, Russian Federation

Trubitsin waited alone in the hotel room. Someone had held vigil every moment of every day since Anya was exchanged by the Americans in the most public spy swap in history. It was his turn to man the room. In reality, it was him most of the time, he determined to be the first to see her. He closed his eyes and pictured her auburn hair draped across her naked shoulders, her head tossed back, her eyes squeezed shut as they made love in the hot tub at the Grand Hyatt in New York City. It was there, three years ago, where he had hatched the final phase of the plan—the retrieval of the arming codes for the missile they had acquired over twenty years before.

A soft knock on the door snapped him from his reverie.

Could it be?

The knock was far too soft for his gruff sergeant. He walked to the door then peered through the peephole and smiled. He opened it and she said nothing, showing no emotion as she walked in. He closed and latched the door, then turned to face her. She threw her purse and jacket on a nearby chair then spun around, revealing a smile as breathtaking as the day he had first seen her. She stepped toward him and slipped her arms around his waist, tilting her head back and closing her eyes.

"Oh, dorogaya, how I've missed you," she whispered.

He leaned down and kissed her soft, full lips, gently at first, then with a growing intensity as a lust from three years of separation took over. There was no love there, but there was something. An animal intensity of desire neither wanted to resist. Her fingernails scratched at his shirt then she reached in front and feverishly unbuttoned it. That was his cue to return the favor, yanking open her blouse then shrugging off his shirt as she let hers fall to the floor. She kicked off her red high heel shoes, unzipped the tight miniskirt and wiggled it to the floor as he reached for his belt buckle.

She wagged her finger "Nuh ah." She dropped to her knees and seized his belt, tugging him toward her. She reached up and loosened the fly, then with her teeth, opened it the rest of the way. "I see you still don't wear underwear."

He smiled down at her. "Not when I know I'm seeing you."

A rap at the door made them both flinch.

"Go away!" yelled Trubitsin.

"But, boss, it's me!"

The voice of his sergeant was unmistakable.

"Go away!" yelled Trubitsin again.

"But, boss, I've got nowhere to go!"

Anya laughed and fell back on her haunches, staring up at Trubitsin. She slapped his pride and stood. "Put that thing away and let him in, there's plenty of time for that later."

Trubitsin stood there for a moment, debating what to do. Yakovski's pounding on the door made up his mind. "Alright, stop making so much noise, you'll wake everybody!" he yelled. He stuffed his waning member back in his pants, zipped up his fly and opened the door as Anya buttoned her blouse nonchalantly in front of the mirror.

Yakovski barged in. "Hey, what's the idea?" Then he stopped as he took in the scene before him. "Oh…" He trailed off then smiled at Trubitsin. "Good thing I took my time, eh, boss?"

"Uh huh."

"So, Anya, how long have you been here?"

"Two minutes."

Yakovski gulped. "Oh." He looked at Trubitsin and whispered, "Sorry, boss."

Trubitsin shook his head, the sexual frustration still in control.

"Down to business, darling?" asked Anya, dragging him reluctantly back to reality.

Trubitsin frowned as he retrieved his shirt from the floor. "Da. You have it?"

Her Cheshire cat grin left no doubt. "Oh yes, my darling, I have it."

"And how did you get it?"

"Oh, I don't know if you want to know that."

"I do!" chimed in his sergeant as he sat in one of the chairs and poured a glass of vodka. He held up the bottle, asking Anya with his eyebrows if she wanted some. She nodded.

"Very well." She took the glass he poured her. "All you really need to know is he was a charming, shy boy, who worked in the Pentagon archives, who had a penchant for gambling and the ladies. The rest was easy."

"You mean *you* were easy," grumbled Trubitsin.

"Are we jealous, darling?" Anya stepped up to him and patted him on the cheek then gave him a quick peck on the lips. "No need. He was a boy." She reached down and gave his crotch a squeeze. "You're all man."

His ego restored, Trubitsin looked at her. "Where is it?"

"Da, how did you hide it from the Americans?"

"Oh, the lengths I go to for Mother Russia, but mostly for you." She stepped over to the mirror and leaned in close. With her thumb and forefinger, she rolled her eyelid up, revealing a tiny string of letters and numbers tattooed underneath. Trubitsin gasped then snatched a pen and a pad of hotel paper, jotting down the sequence. She repeated the process with the other eye and he wrote down the rest.

He looked at the code then at her and smiled. "You, my dear, are a genius."

She smiled then looked at Yakovski. "Boris, beat it. I want to make wild, passionate love to my man, and three's a crowd."

Yakovski looked at Trubitsin as if uncertain what to do. One glare from his former commander removed any doubt, sending him scrambling for the door. "I'll go get a drink."

Arbat Street, Moscow, Russian Federation

Stanislav Ignatev stood in the doorway of a closed bakery, shivering from the cold of a late evening shower. At first, he was excited with his assignment to tail Anya Kushchenko.

She has a great rack, as the Yankees would say!

He gave a single grunt of a laugh as he remembered the hoots in the squad room as they were briefed, he and several others assigned to watch her, to see if she did anything unexpected. The chance she was a double-agent was definite. Most who returned to Russia and saw how terrible things were compared to the West, longed to return to their former assignments.

Ignatev, however, had never been out of Russia. Unless you counted Chechnya, but that wasn't exactly a pleasure trip. After completing his two years compulsory service, in which he had the misfortune to serve six months in that shithole, he had left the formerly glorious Red Army and joined the Main Department of Internal Affairs of the city of Moscow, or more simply, the Moscow Police, an honorable profession, and something that would keep him in his hometown. Tonight his detachment was part of a much larger team he was sure. No way was this given to local cops only. He was certain SKP agents were crawling all over the place. He glanced at a couple kissing on a bench across the street.

He's kissing her neck too much. Definitely SKP.

Kushchenko had entered the Bulgakov Hotel minutes before and Ignatev was preparing to find some place to get comfortable for the rest of his shift, when he saw somebody familiar step from the hotel. The man, in his early fifties with short cropped, graying hair, didn't stand out except for one thing—he had a deep scar running in a jagged pattern from his left eye to the corner of his lip. This he recognized at once from a briefing months earlier. He fished his radio from his pocket and called Dispatch.

"Dispatch, go ahead."

"This is Ignatev. I've just spotted Boris Yakovski on Arbat Street, should I apprehend?"

"Dispatch, stand by."

He waited impatiently, watching the man look up and down the street then hail a cab.

"Dammit!" muttered Ignatev. He spotted another cab coming toward him and flagged it down, climbing in the back as soon as it halted. Before the driver said a word, he pointed at the vehicle containing Yakovski as it pulled away from the hotel. "Follow that cab!"

"Da, da," said the cabby as he glanced in his rearview mirror before pulling a U-turn, falling in behind the other cab.

"Not too close!"

"Da, da." The cabby eased back.

"Dispatch to Ignatev, stand by for communication from HQ, over."

Ignatev started as his phone vibrated in his pocket. He fished it out and flipped it open. "Ignatev."

"This is Agent Dymovsky, on special assignment from the Investigations Committee of the Prosecutor-General's Office. You spotted Boris Yakovski? Are you sure?"

"I saw the scar, sir, it's definitely him."

"Where are you now?"

"I'm assigned to the detail tailing Anya Kushchenko."

"Yes, yes, I know, but where *are* you? Where did you spot him?"

"He got in a cab in front of the Bulgakov Hotel."

"Damn, do you know where he went?"

"No, but—"

"Did you notice the cab number? We might be able to track him!"

"No, but—"

"You didn't get the number!"

Let me get a damned word in!

"Sir! I'm following him in another cab."

A pause.

34

"You left your detail?"

Ignatev gulped. "Y-yes, sir. I assumed since there were three others watching the hotel, it would be better to follow this target."

Again silence.

"Vodka is on me when your shift ends. You call me as soon as he gets to his destination."

Ignatev smiled. "Yes, sir!"

Unknown Location
November 19, 1256 AD

Faisal shyly covered his now raging shame and stepped into the pool of hot water, the steam rising gently into the cooler air above the surface, the scent from the hundreds of rose petals and perfumes filling his nostrils. He breathed a sigh of relief as his waist broke the water's surface, out of sight under the opaque mixture of soap and creams floating on the surface. He looked around, his beet red face revealing his embarrassment, unable to mask the lust forming in his eyes as several women undressed each other, each keeping their eyes on him the entire time.

Faisal was a good Muslim. He had never been with a woman, he had never even seen a woman naked before. His heart pounded as these beautiful creatures revealed their treasures to him, treasures he alone would get to enjoy for the rest of eternity.

Allah be praised!

The one he had awoken to smiled at him, her entire magnificence now revealed. As she took each step into the pool to join him, her eyes remained on him, and it was everything he could do to hold her gaze, his eyes desperate to look upon the rest of her body.

"Does what you see please you?" she asked as she made the final step into the pool.

This was his excuse. He slowly lowered his eyes as she pushed through the water toward him. He dropped his gaze down her face, past her full, painted lips, to her tiny chin, past her slim neck then rounded shoulder and finally her outstretched arm as she neared. He dared to steal a quick, momentary glance at her breasts. He gasped. She smiled.

"I guess you do!"

Several other women giggled as they stepped into the pool. She inched toward him, rolling her shoulders forward, which to his

36

amazement, made her breasts appear even larger, the dark nipples hard, something he had heard was a good thing. He gulped.

"My name is Fatima," she whispered, her voice low, hoarse, seductive. "And I am here to serve Allah's warrior." She pressed against him. He looked back to find some place to retreat to, but found himself against the side of the pool, her warm, naked flesh pushed against his, her soft breasts squeezed against his chest as she reached and took his head in her hands, then kissed him passionately on the lips. Her left hand slowly traced his face as she drew her finger down the center of his chest, over his navel, and then, with a smirk, reached under the water.

He moaned and closed his eyes as she gently kissed his neck, slowly working her way down his chest.

This is truly paradise! Allah be praised.

He looked down as her head slowly went below the water, and a momentary flash of concern over how she would breathe, entered his mind.

Shouting from behind him erupted. He spun his head as a large set of wooden doors burst open and his trainer, Master Hasni, charged through.

He died too?

Somewhere over Maryland
Present Day

James Acton stretched his aching muscles. His back, ass, legs—basically everything—were on fire from having crawled, crouched, knelt and laid on the rocky ground of the dig site every day for months—and to cap it off, he now had this ridiculous flight home to placate the alumni committee at his university. The passengers, not to mention the flight attendants, frowned upon a grown man stretching in the aisles, and his nineteen hours of travel to get *to* this flight, hadn't helped his condition. Ten hours by truck from the dig in the mountains of Peru, bouncing over roads in name only, four hours of waiting at an airport that had more chickens running around the terminal than passengers, all to catch a prop from Lima to Mexico City. Three hours sucking in the filth generated by ten million souls living in close proximity with no environmental laws that couldn't be broken with the right amount of currency, then finally—*finally*—his flight on an American carrier and its promised luxury, promised luxury that had him crammed against the window—even though he had requested the aisle—with an immense man beside him pouring over the armrests. It had left him in a pretty foul mood by the time he boarded his final flight for Maryland.

Landing at last, he departed the flight and arrived at the baggage claim area, exhausted, sore, and ready to swear off airplanes for the foreseeable future.

Yet he grinned.

Waiting for him was his best friend, Gregory Milton, waving from off to the side. The smiling Milton reached for the wheels of his wheelchair but Acton waved him off and hurried over. He leaned over his friend and hugged him around the shoulders, Milton returning the gesture, slapping his friend on the back then pushing him away.

"Have you smelled yourself?"

Acton laughed. "That's not me, that's the livestock that was flying with me." He looked his friend up and down, still unable to get used to seeing him in the chair, but after he thought he had lost him in last year's "incident", it was the most beautiful sight imaginable. "You look good."

Milton patted his stomach, protruding farther than when Acton had seen him last. "Still getting used to this damned thing. I thought life behind a desk was making me fat, but life in a chair is definitely doing it."

Acton winced. It was his fault his best friend of over twenty years, the man who had taken him under his wing as a freshman in college, who had encouraged him to become an archaeologist, and who, as Dean, had given him his current job as head of archaeology at Saint Paul's University, was in this wheelchair.

Milton took his friend's hand and squeezed. "Hey, I know that look. Stop dwelling on this—it wasn't your fault. I chose to help. Knowing what I know now, I still would've done the same thing." He smiled wryly. "Although I might wear a vest next time."

Acton managed a weak smile. "Yeah, well, I guess it's better than the alternative."

"Yes, yes it is. Just remember that."

Acton thought back on that day, receiving the text message his friend had sent him when he thought he was dying from two gunshot wounds. It was almost a week later that he found out his friend was alive, discovered almost immediately by another customer at the gas station who happened to be an ER surgeon. It had saved his life. Dozens had died in those few days, but his best friend had survived. Acton sighed. "So, how goes the therapy?"

"Oh, good days and bad days," said Milton. "Today was a bad day. Tried all damned day to move my effin' toe but it wouldn't budge."

Acton stared at him, about to ask why this was unexpected when his friend smiled.

"Because yesterday I moved it for two friggin' minutes with no problem."

Acton's jaw dropped as he stared at his friend, reading his face to see if he was joking. "Are-are you serious?"

"Trust me, buddy, I'm a joker, but I wouldn't shit you about something like that."

Acton clasped his friend's shoulder and squeezed, tears welling in his eyes. "That's incredible news," he whispered, not trusting his voice.

Milton patted his friend's hand. "My daughter was the first to notice it." His voice cracked at the mention of her. He took a deep breath and smiled. "She was playing some music and I guess I was tapping my toe to it."

Acton wiped his eyes before the tears poured down his cheeks. He laughed and looked at Milton. "Man, are we ever a couple of old women."

Milton laughed and punched him in the arm. "There, that make you feel more like a man?"

Acton feigned a punch to Milton's jaw, laughing. "Better stop, someone'll think I'm beating up on a cripple."

Milton pointed at the carousel. "That your bag?" A beat-up, tan canvas bag, issued to Acton in Desert Storm, tumbled from the chute.

"Yup." Acton jogged over, grabbing it. He didn't bother checking the tag, there no doubt it was his. Although identical to thousands if not millions of others issued over the years, this one had traveled all over the world and had been torn open and patched more times than he could remember. It was his good luck charm. He thought he had lost it after the massacre at the dig site last year, and was delighted to find it when he returned almost six months ago. He pushed the memory away.

Damn, I'm emotional today.

He walked back to where his friend was waiting.

"Come, let's get you home and showered. Sandra has a proper dinner waiting for you if you're up for it."

"Sounds good, I'm exhausted but starving. Just don't be surprised if my head hits the plate."

Milton laughed as he pushed hard on the wheels, surging slightly ahead of Acton. "I'm dying too. The damned woman wouldn't let me eat!"

Acton chuckled and jogged ahead, hitting the handicap button on the door leading to the parking lot. "That sounds like Sandra."

"Speaking of the women we love," said Milton as he squeezed out the exit, "Laura wants you to call her as soon as you get in." He reached into his pocket and retrieved the keys to his van. "I'd suggest you take that shower first, she's liable to smell you over the line."

Acton grunted. "Maybe you think I stink too much to help you in that tricked out van you've got?"

Milton raised his arms in mock apology. "I'm sorry, I'm sorry. You smell like roses. Fertilized roses. But roses nonetheless."

Acton shook his head, smiling. He had missed his friend. After months on the dig, it was great to see him in such good spirits. Milton raised the fob and pressed the button to unlock the doors then pressed another button, the side door sliding open and a wheelchair ramp unfolding.

"Sweet!"

Milton agreed. "Yup, final tricks installed. No one has to help me in or out anymore."

Acton pushed Milton up the ramp, giving an exaggerated groan. "Good thing, you weigh a ton."

Milton feigned hurt feelings. "I'll have you know that once I can move all ten damned toes, I'll start losing this weight, but you'll always be a heartless asshole."

Acton flipped him the bird and slammed the passenger door shut, a grin spread across his face as he climbed into the passenger seat, Milton having already swung into the driver's seat, his friend apparently well-practiced. Milton turned the key and Megadeth roared from the speakers. His hand darted for the volume as he turned it down, but not off.

Acton shook his head in mock disapproval. "Oh, if only the alumni knew."

Titanik Club
Moscow, Russian Federation

Agent Alexey Dymovsky's men took up position outside the bar on Leningradskiy Prospekt. The pounding beats of competing clubs filled the air, drunken patrons stumbled from bar to bar, others leaned against walls as they puked their night's drinks and bar snacks onto the sidewalk, while others tried to convince hookers to offer free samples.

This is a true shithole!

Dymovsky frowned at the sight as one luxury vehicle after another pulled up and whisked young ladies away.

What has this country become?

He agreed with capitalism, and certainly didn't want to return to the old communist days of his youth, but crime was out of control. And now with the puppet master in control in Moscow, he feared it would be used as an excuse to bring back the old ways. Already freedom of the press and freedom of assembly were jokes. Freedom of speech was next. In fact, considering it was now almost impossible to organize an opposition party due to the draconian rules brought in by Moscow's ruling elite, freedom of speech might as well not exist. They had brought back the dictatorship, without anyone realizing they had done it.

Well done, Vlad. I hope too many don't die when the proletariat awakens to the realization of what you have done.

"Everyone is in position, sir," said his second in command over the earpiece.

Dymovsky touched his ear, activating the comm. "I'm going in now."

It had taken him almost a year for his first break. Within several weeks he had enough information to formulate a theory. The July 23, 1985, incident was documented in the Soviet Army archives. The report detailed a successful TACAN spoofing, the downing of a NATO FB-

111F, and the successful retrieval of much of the technology. The report from Major Grigori Trubitsin of the 641st Fighter Aviation Regiment was thorough. Except for one thing. No mention was made of a recovered nuclear missile. And considering the forest was swept for every scrap of metal that could be retrieved, it was inconceivable that a tactical nuclear missile could be missed.

That led him to postulate Trubitsin and his men had stolen the missile for themselves, with plans to sell it on the black market. But something like that on the black market would have been detected years ago, so for some reason, it hadn't been sold yet. The plutonium was valuable in itself, worth millions, but a functioning nuclear device would be worth tens of millions, if not more.

And that required codes.

A call to the Americans had confirmed the compromised launch codes, which is what had prompted the admission in Geneva to the Broken Arrow. Now both the Americans and the Russians knew a tactical nuclear weapon was in play, with launch codes, and no one knew where it was. The unit that had brought the plane down had disappeared after the Cold War ended. It had taken months, but at last he had caught a break. Trubitsin's driver from 1985 was monitored leaving Montreal several months ago on a fake Canadian passport, his photo and those of his comrades, given to Interpol to see if they would have any luck finding them.

As soon as he had heard of the flight, tracking him was easy. They had watched him for several months in the hopes he would lead them to his accomplices, but instead he had spent almost his entire time visiting his mother during the day, then drinking and screwing hookers at night. He was booked on a flight the next day, making it clear he was meeting no one. He had yet to decide whether to grab him before leaving, and risk tipping Trubitsin off.

But Yakovski was a different story. Wherever he was, Trubitsin couldn't be far.

He climbed from his car and crossed the cobbled street, the stones glistening from the light rain blanketing the area. He stepped up to the entrance and glanced around, spotting a few of his men about a block away. The doorman held up a hand, blocking him.

I guess I'm not pretty enough.

He showed his badge, adding several points to his score, the door pulled open without a word.

The roar of the music was deafening.

Certainly no casual conversation happening here.

He descended the curved flight of stairs into the basement club, pushing his way past couples making out, others far beyond that. As he rounded the final bend, he was grabbed by the sleeve of his jacket. He spun to see a girl, bent over as her partner mauled her from behind, staring at him, her lust-filled eyes focused on his.

"Join us!"

Dymovsky yanked his arm away, breaking her grip, and continued down the steps. They laughed, their comments soon lost to the din that greeted him as the steps widened and deposited him into the club. He surveyed the crowd of hundreds, most on the dance floor, others lounging in a series of booths bordering the club. A second level above had more booths with a view of the floor below. Strobe and neon lights illuminated the dance area, augmented with a laser show that played out over the dancers' heads. The bar area was the exception, fairly well-lit so the throngs, about five deep, shouting their orders with Rubles waving in the air, could see the selection of mostly cheap vodkas displayed across the mirrored shelves.

Dymovsky slowly rounded the booths, searching for the man whose image he had burned into his mind. It might be easier to wait for him to leave the club at the end of the night, but the risk they might miss him was too great, and Dymovsky had a plan that needed Yakovski, tonight.

He glanced up at the second level, and there, staring down at him, was Yakovski.

Did he make me?

Dymovsky spotted a drunken girl standing nearby, head flopping on her shoulders, knees threatening to give out, the alcohol long since

45

having done its work. He gripped her hair and pulled her against him, kissing her neck. She moaned, offering no resistance, her arms simply rags hanging by her sides. The support his hand provided as he held her by the neck, her hair tangled around his fingers, was the cue her knees needed to finally give out. Dymovsky wrapped his free hand around her waist, grabbing her ass and grinding his hips into hers. He slowly turned her around, continuing to grind their hips together to the beat as he stared through her hair, up at his target. Yakovski kept his eyes on them for a moment then looked away, losing interest. Dymovsky guided the girl toward a booth with an empty spot and deposited her there, much to the surprise of the three men occupying it.

He climbed the metal staircase leading to the second level, glancing back down at the young girl he had used, now pawed by the booth's occupants. He felt a twinge of guilt, and for a moment debated rescuing her, but resisted—he was after a nuclear weapon that could kill millions. One drunken girl was not his concern tonight.

As he neared the table with Yakovski, he saw him slouch in his chair, his eyes rolling into the back of his head. The table he sat at was covered by a cloth that overflowed to the floor in what at first appeared a poor attempt to add a touch of class to the cesspool they were in, but as he neared, he saw the tablecloth draped over Yakovski's lap move, revealing a flash of short, spiked, blonde hair.

With sluts like this, how's an honest whore supposed to make a living?

Yakovski, his eyes mostly closed, tilted his head to face Dymovsky, and smiled. He whipped his hand out from under the table. As it swung at Dymovsky, he spotted the glint of a pistol. He had nowhere to hide, the wall too close to provide any cover. There was nothing between him and Yakovski's weapon, and he couldn't reach his own in time.

He dove over the railing and tumbled toward the throng of dancers below.

Harry's Irish Pub
Fayetteville, NC

"To BD! Not even a Sidewinder missile can take 'im out!"

A round of cheers erupted from the table as glasses of beer rose in honor of the man of the hour. BD, short for Big Dog, a nickname given to Burt Dawson during basic training years ago, raised his glass in acknowledgment then drained it in one shot as his men cheered him on. Dawson slammed the glass down with a satisfied roar, wiping his upper lip. He looked at the men sitting with him at the long table. Some new, some he had served with for years. But all brothers. Brothers in covert arms. Burt Dawson, Command Sergeant Major, was the leader of Delta Team Bravo, in his opinion, and many others, the best group of operators in what the public knew as the Delta Force, the most highly trained black ops specialists the U.S. Military had to offer. 1st Special Forces Operational Detachment–Delta was America's answer to the growing problem of international terrorism, and had served with distinction in many operations the American public knew nothing about. Dawson had served with Delta for almost eight years, on missions from Iraq and Afghanistan, to Iran and Syria. All successes, all without credit.

And he'd have it no other way.

As events last year in London had proved, their work and their identities had to be kept under the radar otherwise their lives, and those of their loved ones, could be forfeit. He had managed to escape just in time, the explosion from the missile sending him flying away from the helicopter, a gash in his leg that nearly ripped open his femoral artery his lone injury worth talking about, the others simply what he'd characterize as flesh wounds. Over six months of rehab and he was officially cleared again for active duty this very day.

And it was time to celebrate.

Sergeant Carl "Niner" Sung downed his beer and called the waitress over for another round. Niner, whose family moved to the United States after the Korean War, had gained his nickname in a bar fight years before when a redneck had called him "slant-eyed". Niner had proven his wit quicker, slinging his own Asian insults, one of which was "nine iron", then with the help of other Bravo Team members with him, beat the living shit out of the guy and his friends after the rednecks hadn't taken well to the entire bar laughing at them. From then on, he had insisted his nickname be "Nine Iron", which was shortened to "Niner" over the years.

Mike Belme, Dawson's best friend of over ten years, sat to his right. Nicknamed "Red" because of the fiery red hair he kept at bay with a Bowie knife, he was Dawson's second-in-command, if you could call him that, the organization of a Delta unit different from the traditional military unit, with all members of the same or similar rank. There were no officers here.

Mixed in among the long term members were four new members since the events of last year, replacements to those who had lost their lives in that mess. Stucco, who had done drywall before joining the forces, and Casey, whose Casey Kasem impersonation was uncanny, had joined Bravo Team toward the end of the London events, and Dawson was pleased with their performance, especially in the aftermath. Despite being new, the way barbs easily fired back and forth with the long timers, the newest members had fit in well even with Dawson and half the team undergoing some type of rehabilitation after London. With Dawson now back on active duty, the team was fully operational for the first time since last year.

And Dawson was itching to get back into the thick of it.

Sergeant Gerry "Jimmy Olsen" Hudson, named once the team found out he had worked on his school newspaper, stood. "I've gotta drain the main vein." He turned to Niner. "Ready?"

Sergeant Will "Spock" Lightman's eyebrow shot up as the table erupted in laughter. Niner leaned back in his chair and eyeballed Jimmy.

"What are we, a bunch of women?" He turned to the waitress. "Get my friend here a Shirley Temple!"

Jimmy flushed. "But you said—"

Niner threw his hand daintily at Jimmy. "Okay, dear, let's go to the bathroom." He stood and sashayed toward the men's room, the entire bar, filled with servicemen, now laughing.

Jimmy followed, shaking his head and muttering, "But he said he needed to go!"

As Jimmy walked away, Sergeants Leon "Atlas" James and Trip "Mickey" McDonald rejoined the group.

Red elbowed Dawson, and in none too quiet a voice, asked, "So, do you think he struck out?"

Atlas, whose chiseled physique demanded he take a knee and a planet on his shoulders, gripped Mickey by the back of the neck. "This man takes more abuse than any man I know." Atlas shook Mickey's entire body with his massive hand. "He's been buying that girl drinks all night, chatting her up, and what happens? He moves in for the phone number, and she thanks him, tells him she's gay, and plants a huge kiss on her friend that I've been playing wingman with!"

Mickey's ears, the source of his nickname, turned bright red despite his huge smile. "Yeah, but who insisted we keep sitting there for five minutes watching them?"

Atlas nodded, letting go of Mickey's neck. "Damn skippy. I wanted to make sure she wasn't lying to my friend here!"

The table roared with laughter as another round of beer arrived.

Titanik Club
Moscow, Russian Federation

Agent Dymovsky fell silently toward the throng of dancers below, not wanting to warn them otherwise they might scatter and he'd hit the floor without anything to break his fall. Though it felt like an eternity, it was only seconds before he slammed atop several dancers, taking them all into a heap on the floor. With the wind knocked out of him, precursor pains of several new bruises certain to show up in a few hours made themselves felt. He pushed to his knees when he heard a scream, instinctively throwing himself to the right, rolling on the floor and drawing his weapon as gunshots rang out. Several holes ripped through the wooden dance floor as he raised his weapon and fired back at the ceiling, making certain not to hit his target.

I need you alive! Don't make me kill you!

Yakovski dove out of sight then Dymovsky spotted the top of his head as he ran for what might be a door on the second level. Pandemonium had taken over the club. He lay alone on the dance floor, his weapon tracking Yakovski as he made his escape, the remaining club patrons squeezing up the tiny set of stairs leading to the outside. Dymovsky tried his radio but the earpiece had become dislodged in the fall. He was on his own. He jumped up and ran to the metal staircase, forcing past the few remaining patrons from the second level still escaping. Reaching the top, he heard several gunshots and spun to see Yakovski kicking a door open, breaking through the lock he had disintegrated. Dymovsky bolted toward the door and followed Yakovski into a liquor storage area, a single flickering light swaying wildly in the middle of the room, the lone source of illumination. A large garage delivery door was on the far side, closed, another entry door stood beside it, then a large window, painted black so no one from the outside could see the booze stored on the half-dozen long

50

shelves occupying the left and right sides of the room. Several pallets stood in the middle, piled high with boxes of beer and vodka.

Dymovsky hugged the wall, cautiously looking around. All the exits appeared secure—his target was still in the room. He slowly rounded the perimeter, listening for any telltale sign of his opponent, but heard nothing, the music still pounding from the now unmanned DJ booth. He saw the hint of flashing red and blue lights through the painted glass, his comrades in arms obviously having moved in after the gunshots. He rounded the shelves, his gun pointing at the cases stacked in the middle of the room, when he heard a roar and spotted Yakovski leaping from between two rows of Putinka vodka, his outstretched weapon aimed directly at him. Dymovsky ducked, knowing it was too late to avoid taking a hit at this range, but much to his and Yakovski's surprise, nothing but harmless clicks sounded from the weapon.

Yakovski leaped at the now kneeling Dymovsky. Dymovsky raised his hands as he was about to make contact and rose, grabbing Yakovski and propelling him through the window, shattering the plate glass. Dymovsky stepped through the smashed window, hands raised as the police outside screamed at Yakovski to drop his weapon. As he stepped out onto the street, he was greeted by over a dozen Moscow Police, their weapons spinning toward him.

"Take it easy, it's me, Dymovsky," he said in as calm a voice as he could muster.

"Lower your weapons, don't you recognize the scene commander?" yelled the man who had phoned in the tip as he ran up to him. "Are you okay, sir?"

Dymovsky winced. "Might have a broken rib, but I'll live. Your vodka might have to wait, though." He pointed at Yakovski. "Get him into interrogation immediately."

Unknown Location
November 19, 1256 AD

"Master Hasni?" gulped Faisal. "Wh-what are you doing here?" He looked down between his legs as Fatima came up for air. It was then he noticed the other women had stopped what they were doing, looks of concern on their faces as they stared at the new arrival.

"We are under attack, we must go!" said the Master firmly.

"But, but I don't understand!" Faisal's mind raced as he tried to decipher what was happening. "But we're in Jannah. How can we be under attack?" Then Faisal understood. His Master must have just been killed, and didn't know where he was. He turned to face his master, careful to keep his now aching shame under water as Fatima moved away. "Master, it is okay, we are not under attack." He extended his arms and opened them, taking in all of the surroundings. "This is Jannah. You have passed over into paradise! Be at peace and praise Allah for your reward."

Master Hasni strode toward him, apparently unconvinced. He looked at Fatima and snapped his fingers. "Fatima, get you and your girls to safety at once. Take the south tunnel. Do not return until you are sent for."

Fatima bowed then scurried from the pool, grabbing her wrap as the other women hurried out the door the master had entered.

How does he know her name?

"Master?"

"None of it is real, boy," said Hasni, clapping his hands together. "Now get dressed, quickly, there isn't much time."

Not real? How could it not be real? Why?

Faisal stared at his master.

"Now!"

He flinched and looked about, finding his clothes neatly piled on a nearby pillow. He climbed from the water, trying to hide his disappointment, and dressed as Hasni paced in front of the door.

"Come, come!"

Faisal jogged to the door as he tightened his belt and followed his master from the chamber where he heard more voices, then yelling and screaming in the distance.

Where am I?

He followed his master down a long hallway and through another set of doors where he stepped out into a blazing midday sun and a courtyard he was well familiar with.

I'm still in Alamut?

Faisal stopped. "Master, I don't understand."

"Come with me, there is little time!"

Faisal stood fast.

But what about Jannah? I want to be there. I want to go back. I don't understand!

"Faisal, you must come now, we are under attack by the Mongols. There will be time to explain later."

"But I was there. I saw it. Fatima—"

"Is a whore, in our service, who has pleasured many a man before you, and Allah willing, will pleasure many after you."

A flash of anger surged through Faisal, his face flushing red as his heart raced. "She is not a whore!" He barely knew her yet knew he loved her.

It's been less than thirty minutes. How can you love her?

His master stopped and walked back to Faisal, lowering his voice. "Listen, son, it is all part of the ritual. You are now no longer my apprentice. You are Hassassin. You passed your final test. All Hassassins go through the ritual where you are made to believe you were killed and have awoken in Jannah, then after a blissful hour, you fall asleep again after drinking wine, fed to you by a beautiful woman, then wake in our infirmary with a nasty knock on the head. It is the Right of Initiation."

"But why?"

"So you know what you are fighting for!"

"I don't understand."

"Every Hassassin thinks he has died, sees what paradise is like, then awakes, thinking he has been brought back to life by Allah. He then serves Allah without question, knowing that his reward should he die in battle is paradise, a paradise that he has experienced."

"Everyone has done this?"

"Yes."

"And they all know?"

Hasni shook his head. "Of course not, only the training masters know. It is a tradition handed down for over a century, from one training master to the next. I remember when I was told, how shocked I was. I even felt betrayed, as I am sure you do now, but then I realized the brilliance of it. Paradise—Jannah. Few men ever experience anything like it while living. *We* all have. And it is a wonderful thing. Keep it fresh in your mind, boy, for it is something to keep you alive, and something to die for."

Faisal stared at the ground.

It was all a lie.

"Look out!"

Faisal jerked his head up as Hasni grabbed him by the robe and yanked him into a nearby doorway. A volley of arrows cleared the outer wall and rained down on the courtyard they stood in.

Hasni spun Faisal around to face him and stared him in the eyes. "We are under attack. Are you Hassassin or are you a coward?"

Faisal took a deep breath through his nose, the scent from the pool still fresh on his skin, filling his nostrils, the memory of what had almost happened sending a surge through his loins. Then he realized what it all meant. "I am Hassassin!" he said with a surge of pride. "I am no coward."

Hasni smiled and squeezed Faisal's shoulders. "Good, good. Now let's get in this fight, brother."

Milton Residence
St. Paul, Maryland
Present Day

Acton tapped his steak with his fork, his eyes rolling up as he chewed. "You have no idea how good this tastes. I've been eating campfire food for so long, I forgot what a home cooked meal tastes like."

Sandra Milton smiled at him. "Thanks, Jim, glad you're enjoying it. Compliments like that will get you seconds." She turned to her husband. "Silence won't even get you to first base tonight, mister."

Greg Milton nearly choked, his eyes bulging slightly. He took a drink of water then gave his wife a look. "Honey, I was just being polite and letting our guest pay you the first compliment."

"Good one," whispered Acton.

"Don't encourage him."

Their young daughter, Niskha, giggled, her head pivoting as each of them spoke, a mouthful of mashed potatoes going forgotten.

"But if it's compliments you want, may I just say that this steak is cooked to perfection, and is just as good"—raised eyebrows from Sandra—"nay, I say *better*, than anything I've barbecued in all our years together."

"Better. You may take first base tonight."

Milton's eyebrows bobbed up and down. "Baby, I may not be able to walk, but these elbows will drag me all the way to home plate if you let me."

"It wasn't that good a compliment."

"Denied!" laughed Acton, taking a drink of his wine.

Niskha giggled, swallowing her potatoes then her own drink of grape juice.

The phone rang and Sandra rose. "Excuse me." She stepped into the kitchen. "It's Tom. Do you want to call him back?"

Milton's eyes narrowed slightly as he checked his watch. "You better take it, he never calls at this time."

Acton wiped his mouth with his napkin. "Where's your brother now?"

"Hong Kong. His job has him all over the place. He said he's thinking of quitting, though. He never gets to see his family and his son has barely said a word to him in a year."

Acton frowned. "That's not good. How old is he now? Must be eighteen? Nineteen?"

"Eighteen. Just graduated." Milton turned in his chair, listening to Sandra as she talked to his brother, returning to the dining room.

"Here, I'll put him on." She handed her husband the phone.

"Hey, Tom, how are ya?"

Milton listened, grunting several times as his eyes widened with each passing moment. "Are you sure?" More one-sided conversation then a crestfallen expression. "I-I don't know what I can do. I'm in this damned chair. You know if I wasn't I'd help you out, but—" Milton's chin dropped to his chest and he closed his eyes, the hint of a tear forming in the corner. Sandra reached over and put a hand on his arm, squeezing gently.

"What's wrong, dear?"

"Tom, let me think about this, I'm going to call you back."

He ended the call and drew a deep breath, exhaling with a loud sigh. He wiped his eyes dry and looked at his wife, patting her hand. "It's Jason. He's run away and apparently joined some white-supremacist group or something."

Sandra gasped and Acton's eyebrows popped. He had met Jason on several occasions, a nice young boy who had withdrawn from those around him over the past few years, as many teenagers were apt to do. And with his father rarely home, life had only grown more difficult. Milton talked of the young man often, and how his brother and sister-in-law were at their wits' end as to what to do with him. And if Tom was looking to quit his *very* lucrative job, then things must truly be bad.

"A white-supremacist group? Did he ever show any signs of that?"

Milton shrugged. "Not that I know of. Certainly nothing Tom or Mel mentioned." He pushed his plate away.

"What's Tom going to do?" asked Sandra, Niskha now in her lap, her happy smile replaced with one of concern as the adults' mood changed.

"There's nothing he can do. He's stuck in Hong Kong and can't get a flight for two days, apparently there's some sort of festival and everything's booked." Milton stared at his legs. "He asked me to help." His voice cracked. "But I can't."

Niskha squirmed from her mother's lap and climbed in her dad's, hugging him. "It's okay, Daddy, don't cry."

That was the catalyst triggering a single, uncharacteristic sob from Acton's friend, and at that moment he knew how helpless the crippled man felt. He had always kept a positive attitude through his ordeal, though Acton had no clue how his friend was in his private moments. He could only imagine how the man felt, unable to act to help his only brother and his only nephew.

"I'll go."

Milton wiped his cheeks, kissing the top of his daughter's head. "Sorry, what did you say?"

"I'll go. Jason knows me, maybe I can reason with him."

Milton shook his head. "No, it could be dangerous. These are white supremacists. They might kill you."

Acton grinned. "After what I went through last year, I'm bulletproof."

"Apparently I'm not."

"Ha ha. Call your brother back, tell him to email you all the information he has then I'll go see if I can find Jason and talk some sense into him."

Milton's shoulders dropped, a sigh escaping as he closed his eyes, nodding slowly. He looked at his friend.

"Thank you."

Interrogation Room 1, Southeast District Police Headquarters
Kashirskoye Street, Moscow, Russian Federation

The interrogation room at the Southeast District Police Headquarters would have horrified any tourist unfortunate enough to find themselves in it. A single incandescent bulb burned hot in the center of the room, its cheap shade serving to focus the light down over the lone table. The table, made from a sturdy oak, was a fixture in the station house for years. Hit with weapons, fists, prisoners' heads, and more, tossed over and thrown on too many occasions to count, pockmarks, splinters, and chips now covered its surface. The times it was broken, the men at the precinct would repair it rather than have it replaced. It had been there as long as the precinct had been, and it brought them good luck. More cases broke at that table than any other in Moscow. Whether true or not was irrelevant, but it was the story they told the rookies, and the myth was perpetuated. It had been there so many decades the story very well might be true by now.

Yakovski was handcuffed, sitting in an uncomfortable metal chair, staring at the floor. He raised his foot and dropped it on a cockroach unfortunate enough to pass within his field of vision. He twisted his boot, grinding the insect into the filth-covered floor, its original color anybody's guess.

Agent Dymovsky watched the proceedings through the two-way mirror. They had run the man's fingerprints and confirmed he was Yakovski. Dymovsky had refamiliarized himself with the man's military history, the last information they had on him. In August 1991, he had disappeared along with the rest of his unit from 1985, never to be seen again.

This one will be tough to crack.

Dymovsky left and paused before the door to the interrogation room. He took a deep breath and raised his hand before dropping it on the handle, yanking the door open quickly. If he had hoped to startle

Yakovski, it hadn't worked. In fact, Yakovski didn't budge, giving no outward sign he was even aware Dymovsky had entered.

Dymovsky walked around the table and laid out his files deliberately, taking his time, saying nothing. Finally done, he sat down across from Yakovski, leaning back in his chair as he folded his arms, then stared.

This continued for ten straight minutes. Dymovsky didn't move, didn't say anything. Yakovski, slowly sobering up, fidgeted, using the nail of one thumb to pick those on his opposite hand clean.

Dymovsky abruptly leaned forward and flipped open one of the files. "Boris Yakovski, born September 23, 1958, in Morshansk, Russia. Parents Mikhail and Devora, both deceased. Only child. Joined the Soviet Army on September 23, 1974, your sixteenth birthday I see, Service Number 3-741187, served with distinction in Afghanistan, Angola, and Ethiopia until disappearing August 21, 1991." Dymovsky glanced up from the file. "Interesting date that. Not happy with Mr. Yeltsin?"

No reaction.

"I have here a mission report," continued Dymovsky as he opened another file and placed it in front of him. "This is from July 23, 1985, filed by Colonel Grigori Trubitsin, Major at the time. Would you like me to read it?"

The fidgeting had stopped. Yakovski shrugged.

Got you!

"Very well, I won't. There's no need. Both you and I know it's a fabrication."

Yakovski was now still.

"Well, perhaps not a *complete* fabrication. You *did* successfully 'spoof the TACAN' as they call it, shoot down a US Air Force FB-111F fighter-bomber, kill the crew when they tried to resist, and recover invaluable technology for Mother Russia. Do you deny this?"

A slight smile flashed for a brief instant on Yakovski's face.

"I see you don't." Dymovsky closed the file and placed it back on the stack he had taken it from. He picked up another file and placed it in front of him, but didn't open it. "The problem with this report is that it is incomplete."

No smile this time.

Is that vein in his neck throbbing harder than it was a minute ago?

"We both know that you recovered a nuclear weapon and didn't report it."

It looked like the vein would burst through the skin at any moment.

"You recovered this missile, failed to report it, and just recently, acquired the arming code."

Yakovski sat still, the only movement the vein.

"You orchestrated the theft of this code, and knowing the Americans were closing in, deliberately betrayed one of our spy networks in the United States in order to have the code transported back without trying to transmit it electronically where it might be detected and blocked."

Yakovski glanced up, briefly making eye contact, then stared at the door.

This last part Dymovsky had made up, but it was a likely guess. The Americans said the code was stolen, and Yakovski was seen exiting a hotel Anya Kushchenko had entered minutes before. Dymovsky didn't believe in coincidences.

Yakovski tilted his head toward him, revealing the long scar occupying much of the left side of his face. "When do I get my phone call?" he snarled.

Dymovsky laughed. "You watch too many American TV shows." He pushed his chair out, stood, then left the room, quickly returning to the observation room where several watched. Yakovski had resumed staring at the floor, giving no indication anything from the last few minutes bothered him.

"Thoughts?" asked Dymovsky as he stared at his adversary.

"I don't think you'll break him, sir. He's not the type."

"Da," agreed another. "He's ex-army. A sergeant. They are the toughest of the tough."

Dymovsky nodded. "Agreed, we can't scare him or threaten him with anything. He has no family and we don't even know where he lives. Taking his freedom away means he wins. He knows we need that missile and he knows he's our only lead."

"What are you going to do, sir?"

Dymovsky remained silent as he stared at the man on the other side of the glass.

"We let him go."

Alamut, Persia
December 15, 1256 AD

"It is time."

Hassassin warriors filled the chamber, dressed from head to toe in black robes, their faces, normally covered, bared without fear among their brothers. Many showed the scars of long ago, even more revealed the fresh wounds of a bloody, hopeless battle, a battle they knew they could not win. They turned as one to face the Grand Headmaster of the Hassassin Order, Ruknuddin Khurshah, who stood on a raised platform at the head of the chamber.

The battle hadn't gone well. It had raged for almost a month, the Mongol hordes surrounding them unleashing never-ending volleys from their ballistae and scorpion siege weapons. The enemy hadn't had the courage to fight the Hassassin man to man, instead relying on the weapons of cowards. The Hassassin had killed many, but so outnumbered, it was clear in the end there would be no victory.

Faisal had fought by the side of his master, Hasni, never flinching, never questioning his orders. He did what he was told, participating in nighttime raiding parties, sometimes to take prisoners for interrogation, other times to silently kill the enemy while they slept in their tents, sowing fear among them. Despite the success of these missions, the numbers they faced remained too great, and they all knew it.

"It is time to think of the future, rather than the present." Grand Headmaster Khurshah's voice was strong, firm, reassuring—but tired. Though exhausted, their pride had never wavered—not for an instant. Faisal glanced at Hasni, his master's chin held high, a slight smile evident as he gazed upon the man who had trained him years before. Faisal wondered what was going through his master's mind. Did he feel fear? Did he feel desperation? Did he *feel?* He rarely revealed any emotion except anger, and that was usually when an order wasn't followed, or he was in the thick of battle. But this thin smile, this hint of pride, was the first sense of emotion Faisal had seen that made Hasni seem less than super-human.

"This battle will be lost. This battle will be lost though we will continue to fight, for we are Hassassin, and surrender is not an option." Nods of assent spread among the gathered throngs of rugged warriors. "The Mongols claim they will let us live if we simply surrender. We know that to be a lie. The Mongols are without honor, without courage. The moment we lay down our arms, they will slaughter us. There is not a man here who fears death, there is not a man here who would not die for the Order, die for his beliefs, die for Allah."

More murmurs filled the room then someone screamed, "Allahu Akbar!" The room erupted into a roar, the entire crowd chanting "Allahu Akbar!" at the top of their lungs, fists pumping.

Faisal's chest swelled with religious ardor as his own fist punched the air in defiance of the hordes outside the walls. "Allahu Akbar!"

Khurshah raised both hands and quieted the crowd, bowing slightly. "And it is in the name of Allah that we must make the next sacrifice. For death is not to be feared, for Jannah awaits all those who sacrifice themselves in service to Allah. However, death of the Order is not acceptable. To maintain balance between Islam and Christianity, the Order must survive. And for the Order to survive, some of you in this room must survive."

Faisal looked around him. He was the youngest there, the last to have passed the rigorous testing, the last to have gone through the Rite of Initiation, or as it was called among the select few in the room who knew the truth, the Ritual of the False Jannah. Over the past days of fighting, he had come to understand the reasoning behind it, to realize the genius behind it, and he no longer felt betrayed. He had come to accept it, to romanticize it, romanticize it to the point where part of him was now convinced it had indeed been real, and it warmed his heart to know the wonder of Jannah, in reality, must be far greater than any fantasy created by man. He knew when he died, should he be granted entry to Jannah, it would be even more wonderful than the few moments he had experienced.

And his time would come shortly, for he was the youngest and had no reason to expect to be among those who would survive. Why should he? He knew little of the Order, of its ways. How could he, one so young, be expected to continue the Order? Yes, he was well trained, but he lacked experience, experience the rest in the room had in abundance. He looked at Hasni and his heart turned heavy as he thought of how little time he had left to learn from his master.

"I have decided that to survive, those who remain must be swift of foot, strong in mind and body. And it is for this reason that I will remain here, with the defenders, to delay the Mongol hordes for as long as we can, while younger men make their escape to preserve the Order."

The room filled with cries of outrage, of disappointment, shouts of "No! Not you master!" echoing off the stone walls. Their grief was palpable, the dismay on their faces speaking more than their words could convey. Faisal shouted with them, and a glance at Hasni shocked him as he watched a tear roll down the weathered face, leaving a trail in the dirt and dust caked upon its cheek.

Khurshah again raised his hands. "My heart leaps with your outpouring, but I am old, and will only slow you down. There is one among us who can take my place, and who will lead to safety those that have been chosen to preserve the Order."

The crowd looked around at each other, and one near the front raised his head, looking up at their leader. "Grand Headmaster, who among us is worthy enough to take your place?"

The room fell silent, all eyes on Khurshah, whose eyes slowly surveyed the audience then settled on Faisal. Faisal gulped.

Why is he looking at me?

Khurshah descended the platform steps and walked toward Faisal. The thick crowd parted to let him pass, all eyes turning to see who the successor would be. Faisal took a slight step to the side, shifting behind his master.

Khurshah paused in front of Hasni. Hasni bowed his head, his master returning the gesture, and then taking Hasni by the hand, he

65

turned to face the crowd. "Brother Hasni will be your new Grand Headmaster. Honor him with loyalty as you have honored me over the years. Let us all put our faith in him, and in Allah, to preserve the Order. All hail your new master!"

The crowd erupted in applause and cheers, shouts of "Allahu Akbar!" again filled the chamber. Faisal joined in, reveling in the fact it was *his* master who was now the master to all, and embarrassed that for a moment he had thought Khurshah was speaking of him. He patted Hasni on the back as the crowd surrounded their new and old masters, their troubles beyond the walls momentarily forgotten.

Cellblock C, Southeast District Police Headquarters
Kashirskoye Street, Moscow, Russian Federation
Present Day

"Hey! Wake up!"

The cot Yakovski was sleeping on shook again. He opened his eyes and stared up through the fog of the first glance at a new day, and a hangover, made all the worse by the bright light in the middle of the small cell he was transferred to after the interrogation.

His interrogator kicked the cot again. "Wake up, unless you want to stay here!"

"Da, da, I'm up, I'm up," he mumbled as he swung his stiff legs from the cot to the floor. He stretched and looked around.

"Come on, I haven't got all damned day to wait for you!"

He eyed the cop. "Dymovsky, wasn't it? Did you ever serve?" He smiled slightly. "You must have, you have balls of steel."

Dymovsky nodded. "Chechnya."

Yakovski's eyes opened slightly wider. "Now that's a place I'd like to have gone to."

Dymovsky frowned at him. "I don't know anyone who'd want to go there."

Yakovski stood and faced him. "That's because you don't know anyone who likes to kill camel jockeys!" Yakovski laughed heartily then coughed.

I need vodka.

"What time is it?"

"Time for you to go."

"What?"

"You're free to go."

Yakovski smiled, knowing he was being played. "Really? Do you think I'm stupid?"

Dymovsky yawned. "Listen, I just follow orders. I was told to let you go, so I let you go. If you want me to ask again, because believe me, I asked them to confirm the order several times, then I will."

Now *that* story Yakovski did buy. Someone, somewhere, had pulled strings. He could only think of the Colonel, but wasn't sure how he would have found out about the arrest. He seemed to know everything, though, so it was possible. "Nyet, let's go."

Dymovsky led him from the cell and down the long corridor leading out of the cellblock. He rapped on the metal door at the end. A small window slid open and the officer on the other side glanced around before nodding then shutting it. The door opened and they stepped through to the main control area.

One man Yakovski recognized from the arrest the night before stood there, his steeled jaw and glaring eyes telling him he was not happy about the situation.

"I can't believe we're letting this piece of garbage go."

"Orders," said Dymovsky firmly.

"Yes, but—"

Dymovsky cut him off, pointing at a brown manila envelope. "Is that his stuff?"

The man nodded and handed it to Yakovski. He looked inside, taking a quick inventory. "Don't I get my gun back?"

The man's fists clenched into balls and his face turned Soviet red. Dymovsky shoved Yakovski forward before he got belted, herding him toward the exit. "Don't push your luck. We have orders to release you, not what condition to release you in."

Yakovski kept his mouth shut, not feeling like a beating today, not before a healthy dose of vodka.

Dymovsky opened the door in front of him then shoved Yakovski out into the cool morning air. "Now piss off!" He slammed the door shut.

Yakovski looked around the alley he was in, got his bearings, then headed toward the street. He wasn't an idiot. Even if there were orders to release him, he would be followed or tracked somehow.

Now it was time to lose them.

Knoxville, Tennessee

Edison Cole sat in a green and white lawn chair, manufactured long after it went out of style, the plastic lattice torn, faded and stained by years of abuse. But it was American made.

Built tough.

He sat with three of his trusted advisors in the back room of a rented warehouse, a staging area for the upcoming action. Beyond the tin and frosted glass walls, the bustle of activity could be heard as the men prepared for the next phase of the operation. He re-read the email he had received then snapped his laptop shut, a stack of milk cartons it sat atop, swaying. "They're up to something."

"What?" asked Charlie Parker, the man who had recruited him into New Slate twelve years ago and now his second-in-command.

"This is too easy."

"Easy?" Chip McConnell yelped. "Are you kidding me? The amount of hoops we've had to jump through with these Rooskies and now these goddamned pull-starts has been ridiculous!"

Cole smiled. Chip was extremely excitable at the best of times. "Easy, Chip, or you'll burst a blood vessel before you get to see that beeyewteeful mushroom cloud."

Chip laughed, his face dropping a couple of shades of red. "Sorry, Ed. You know me, I just can't stand any of these sonsabitches, especially those commie bastards. As far as I'm concerned, Moscow's a good enough target."

Cole chuckled. "One problem at a time, one problem at a time!" He sat forward, the chair's metal frame squeaking loudly. "In all seriousness, them wanting two of their people at the exchange is a problem."

"Why? Two sandtards should be easy to deal with," said Mitch Fawcett, their computer and communications expert.

"It's not that. It's the fact that there are only two."

70

Chip nodded. "You were expecting more?"

"If I had just agreed to hand over twenty-five million dollars to shady arms dealers I had done business with only a few times, I would be insisting on a lot more of my men at the delivery site."

Parker stood and stretched, his chicken and ribs enhanced rear momentarily sticking in the chair before his legs popped it off. "Part of me thinks we just take the twenty-five mil and use it here at home."

Chip's eyes widened. "You kidding me? And miss the chance to go to war with these sons-a-bitches?" He looked at Cole. "You're not considering this, are you?"

Cole shook his head. "No, this is too great an opportunity. In fact, it's a once in a lifetime opportunity. When have we ever, throughout history, had a chance to destroy a religion, in one push of a button?"

"Metaphorically, of course," said Parker. He turned to Chip. "Don't worry, Chip, I'm completely on board. I just get frustrated when we're so close to the end game."

"We all are," agreed Cole. "But when we're finished, we'll be running on adrenaline for the next twenty years as we mop up the mess."

"So when's their little shin-dig over there start?"

"October."

Inebolu Sokak Street, Istanbul, Turkey

"The weapon is in play."

Abdullah bin Saqr hung up the phone and leaned back in his chair, surveying his office and the artifacts lining its walls. Mounted on the far wall, as it had been for over five hundred years, was the sword used by the first Grand Headmaster when he conquered Alamut, the fortress that housed the Order of the Assassins for over 150 years, a battle that shed no blood, the conquerors hailed as heroes by their Ismaili brethren. Several of the original texts salvaged before the Mongol hordes sacked and burned the great library in Alamut, sat on pedestals, encased in vacuum-sealed glass, others entombed below the complex, protected from all manners of damage.

The revered Grand Headmaster Hasni bin Saeed Al-Maktoum, who had led a small band of the Order to survive the Mongol onslaught, had continued the teachings of the great Sabbah and had led the Order in secrecy for almost thirty years. His pupil and trusted companion, Faisal bin Sabah, succeeded him as Grand Headmaster, and the Order had survived, constantly moving, constantly keeping the ancient beliefs alive from generation to generation, continually spreading through society, and eventually making their headquarters in Istanbul.

The great city spanning the Sea of Marmara, separating Christian Europe from Muslim Asia, was a symbolic home, and a safe home, from where they could play their part in maintaining the balance between the world's two greatest, and conflicted, religions. The balance between Islam and Christianity had to be maintained until both sets of adherents could learn to live as one. And now one of the greatest threats to that balance needed to be faced head-on and defeated without mercy.

The weapon is in play.

One of their agents, a recent convert, had provided them with invaluable intelligence using the American's own Echelon system. They knew about the weapon, they knew about New Slate. And they knew something the Americans didn't. They knew where New Slate was getting the money to purchase the weapon.

From the Hassassins themselves.

Knoxville, Tennessee

"Crusade! Crusade! Crusade!"

The roar of the crowd filled Edison Cole's ears. The rush of adrenaline at the excitement of hearing several hundred men chanting, arms extended in salute, salute to him, gave him goose bumps. His heart thumped as he smiled back at them, his head nodding in approval. He let the chant continue for another minute before raising his hands to silence them. He leaned forward and gripped the podium edge with both hands.

"My friends, the Muslim scourge on our land must come to an end. It *is* them or us. There is no in between. Peaceful coexistence? We tried that. And what did we get in return? Nine-eleven!"

"Death to Islam!"

The crowd roared in approval at the spontaneous outburst from the back of the crowd.

Cole smiled. "Indeed. Death to Islam. I'm just as sick and tired as you are of hearing these fanatics yelling 'Death to America' day after day, night after night. And what do our politicians do about it? Nothing! Free speech? Bullshit! What about our freedom to exist? Our freedom to exist as free men? Free men who can say and do what we want, when we want, without government interference? If these camel jockeys had their way, our women would be wearing burqas and we'd have to bow down and pray to their *Allah* five times a day!" The crowd laughed at the way he drew out the word. "Their nutbar Imam's would be screeching their hate over speakers throughout our country, and if we stood up to them, our women, our sons, our daughters—we—we would all be slaughtered under the sword of Islam, all in the name of peace!" He paused to take a breath as his words sank in, then lowered his voice.

"Did you know that a recent survey of Muslims found ninety percent of them wanted to live in peace with us? Sounds pretty good,

74

huh?" A few guffaws burst from the audience. "Good, I'm glad to see some of you get what the sheep leading our country don't. If ninety percent want to live in peace, then that means ten percent don't. And there's a billion of those bastards out there. That means one hundred million of them want us dead, want our way of life wiped from the face of the earth, want to take us back with them to the goddamned Dark Ages!" His voice was now a fevered pitch, his face red with anger, the veins throbbing on his neck and temples threatening to burst through the skin. "I say enough is enough! It is time to act! Time to act to preserve our way of life before it is taken away from us while our government watches, tail between their legs, concerned only with political correctness, a political correctness that if this scum had their way, would be tossed to the wayside."

He sucked in a lungful of air as he gazed out at the throng, now as angry as him, some punching their palms with a clenched fist, others as red as he felt, their anger palpable.

If one of those bastards came in here now, he'd be torn to shreds.

He smiled. "But what can we do?" he asked quietly, shrugging.

"Kill 'em all!"

Thunderous applause erupted and they chanted, "Kill 'em all! Kill 'em all!"

Cole smiled and shook his head, raising his arms. The crowd drew silent. "As much as I'd love to kill every last one of those sons of bitches, that would take too long." He chuckled and smiled, leaning forward with one elbow on the podium. "Besides, I don't think we have enough bullets."

The crowd roared in laughter.

"I'll make 'em!"

The crowd laughed harder, the man who said it getting ribbed by the people around him. Cole laughed and stood straight.

"And I'll help you," he said, still laughing. Then his face became serious. He leaned forward again. "No, my friends, we don't need to kill them all." He leaned even closer to the microphone, his knuckles whitening as he gripped the podium. "We need to kill their faith." He

75

lowered his voice until it was almost a whisper. The crowd leaned forward in anticipation. "And I know how we're going to do it."

Professor James Acton sat near the back of the packed hall, his fist pumping the air with the others as he cheered, despite the sickening pit forming in his stomach. The hatred spewing from the leader of New Slate, Edison Cole, was uncomfortable to say the least. He personally had no problem with Islam, though he had serious problems with Islamic fundamentalism, something he considered distinctly different. While he wasn't sure how Islam in its current state could peacefully coexist with anyone, he could never believe that an all-out war like Cole espoused was the solution to anything.

But that was neither here nor there. He wasn't here to be informed or misinformed, he was here to make contact with young Jason Milton, his best friend's nephew. After last night's phone call, they had put Niskha to bed, then the three of them hit the Internet, researching everything they could on New Slate, discovering mostly hate filled propaganda websites, but little more. They were headquartered in Knoxville and appeared unconcerned if people knew where they were located. In fact, their website invited corrupt government officials to join them for their weekly meetings.

Perhaps you'll learn something.

The weekly gathering was today, so a flight had been booked along with a hotel room, it less than 24 hours since the desperate phone call from Milton's brother. They were counting on Jason being in the crowd, but Acton hadn't spotted him yet and was growing concerned. The gathering was far bigger than they had anticipated, which in itself was tragic, but more critically, the crowd made it hard to spot Jason.

A boy—or young man—he hadn't seen in a couple of years, who may look completely different now, there a lot of tattoos and shaved heads among those gathered.

And a lot of completely average looking people, including black, white, Hispanic and Asian.

It was a cross section of America who ate up the continued rantings from the front of the room.

There he is!

Jason was in the front row, Acton spotting him a near miracle, the boy having turned to look behind him for a moment.

A moment that to Acton suggested fear in the boy's eyes.

It gave him hope.

If Jason were scared, if he were here against his will, then he may not have to convince the boy to leave, instead only give him the opportunity. He glanced around the room, the exits all guarded with men who would look equally at home in a biker bar as they would here.

And they all had guns.

You're in over your head on this one.

His stint in the National Guard had trained him decently. He knew how to use a gun and was a pretty good shot, but he had no weapon and was hopelessly outgunned even if he did.

This would take finesse with a little luck.

But first Jason had to know he was there so that he'd act when opportunity struck.

The rant ended, sending everyone to their feet, some rushing toward the stage to shake Cole's hand.

This is it!

He pressed forward with a forced smile, his eyes wide to match the zeal of the others, but glued to Jason who stood halfheartedly clapping. Acton pushed out of the aisle and down a row of chairs behind the boy, clapping hard as he stared up at Cole and the other leaders on the stage, inching his way past the throng.

Jason turned and their eyes met.

And then there was true fear.

Jason shook his head rapidly, catching himself before turning away. The boy was scared and had warned him off.

But now he knew help was here.

Cole left the stage and the crowd quickly broke up, Jason led to a back exit, Acton leaving through the front. He climbed in his Chevy

Equinox rental, his phone to his ear to allay any suspicions, his rearview mirror on the front of the building. It was a seedy area of town from all outward appearances, and he was tempted to call the police, but for what? The meeting was over, those with the guns probably gone or all packing permits, and Jason, if he was that scared, likely to deny being held.

His heart slammed as he saw the boy exit the building with two men, all three climbing into a pickup truck. The engine roared to life and pulled away from the curb, executing a quick U-turn before thundering away, its custom pipes designed to annoy. Acton followed, keeping a good distance, the traffic light and the roar of the truck distinct. They were quickly out of town, and as he was painfully aware, getting farther from help should he need it.

Headlights blazed in his rearview mirror, filling the cabin. He squinted, looking in his side mirror to see a truck behind him, lit up like a ballpark, a large array of lights blaring at him from a roof rack.

Then they rammed him.

He swerved, his backend fishtailing as he struggled to keep control. He had been made, that much was obvious. Whoever New Slate was, they were good, they having spotted him at some point during the evening. And now they meant to have a conversation.

Or worse.

He glanced ahead at the truck carrying Jason and cursed, its brake lights on as it came to a halt.

They're going to box you in.

He was hit from behind again, but this time he anticipated it, hammering on the gas and receiving a love tap compared to the first hit. He swerved to the right, the truck matching his move. He jerked the wheel to the left and slammed on his brakes, straightening out as the truck behind him blew past, sideswiping him. He put it in reverse and rapidly backed away, then jerked the wheel to the right, hitting the brakes. He shoved it in gear and floored it.

He checked his rearview mirror and watched the two vehicles fade into the distance, they apparently not interested in pursuing him. He eased off the gas, bringing himself down to just above the speed limit as the lights of Knoxville came into view.

And wondered if he had made things worse for Jason.

Ochotny Riad Shopping Center
Red Square, Moscow, Russian Federation

Yakovski closed the changing room door and quickly stripped naked. He sat down on the bench, pulled on a pair of black socks, then stood and removed all the tags from a pair of Levis. He put them on, sans underwear. Buttoning then zipping the fly, he cleaned a t-shirt of its tags and yanked it down over his neck. He stuffed his arms in the sleeves, tugged the cheap cotton-polyester blend over his torso, then shoved his feet in a pair of sneakers he had tried on moments before. He bundled up his old clothes and placed them in a shopping bag, depositing his watch, wallet, and cigarettes, including his prize lighter he had taken off an East German Colonel in a poker game in Dresden over 25 years ago. He left nothing to chance, knowing they could have planted a tracking device on anything. He fetched an FC Spartak Moskva ball cap from the bench and pulled it over the top of his head as he gazed in the mirror. He yanked it off, molded the brim with his hands into a gentle curve, then with one hand gripping the brim, the other the back, drew it into place. He smiled in the mirror, satisfied.

Ladykiller!

He unlocked the changing room door then opened it slightly. Then he waited. He was sure he was watched entering the store and was certain only one of the two men tailing him had followed. And if he knew his quarry, they would be watching the door like a hawk. And an open door begged investigation. It would be irresistible.

Is he still in there? Did I miss him?

Yakovski pictured what must be going through their minds. He stood, back to the wall behind the door, and waited. It took a few minutes before it moved slightly, then a little more, a hand wrapping around the edge of the door.

Yakovski reached forward and seized the hand, yanking his pursuer inside then pushing the door shut with his knee. He placed the man in a chokehold, cutting off the flow of oxygen, the man's struggles soon becoming weak, and in less than a minute, he was unconscious.

Yakovski tied the man's hands and feet with his old pants and shirt, then with some satisfaction, stuffed his old socks into the man's mouth. Peering out the door, he saw no one. He took up a position near the entrance, out of sight, and waited for the second tail to check on his partner. It took only five minutes before he saw a man casually stroll in with an anxious look. Yakovski ducked behind a rack of women's slacks, then as soon as the man entered the changing room area, slipped out the front door of the shop and into the throng of shoppers.

Bulgakov Hotel
Moscow, Russian Federation

Trubitsin lay on the hotel bed, halfway through a cigarette and his morning coffee, feeling totally relaxed. He loved morning sex. Two bodies, barely awake, no kissing, none of the foreplay or intimacy two fully awake lovers demanded. This was basic. Primal. Instinctual. The rawness of it was a pleasure in itself. No tricks, no pressure, just plain old teenage style sex. Get in there, do your business, get out.

He looked over at Anya, sleeping softly beside him, her naked body half covered by the sheet, her left leg draped over his. He ran his eyes over her form and a little life sprang back into Grigori, Jr. He chuckled and turned, stubbing his cigarette out.

Where the hell is Yakovski?

As if on cue, the hotel phone rang. Anya stirred and rolled off him, turning away from the phone. He swung his legs out of bed and grabbed the black, rotary style phone dating from Breshnev's days as Chairman. He picked up the receiver and held it to his ear. "Da."

"We've been compromised."

Trubitsin's heart thumped as adrenaline raced through his veins. "Da. Plan Foxtrot." He hung up the phone, quietly got out of bed, and began to dress. Anya rolled over.

"Who was that?"

"Yakovski."

"Problem?"

"Da. They found us."

She propped her pillow against the headboard and shuffled her body to a sitting position. "They probably followed me here."

"No doubt." He looked around for his shirt.

Anya pointed behind a nearby chair. "Over there, darling."

"Thanks." He picked it up off the floor and shoved his arms in then quickly buttoned it up. Finished, he slipped on his pants, socks and shoes, tossed his few belongings into a carry-on bag, then returned to the bed, climbing on with one knee and positioning himself in front of her. "It's best if we aren't seen together." He kissed her then pushed up off the bed.

"I understand. Where shall I meet you?"

"Cyprus, as discussed." He headed to the door.

"Bye, darling, it's been fun!"

Trubitsin smiled at her, peered out the peephole and opened the door carefully. He glanced out into the hallway, and finding it empty, quickly made his way out a little-used employee exit he had scouted months before.

Knoxville, Tennessee

Acton looked both ways, the alley behind the New Slate building empty, though any number of homeless could be hidden under the copious amounts of trash that littered the failed commercial area. He had dumped the rental and took a taxi to his hotel last night, renting a new vehicle this morning before setting up camp across the street.

Then waited.

Jason had arrived a few minutes ago, a steady stream of men having entered the building during the time he watched. From what he could see, nobody was using the rear, so he had taken a chance. Milton was waiting at home by his phone, and if Acton didn't call his friend back within ten minutes, the police were to be called.

Milton wasn't happy and had told him so. "This is too dangerous. Let's leave it to the police."

"If we do, and he's too scared to tell them the truth, it could get him killed. The boy is terrified and he needs help."

Milton sighed. "It's not your job to help him. You're not even family."

Acton had to admit that hurt a bit. "Funny, I've always considered *you* family."

"You know what I mean. You're like a brother to me, hell, I'm closer to you than my own brother, you know that. But you barely know Jason, and it should be me there, not you."

And that was exactly why Acton was there, because his friend was in a wheelchair, and it was *his* fault. If he hadn't discovered that damned artifact, none of what had happened would have occurred. His friend would be walking, his students would be alive, and he wouldn't be the one standing here.

And you never would have met Laura.

He loved that woman. Hard. And of all that had happened, all the death and mayhem and terror, it was the only good thing to have come of it all. But he would trade his happiness in a heartbeat for all those lives.

Yet that was beyond his control.

And *this* wasn't.

He was here, his friend trapped in a wheelchair, and a boy, barely a man, was trapped on the other side of the door he now jimmied open.

He listened, the door open slightly, but heard nothing. Opening the door all the way, he stepped inside, closing it behind him, then quickly ducked behind a stack of boxes, continuing to listen. Sounds of men working deeper inside the building echoed down the short hall he found himself in, but nothing else.

A door creaked to his right and his heart leaped into his throat. He ducked lower, peering out to see someone exit a bathroom.

It was Jason.

"Psst!"

Jason spun as Acton stepped out from his hiding place, the boy's eyes bulging. He looked around then tiptoed over to Acton.

"Uncle Jim, what are you doing here?"

"Your Uncle Greg sent me. I'm here to get you out."

Jason shook his head emphatically. "I can't leave, they'll kill me."

"Why?"

"I overheard a conversation my first week here that I shouldn't have." He tossed a glance at the bathroom. "In there. Now they say I can't leave until after they do."

"When's that?"

"October."

Acton shook his head. "No, we can't wait, and besides, you don't know if they'll actually let you go. Your uncle and your dad want you out, now. They're worried sick about you."

Jason grunted. "My dad hasn't worried about me in years."

Acton put a hand on the boy's shoulder, the pain in his eyes obvious. "That's not true. Your dad's on his way back from Hong Kong right now, and he's going to quit his job so he can spend more time with you."

85

"Hey, where the hell are you!"

Jason paled, spinning toward the shouted voice. "J-just tying my shoe, be right there!" He turned back toward Acton, pushing him toward the rear door. "You've gotta go, now, before they catch you." He paused, his eyes glistening. "Tell my mom—and my dad—I'm sorry. I screwed up."

Boots pounding on concrete echoed in the hall and Acton yanked open the door. He reached for Jason, to pull him out with him, but the boy avoided his hand and stepped back, rounding the corner and disappearing.

"What the hell are you doing?"

"I thought I heard something."

Acton closed the door carefully behind him then sprinted for a nearby garbage bin, ducking behind it, his back pressed against the filthy metal. The stench was almost overwhelming, in fact it was, as he sucked in lungful after lungful. He peered around the corner and saw the door close, Jason's captor obviously having looked to check out his story.

I'm going to have to force him to leave.

He shook his head, his lips pursed. These men were armed and dangerous, and yes, he could get his own gun, but he was still outnumbered, and it would be illegal.

He looked at a Coke bottle lying on the ground beside him.

And smiled.

Briefing Room A, Southeast District Police Headquarters
Kashirskoye Street, Moscow, Russian Federation

"Are you kidding me? It hasn't even been an hour!"

The men mumbled their apologies, their heads hung so low in shame they threatened to tumble to the floor they stared at. Agent Dymovsky glared at one and then the other, not sure which one he was madder at. He shook his head then pointed to the one who was assaulted. "Get yourself checked out, make sure he didn't damage any of the few remaining brain cells you have left. Judging by today's quality of police work, I'd say he may just have cost you your last few."

"Yes, sir." The man left, leaving his partner to take the heat for both.

"And you!"

The man snapped to attention, his eyes longingly following his partner from the office before turning to face Dymovsky. "Yes, sir!"

"You and I, Ivan, will go pick up Anya Kushchenko. There's no way that is a coincidence."

"Yes, sir!"

Dymovsky headed for the door and pointed at three uniforms sitting at their desks. "Come with us."

They drove to the hotel in two cars, and mostly silence. As they pulled up, Ivan cleared his throat as if he had something to say.

"What is it?" asked Dymovsky.

"Well, sir, should we be doing this? I mean, isn't she FSB's responsibility?"

"And what if she is?"

"Well, sir, won't they be mad?"

"Most likely."

Ivan gulped and with a hint of panic in his voice, whispered, "But you don't want to piss those people off, sir! You're liable to end up in Siberia!"

Dymovsky brought the car to a halt and threw open the door. He glanced back at his scared underling. "My orders come from higher than you can possibly imagine."

Ivan's eyes shot up at this, seeming to rid him of some of his fear. They climbed from the car and headed to the hotel entrance. Joined by the other three men, he ordered two to the back of the hotel, one to remain at the front, and he and Ivan entered the lobby. Dymovsky strode up to the desk clerk and flashed his badge. "Agent Alexey Dymovsky, Prosecutor-General's Office. What room is she in?"

The desk clerk stared at him, a look of terror that reminded Dymovsky of what the old days must have been like, and how much of their hard-fought progress had been lost. "Wh-who do you mean?" The clerk's hands gripped the counter in front of him.

Dymovsky leaned in. "You know who I mean."

The man trembled. "Three-fifteen."

Dymovsky smiled. "Thank you."

He strode to the elevator, Ivan following, and rode to the third floor, silently anticipating what was to come. The bell chimed their arrival and the doors slid slowly open. He stepped out and checked the sign in front indicating 315 was to the left. Three doors down they found the room.

Deciding speed was the safest course of action, he drew his weapon and Ivan did the same. He stepped back then rammed the door with his shoulder, splintering the lock and sending the door flying open. He fell into the room but regained his balance, and with gun drawn, stormed inside.

"Moscow Police, nobody move!" he yelled to what turned out to be an empty room.

"Are we too late?" asked Ivan.

Dymovsky raised his finger for silence. The sound of a shower came from the other side of the room's lone interior door. They took up positions on either side then Dymovsky gripped the doorknob and slowly turned it. He pushed the door open and they both burst into the small bathroom. He stepped toward the shower and yanked the curtain aside, his weapon extended in front of him.

The woman on the other side yelped in surprise, her hand flying to her chest.

"Agent Dymovsky, Prosecutor-General's Office." He raised his badge. "And you are Anya Kushchenko."

She turned to face him, placing both hands on her hips as the water drenched her naked body. "More questions?"

Dymovsky couldn't help but stare. He reached blindly past his gawking younger partner and snatched a towel off the nearby rack. He handed it to her. "Yes, more questions."

She didn't take the towel for a moment, then finally reached down and turned off the shower, wiping the beaded water off her body slowly, sensually, running her hands over each opposite arm then down her chest and over her breasts, all the while staring at Dymovsky. He met her stare, knowing she was trying to make him uncomfortable. It was working, but he wouldn't let it show. He tossed her the towel and snapped his fingers. "Hurry up, we haven't got all day."

Knoxville, Tennessee

Acton gripped the bottle tight as he watched Jason and his two "companions" climb into the pickup truck he had followed the night before. It roared to life and pulled away from the curb.

With the distinct thump of a flat tire filling the still of the evening.

Curses erupted and the truck pulled over, the driver jumping out then slamming his fist against the side panel as he spotted the flat rear tire. He leaned back in. "Hey, kid, you know how to change a tire?"

Acton couldn't hear the reply.

"Well, it's time to learn. Get out here."

The other man climbed out the passenger side and lit a cigarette, nonplussed by the event, the driver making up for it. Cancerman turned his back and Acton stepped forward, emerging from the shadows. He crossed the street as quietly as he could then jammed the mouth of the bottle into the driver's back.

"Move, you die."

The man's hands slowly went up. "Okay, buddy, take it easy." His partner swung around, reaching for what Acton assumed was a gun tucked into his belt.

"Uh-ah, if I see that thing, your friend gets a bullet in the back."

A second set of hands went up.

Acton handed a plastic tie to Jason who stood trembling, his own hands up. "Tie his hands." Jason didn't move. "Now!" Startled, Jason nodded, taking the tie and tightening it around the driver's wrists.

"You're a dead man," said the passenger, rounding the back of the truck. "Both of you."

Acton jammed the bottle harder against the driver's back. "Keep moving and your friend's dead, then so are you."

The man stopped, fuming, a prominent vein in his forehead pulsing rapidly.

Then he smiled.

Something pressed into Acton's back. "I think the only one dying tonight is you."

Acton's heart slammed into his rib cage, his pulse racing even faster than it already was, as he recognized the voice behind him.

Edison Cole.

"Let's see the gun. Slowly."

Acton raised the Coke bottle and Cole laughed, the others joining in when they saw what had been used on them.

"Buddy, you've got balls." Cole flicked his gun toward Jason. "What do you want with him?"

Acton knew he had to play it cool and keep Jason safe. How *he* might keep himself safe, he had no clue. "I'm a friend of the family's. They're worried about him."

Cole grunted. "Well, now they've got two things to be worried about." He raised his weapon and pressed it against the back of Acton's head.

"Listen, they know I'm here, and if I don't check in, the police are going to be all over this place."

Cole shrugged. "So, we've got nothing to hide."

"Really? You don't think they'll be interested in all those guns you were moving in there?"

Cole frowned, stepping back slightly. "How do you know about that?"

"I was in there earlier and took some pictures. Don't worry, they're not on my phone, I uploaded them and my friends have them, just in case I don't leave here safe and sound with Jason." He turned to face Cole. "Kill me, and they get sent to the Feds. Let us go, we forget everything."

Cole reached forward and pulled Acton's wallet out of his pocket. He flipped it open, removing the driver's license. "Well, boys, meet James Acton from St. Paul, Maryland." He stuffed the wallet into his pants then flicked Acton's forehead with the license. "Now I know who you are and where you live, which means I can find your family and friends."

The squawk of a police siren had them all spinning toward the sound, the lights of a squad car flicking on, bathing the entire area in a blue pulsating glow. Cole bolted, the others following, leaving Acton and Jason to deal with their saviors.

"Tell them anything, James Acton, and you're a dead man!"

Cole eased up, there no sign of pursuit, then pointed at Gabriel Atkins. "Call for a ride." Atkins pulled out his phone as Cole contemplated the situation, pacing back and forth, pinching his chin. He spun on the other two. "We should have killed that kid the first damned day he overheard you two idiots talking."

Atkins ended his call. "Five minutes."

Chip McConnell shook his head. "He was just a kid and looked like a promising recruit. We all agreed to just hold him, so don't try and hang this shit on me."

Cole's eyes bored into Chip, his jaw clenched tight as he fought the desire to draw his weapon and remove Chip from his circle of friends.

But he *was* a friend.

They had been through a lot, and they were all instrumental in planning the current mission. He closed his eyes and sucked in a deep breath, blasting it out through his lips. "Who the hell is this James Acton guy?"

Chip shrugged. "Said he was a friend of the family. I'll have one of our FBI contacts run his name."

"Do it."

"What do you want us to do about them? We know where they both live, we could take care of it tomorrow."

Cole shook his head. "No. If we kill them now, they'll know who it was, and we're too close to pulling this off."

"But if he talks, the Feds could come down hard on us."

Cole nodded, a decision made. "Call Jason, tell him his parents are dead if he breathes a word."

"And this Acton guy?"

"Find out who he's close to, then we'll deal with him."

BRASS MONKEY

Interrogation Room 1, Southeast District Police Headquarters
Kashirskoye Street, Moscow, Russian Federation

Agent Dymovsky stared at Anya through the two-way mirror as he waited to be connected to the Minister in charge of his investigation. He had met the man once, when he was given this assignment. "Find the missile, no matter what the cost." Simple, concise. In the old days that would have meant a lot more than it did now, but with the swing back to the old ways over the past few years, he had a lot more leeway than he was willing to take. He was part of the new Russia. He was young when the Soviet Union had collapsed so he had no real memory of it. He had survived the chaos afterward and had vowed to help clean it up so Russia could take its place on the world stage as a free, democratic, strong country. Well, they were barely free, barely democratic, and if it weren't for the price of oil and an aging nuclear stockpile, hardly strong.

And the last thing Russia needed now was a rogue ex-army colonel with an American nuke, selling it on the open market, then having that weapon used in a terrorist attack. The Americans would go public, blaming the Russians, and with the way Russian luck seemed lately, it might just get sold to the Chechens and used on Moscow.

There was a click on his cellphone as someone on the other end picked up. "This is Silayev, speak."

"Sir, this is Agent Dymovsky."

"Da, what is it?"

"I found one of Trubitsin's men, and it appears they are connected to Ms. Kushchenko somehow. I have picked her up—"

"You did what?"

Uh oh.

The voice didn't sound at all pleased.

"I believe she knows where Trubitsin is."

A grunt. "What makes you think that?"

94

"She told me so."

This time, there was silence for a few moments. "She told you so?" repeated the Minister, saying each word as if a sentence of their own.

"Yes, sir, she says she knows where Trubitsin and his men will be, but—"

"Yes?"

"Well, sir, she wants to make a deal."

"Of course she does." He heard a burst of static at the other end of the line. "What does she want?" Silayev asked, sighing out the words as if talking about a child.

"She wants to be given a new identity and sent back to America or Canada."

The minister chuckled. "Put her on."

"One moment, sir."

Dymovsky stepped from the observation room and entered the interrogation room, closing the door behind him. He handed Anya the cellphone. "Minister of the Interior, Mr. Silayev."

She took the phone. "Mr. Minister."

Dymovsky watched as Anya listened to the Minister, saying nothing. Finally, after barely a minute, she handed Dymovsky the phone. "He wants to talk to you."

Dymovsky placed the phone to his ear. "Yes, Minister?"

"We have a deal."

"Yes—" The line went dead before he had a chance to finish his sentence. He flipped the phone shut and clipped it on his belt. He looked at Anya. "So?"

"Cyprus, Livadhiotis City Hotel, room four-oh-nine."

"When?"

"Two weeks from now."

Baltimore–Washington International Airport, Maryland

Acton stepped through the doors and heard a woman cry out, a bundle of tear stained cheeks and worry charging toward them. He stepped to the side as Jason was grabbed by his mother and hugged hard, renewed sobbing causing everyone in the immediate vicinity to stare.

Jason's father, Tom, walked over and wrapped his arms around his family as Milton rolled up, shaking Acton's hand. Melanie Milton let go of her son then turned to Acton, wiping tears from her eyes.

"I don't know how we can ever thank you enough," she cried, collapsing into his arms. Acton held her, patting her back as Tom held his son, neither saying anything, a bond long broken slowly being reestablished. The fact Jason was hugging him back suggested they might work things out over time.

Acton gently pushed Melanie away and smiled at her. "I've been Uncle Jim to him since he could talk. Of course I was going to help, and there's no need to thank me."

She smiled, shaking out a nod. "You're a good man, Jim."

"The best," agreed Milton, his own eyes glistening.

Tom shook Acton's hand. "Thank you for bringing my son back."

"No problem." Acton leaned in, lowering his voice. "But we need to talk about what happened."

Tom's face clouded, his eyes narrowing. "Come by the house in an hour?"

Acton nodded and the reunited family left, there no luggage to gather.

Milton rolled toward the parking lot, Acton at his side. "So, what happened?"

"You don't want to know."

"That bad?"

"Could have been worse."

"You look worried."

Acton paused, looking down at his friend. "They have my driver's license. They know where I live."

"Did they threaten you?"

"Oh yeah."

"What are you going to do?"

Acton sighed. "I'm not sure what I *can* do. They said if I told anyone they'd kill me, and they threatened my friends and family. But they think I've got pictures of what they were doing, so I might be safe."

"Do you?"

"No, I was bluffing."

Milton pushed ahead. "It's probably all talk, though, right? I mean, they're just some neo-Nazi group, aren't they? All talk and no action?"

Acton shook his head. "No, they weren't like that. Some of them were, but their leader looked like a normal guy, just filled with hate. From the little bit I did see, I think they're planning something, something big. And I got the distinct impression they were prepping to go somewhere."

"Where?"

Acton frowned. "I have no idea."

Sahara Desert, Egypt

"If they are successful, the war that will result will never end. We must do everything in our power to stop this from happening." As if to punctuate Abdullah bin Saqr's point, a gust of wind blew through the tent, bringing with it the delicious aroma of Turkish coffee brewing in the hearth on the other side of the black goat and camel hair cloth. "With the target they have chosen, we cannot afford to fail."

"What will the Americans do?" asked the youngest of the ruling council gathered today, all resting comfortably on silk pillows and thick carpets, luxury not requiring four permanent walls.

"They do not know the target, our operative erased it from the record."

"Is that wise? With their resources, they might be able to find it first!"

Several members' heads bobbed in agreement.

"And what would they do?" asked Abdullah. "If the Americans told them the target was in their country, the regime there would use it to their advantage. They would twist the American's help into something evil, something to further their cause." He shook his head. "The Americans must not know the target. We will handle this as we have handled innumerous threats to Islam and the Prophet's teachings, peace be upon him, and we shall emerge victorious."

The laptop sitting by his side sounded a tone. He glanced at it and clicked to open the new message that had arrived via the satellite link. He smiled then turned to the expectant group.

"Good news, my brothers, our conditions have been accepted."

Tom Milton Residence
Randallstown, Maryland

Acton helped Milton over the threshold and into the elder brother's home. Hugs were exchanged, Jason giving an awkward handshake to Acton and his uncle.

"How are you doing?" asked Acton quietly.

Jason shrugged. "Okay, I guess."

"What have you told them?"

Another shrug. "Not much, I guess."

Acton smiled, patting him on the back. "Don't worry, I'll fill them in, okay?"

Jason looked up at him, a flash of a smile, he clearly relieved. The boy appeared embarrassed and ashamed, and it was understandable. He had screwed up. Royally. But he was safe.

At least Acton hoped he was.

The past hour had been a frank discussion with Milton about what had happened, including a lot of Googling about New Slate and whether there had been any violence linked to them. They seemed to have kept their noses clean over the past few years, ever since Edison Cole had taken it over, apparently trying to appeal more to the mainstream.

The phone rang as everyone sat down, Melanie picking up the cordless receiver from the end table. "Hello?" Her eyes widened in surprise then narrowed. "Who may I say is calling?" She paled then looked at her husband. "Th-they say they want to talk to Jason."

Tom leaned forward in his chair. "Who is it?"

"They just say it's a friend."

Acton looked at Jason then Milton, they all knowing exactly who was calling. "Let him take it," said Acton, jumping up and heading into the kitchen where there was a hardline he could listen in on. He picked up the receiver, cupping his hand over the mouthpiece.

99

"Hello?"

He could hear the fear in Jason's voice, he even feeling it himself. It had been less than a day since they escaped, and now they were already hearing from them.

And the timing couldn't be coincidental.

Do they know I'm here?

"Jason?"

"Y-yes."

"Do you recognize my voice?"

Acton didn't—it wasn't Cole.

"Yes."

"If you say anything, we will kill your parents, understood?"

Jason's voice was barely a whisper. "Y-yes."

"And tell your friend, Professor James Acton, that the same goes for him. If either of you say anything to anyone, you're all dead. Keep your mouths shut, and you'll never hear from us again. Got it?"

"Y-yes."

The line went dead and tires squealed outside. Acton raced to the kitchen window and peered out, but saw nothing.

They're here already!

A shiver raced up his spine as he stepped back into the living room. Jason placed the phone on the table then broke down. "I'm so sorry!" he cried, his head dropping into his hands as he was overcome with sobs, his shoulders shaking as his mother leaped to his side, wrapping an arm around his shoulders as she comforted him. She looked up at Acton, desperate for an explanation.

"Who was that?" asked Tom.

"It was them."

"Them? You mean this New Slate group?"

Acton nodded.

"What did they want?"

Acton sat down, sucking in a deep breath, there no easy way to tell them what they needed to know. "They threatened to kill all of us if we told anyone what had happened or what we had seen."

Melanie gasped, even a yelp escaping from Tom.

Jason's sobs and apologies grew louder.

"Wh-what should we do?" asked a stunned Tom.

"Nothing." Acton held up a hand, cutting Tom off. "If they're smart, they've already moved their operation or hidden any evidence. If we call the police and they find nothing, then they're still free, and they'll know who reported them."

Mel looked at him. "Do you really think they'd kill?"

Jason sat up, nodding. "Y-yes. I think so."

"What makes you say that?" asked his father.

"These guys are nuts." Jason sucked in some courage. "They're dealing in stolen weapons from a military base. They've got some inside guy there. That's what I overheard. It was an accident. I was using the bathroom when two of the guys came in, talking about it. I guess they didn't know I was there."

"We need to call the police," said Mel, reaching for the phone.

Tom reached forward, grabbing it. "Absolutely not. We keep our mouths shut like they said, and we go on with our lives. Let's just be thankful that everyone is safe now and forget all about this."

Acton agreed it was the safest option for the moment.

But he wasn't sure if New Slate would be willing to forget about them so easily.

Knoxville, Tennessee

"So, I've been looking into this James Acton hero and you'll never guess what I found."

Cole looked up from his laptop at Chip McConnell, the final arrangements having been made, their equipment already on its way—it was incredible what a bankroll of millions afforded you. The excitement he felt was now uncontrollable, and he could only imagine how insane it would be once the mission began.

I can't wait!

The very idea that they might succeed in his dream was intoxicating, and at this moment, he could see nothing that could screw it up.

Except Jason and his nosey friend.

"What?"

"He's got a girlfriend."

Cole's head dropped slightly, his eyebrows popping up as he gave Chip a look. "So?"

"So, she's an archaeologist like he is."

Cole frowned. "Again, so?"

Chip smiled. "Guess where her latest dig is."

Cole's eyes narrowed. "Where?"

"Egypt."

Cole smiled, leaning back in his chair, folding his arms across his chest. He looked at the ceiling for a moment then back at Chip. "I think maybe we'll kill two birds with one stone."

Chip grinned. "That's exactly what I was thinking."

"How far is she from our planned location?"

"Less than one hundred miles."

Cole's smile broadened.

"Make the arrangements."

Larnica, Cyprus

"Sir, infrared shows the same two targets in the room. No one has come in or out in the past twenty-four hours except for room service," said Lt. Colonel Kolya Chernov, commander of Alfa Group Six, Spetsnaz, Russian Special Forces. He and his team were stationed on a yacht offshore from the beachside resort of Livadhiotis City Hotel. They had room 409 under surveillance now for over a day, waiting for confirmation their target was inside. They had every type of camera and listening device at their disposal trained on the target, but with the curtains closed, they didn't have confirmation of *who* was in the room. The two men simply talked about football when not sleeping, and called each other by anything but their names.

"Recommendation?"

"I recommend two of my team get eyes on the targets."

There was a moment's pause. "Proceed," came the order over his earpiece.

"Yes, sir." He turned to his second-in-command, Major Anton Koslov. "We're going to get some eyes inside that room."

Chernov, very hands-on for a senior officer, led most of the missions his men were tasked with, begrudgingly agreeing to take this last promotion only when promised he would still be operational. "We have good men, but not enough good leaders!" his commander had said. Chernov had to concede that point, agreeing to the promotion and never regretting it, the leeway it provided him on missions more than he had ever imagined. He grabbed a small duffel bag and they both climbed over the side of the yacht, into a rubber dingy floating lazily in the water below. Dressed in beach attire, they headed for shore and tied up to the pier in front of the hotel. It was almost dark, the beach thinned to a few couples out for romantic walks. They strode down the pier and headed to the hotel. Chernov touched his earpiece.

"Which rooms are unoccupied?"

"You've got one directly above and one to your immediate left of the room," came the response from one of his men on the yacht.

Koslov turned to him, having heard the same intel. "So, which is it? Top or left?"

"Let's go top, more options."

Koslov agreed and they entered the hotel, making directly for the elevators as if they belonged there. A short trip to the fifth floor had them at the door, Koslov making quick work of the keycard lock.

Chernov already knew the layout of this room was exactly the same as the one below, having studied the hotel plans when the mission began. He pointed to a corner. "Get a snake cam in there, that should give us a look at their faces without them noticing."

Koslov nodded and pulled a hand-cranked drill from his bag, silently boring a hole through the floor, the specially designed device gently sucking up any debris, preventing anything beyond a few dust particles from falling to the room below. In less than two minutes he was feeding the flexible camera through the hole while watching a display. With the head poking through slightly, he twisted the camera to aim at the two chairs their targets had positioned in front of the television. Zooming in on both their faces, he clicked a button on the control pad and took pictures of each, transmitting them to Moscow for identification.

On the screen, they saw one reach for his cellphone.

Chernov activated his comm. "Let me hear the room audio."

He heard a burst of static then muffled background noise as the gain was cranked up. The laser guided device, trained on the window glass, picked up the vibrations of every sound inside the hotel room. They watched the display as the man answered the phone.

"Da." There was a moment's pause then he leaped to his feet, searching the ceiling. "What? Where?"

His partner joined him, looking confused. "What is it?"

"The Colonel says someone is watching the room!"

"What?" Now both searched, the one with the phone nodding rapidly as he listened to the person on the other end.

"Understood, Colonel, we'll meet you at the rendezvous point." He flipped the phone shut and pointed to the bedroom. "Grab our gear, we have to get out of here, now."

Chernov had seen enough. "Move in now!" he yelled over his comm. He ran to the balcony door, threw it open and launched himself at the railing. He flipped over the side and slid down the metal bars, swinging onto the balcony below. He yanked the door up and to the right, lifting it out of its track, and pushed it aside as Koslov swung down behind him. They both burst into the room, drawing the weapons tucked into their shorts.

Charging forward, Chernov pistol-whipped the first man who had the phone, knocking him out cold, then continued to advance toward the bedroom with Koslov.

The other man burst through the door. "What's going—"

He stopped as soon as he saw the two guns pointed at his head. "On the ground, now!" ordered Chernov.

The man dropped to his knees, clasping his hands behind his head as if he had done this before. Koslov used plastic ties to secure both prisoners then taped their mouths shut as two men slid over the balcony railing to join them.

"The room is secured," said Chernov to the new arrivals. "Grab any intel then join us on the beach. Sixty seconds." They nodded and split up, grabbing every piece of paper and technology they saw, stuffing them into small black gym bags.

Koslov and Chernov hustled their two prisoners to the balcony. Koslov leaned over the edge and whistled. One of his men below looked up. Koslov signaled for a rope and the man removed a long coil from over his shoulder then swung it up to the balcony. Koslov secured one end to the railing then tied the other end around the first prisoner's ankles. The man, still unconscious, didn't protest as he was thrown over the balcony edge, Koslov letting the rope play out quickly, but controlled. The men below snagged the first prisoner, untied him and Koslov quickly wound the rope up and secured the second prisoner, who struggled. Chernov hit him with a right cross, sending the man over the railing, screaming into his taped mouth. Koslov gripped the rope and slowed the descent, slightly, the man hitting the ground with a thud. Chernov flipped over the railing and quickly slid down the rope, Koslov and the rest of his team behind him.

They grabbed their two captives and rushed them to the waiting dinghies then back to the yacht. The entire operation had taken less than ten minutes, the yacht now heading for international waters at high speed.

Chernov activated his comm. "We have two targets. They were warned. Somehow they knew we were there."

"How?"

"Unknown. The occupants received a phone call from someone they called 'Colonel'."

"Very well, prepare for extraction."

"Roger."

Chernov turned to his men. "Hook them up!"

His men quickly attached a crotch and shoulder harness to the two prisoners, now wide awake but no longer struggling, recognizing their position as hopeless. Koslov and Chernov were then strapped into the same harnesses, and the men hooked all four to a long, thick, steel reinforced rope they pulled from a container on the deck.

All four now connected, they hooked onto a metal clasp of a larger orange bag his men had retrieved from below decks. The two prisoners stared at it, their eyes questioning what was going on. One of his men turned a knob and a hissing sound filled their ears as the bag rapidly expanded into a balloon. As it filled with air it floated, then once full, his men disconnected it from its air supply and let it rise up into the night sky, two beacon lights flashing rhythmically as it raced into the darkness. The long rope attached to it quickly played out, and as less and less of it lay coiled on the deck, the two prisoners realized what was about to happen, and screamed again into their muzzled mouths. One ran to the boat edge, but a gun to his temple quickly silenced him.

Chernov dragged the now unconscious man to the water's edge of the floating harbor located at the rear of the boat, as Koslov shoved his partner into position. Overhead they heard the rumble of a large aircraft. Chernov looked up and saw a dark mass pass in front of the stars, the only evidence it was there, all of its running lights turned off. "Brace yourselves!" he yelled. A snap was heard above their heads then the first prisoner was pulled into the air as if on an elastic band. Chernov smiled as he saw the second prisoner's eyes shoot open a moment before he too was yanked from the boat and into the night sky. Koslov was next, followed by Chernov. He had used this method of extraction many times before, and the initial jolt of going from zero to two hundred miles per hour always took your breath away, but once over, it was riotously fun.

The muffled screams above him suggested not everyone agreed.

Somewhere over the Mediterranean

Agent Dymovsky watched the Spetsnaz commander, Lt. Colonel Chernov, unbuckle his harness as the wind howled through the hold of the Antonov An-70 transport plane, its cargo ramp still down as the crew hauled in the final Spetsnaz operative. The two prisoners huddled against the wall, still recovering from the shock of being yanked into the sky. Dymovsky stood in front of them, gripping a handhold above him as the plane buffeted during the recovery.

A crewmember shouted over the din. "All clear!" Another leaned over and hit a large red button on the side of the hold, beginning the process of raising the ramp. As it closed, the wind died down, its howling slowly replaced by the turboprop engines' dull roar that seemed comparatively quiet after the last fifteen minutes.

Dymovsky turned to the prisoners. "I am Alexey Dymovsky, Prosecutor-General's Office." He sat down in a row of seats along the outer fuselage and opened a file he had been gripping. He flipped through it, looking at the prisoner's faces and back at the file. He nodded at the first. "You are Corporal Konstantin Lukin, and you," he motioned at the other man, flipping through the file. "You are Private Misha Mayorsky." Dymovsky closed the file and looked at both men. "Who will talk first?"

The men remained silent. Mayorsky stared at the floor, clearly still scared, Lukin met Dymovsky's gaze with a glare of defiance.

"I see." Dymovsky stood and grasped a handhold again. He leaned toward the men. "Let me make something perfectly clear. We are in international airspace. You have information about a nuclear weapon that I need. There are no laws to protect you here." He lightly kicked the shins of Mayorsky. "You, where is Colonel Trubitsin?"

Mayorsky glanced up momentarily, then returned his gaze to the floor.

Dymovsky looked at the other. "Tell me where Trubitsin is. I don't care about you two, I only care about the weapon."

"Screw you."

Dymovsky frowned. "Screw me?" He jerked his thumb at Chernov. "If you don't tell *me*, you *will* tell him." Dymovsky took a knee. "You see, I'm the nice guy. You tell me what I want to know, everybody finishes the day with all their body parts intact." He glanced at Chernov who stood near the far wall, staring without expression, arms crossed, somehow keeping his balance effortlessly in the buffeting aircraft. Dymovsky looked back at the prisoners. "He, on the other hand, is not a nice guy. If he has to interrogate you"—Dymovsky shrugged and raised his hands palm upward—"well, let's just say I can't be responsible for what happens." He stood and grabbed the handhold. "So, what's it going to be?"

Lukin glared at Chernov. "Go to hell."

Dymovsky shook his head. "Tsk tsk, now look what you've done." He glanced over at Chernov, who continued his expressionless stare. "I think you've made him mad." Dymovsky headed to the front of the plane where the passenger cabin was located. He turned back to face Chernov. "They're all yours."

Chernov waited for the passenger cabin door to close then looked over his two prisoners without moving. Major Koslov stood on the other side of the fuselage, his weapon trained on the two men. Chernov raised his hand and snapped his fingers, pointing at the rear door mechanism. Koslov smiled, then stepped over to the control panel and hit a large green button. An alarm sounded and a flashing red light cast its warning across the cargo area. A few seconds later the rear door opened, filling the cabin with a roaring, bitter cold wind. The file Dymovsky was holding earlier flew from the seat he had laid it upon, scattering its contents around the cabin, some pages flying out the now open access ramp.

Chernov walked over to the two prisoners and yanked them to their feet. Mayorsky was clearly terrified, however Lukin still had a look of defiance on him. He turned to his partner and yelled over the wind, "Don't worry, he's just trying to scare you." Mayorsky nodded, his shaking betraying his lack of belief in his partner's assessment of the situation.

Chernov positioned the two men in the center of the cargo area with their backs facing the open access ramp. "Tell me where I can find Trubitsin, or the missile, and you both live."

Mayorsky stared at the floor, shaking in terror. Lukin met Chernov's gaze and said, "Kiss—"

Chernov leaned back to his side and planted a kick square in the middle of Lukin's chest, sending him sailing toward the back of the plane. He was silent at first until the realization of what had happened sank in. Then he screamed as he discovered his hands, still secured behind his back, had nothing to grab onto as he tumbled from the rear of the plane. His cries as he began his fall were lost amid the howling wind and the roar of the engines.

Chernov seized Mayorsky by the face and twisted his head around to see that his partner was gone, then twisted it back to look directly at him. "Talk!" yelled Chernov.

Mayorsky flinched. "I'll tell you everything, oh God, please, don't kill me, I'll tell you everything!" Mayorsky's eyes filled with tears, his face pale, his pants newly soiled.

"Where is Trubitsin?"

"I-I don't know!"

"Bullshit!" Chernov pushed Mayorsky by the head, toward the back of the plane.

"No-no, I swear, I don't know, but—"

Chernov stopped, still having a firm grip on the man's jaw. "But?"

"But I know where we are supposed to meet."

"Where?"

"A-a cargo ship, in the Red Sea."

"What ship?"

"The MS Sea Maiden."

"When?"

"Tomorrow."

"Are you sure?"

Mayorsky nodded furiously. "Yes, I swear, that's all I know."

Chernov leaned within inches of Mayorsky's face, staring into his eyes, then pulled away, nodding. "Yes, I believe that *is* all you know." He shoved the man away from him and spun around, hitting him full force in the chest with a side kick. The wind knocked out of him, Mayorsky sailed through the air without a sound, his feet never making contact with the cargo area floor as he flew out the back of the plane.

Koslov hit the button to close the cargo bay door then turned to his commander. "There's only one problem with your technique."

"What's that?"

"Now we have nothing to show for all our hard work."

Chernov chuckled. "Less paperwork?"

Koslov snapped his fingers and pointed at Chernov as he raised his eyebrows, smiling. "Ah, so there is method to your madness."

Chernov smiled and headed to the passenger cabin. "Now let's hope this MS Sea Maiden is real."

CIA Headquarters
Langley, Virginia

"Sir, you need to see this."

Leif Morrison, the Central Intelligence Agency's newly anointed National Clandestine Service Chief, glanced up at one of his analysts, Chris Leroux, and rubbed his eyes, the strain from the computer screen he'd been staring at for far too long taking its toll. "What is it?"

Leroux handed him a file. "You know that chatter we've been following about a possible nuke being on the market?"

Morrison nodded, flipping open the file. "What's this?" he asked as he ignored the cover page warning him of severe jail time if he were unauthorized, and proceeded with reading the document.

"Echelon intercepts."

Morrison leafed through the lengthy transcript and looked up. "Give me the skinny on it, I don't have time to read all this."

"Well, not sure if you remember, but one of the intercepts I brought to your attention last week had a conversation between two members of a white supremacist group, New Slate, talking about going to Egypt as part of an NGO."

Morrison vaguely remembered the conversation, but Leroux had a habit of bringing him a lot of relatively weak-linked intelligence. The problem was that more often than not the kid was right.

"And why were we watching these guys?"

"A tip on a speech their leader gave in Knoxville awhile back, where he said he knew how he was going to kill the Muslim faith."

Morrison nodded as the conversation came back to him. "Now I remember. Go on."

"Well, like I said last week, what the hell is a white supremacist group going to Egypt for as part of an NGO?" Leroux was clearly getting more excited as he conveyed the information, his voice rising in pitch. "Let's be frank. These guys hate Muslims. Why would they go to Egypt to help them?"

Morrison agreed the conversation was odd, but failed to see how it tied to their nuke investigation. Apparently Leroux read his mind.

"I know what you're thinking, how does this relate to the nuke investigation?"

Morrison nodded.

"Well, sir, I've had Echelon flags in for various keywords relating to nukes and terrorism, so things have been hitting my desk for months. I've found several conversations between members of New Slate suggesting they wanted to take the fight to the Muslims. It concerned me a bit, so I had all their convos flagged and found some chatter suggesting something big was going to happen soon."

Morrison sipped his coffee, settling in for a long conversation. He had found over the two years the kid had worked for him, that it was best to let him ramble, the intuitive leaps he made fascinating, if not quick to convey.

"So when I found the convo about them going to Egypt, I had anything odd in Egypt sent to my desk, and guess what I found."

Morrison spun his fingers in a circle, urging Leroux to continue.

"An intercept from the Russians, requesting permission for one of their military transports to refuel in Benghazi, Libya, then a flight plan taking them over the Red Sea."

"So?"

"So?" Leroux appeared perplexed then his eyebrows shot up. "Oh! Well, that's just it. The flight plan ends at the Red Sea, with them returning the same route, no deviation in altitude."

Morrison cocked an eyebrow and leaned back in his chair, steepling his fingers. "That's odd."

"And here's something even odder."

Morrison waited patiently for what he knew would be Leroux's 'Pièce de résistance'.

"The Russians re-tasked a battlecruiser deployed to monitor the Somali coast for pirates, and sent it steaming north into the Red Sea at the same time as the request to Libya went out."

"It's thin," said Morrison, his eyes gazing at the ceiling as he processed this new information. "So we have a white supremacist group claiming something big is going to happen, that they are going to go to Muslim Egypt as an NGO. The Russians seem to do a meaningless flight at thirty plus thousand feet, calling in political favors—"

"*Major* political favors," interrupted Leroux.

"—*major* political favors, to do it, and re-task a battlecruiser at the same time, sending it into the same geographical area as this flight." He closed his eyes. "Damn, it's really thin," he muttered.

"We've gone on thinner," said Leroux, some of the eagerness out of his voice, replaced with a more hopeful tone.

Morrison opened his eyes and snapped forward in his chair, startling Leroux. "Yes, yes we have." He reached for the phone. "When's this flight supposed to be over the Red Sea?"

"Tomorrow night, local time."

Shit!

He picked up the phone and hit the intercom to his assistant.

"Get me Delta."

1st Special Forces Operational Detachment - Delta HQ
Fort Bragg, North Carolina
A.k.a. "The Unit"

Burt Dawson buffed the last bit of wax off the rear quarter panel of his 1964½ Mustang convertible, in original poppy red, then stood back to admire his handiwork.

Damn, she's beautiful.

He loved this car. It was his dad's dream car, and when he had died a few years ago, it was handed down to him. With no children of his own, and none likely with his lifestyle, he sometimes wondered who he'd leave it to.

"Can I sit in it, Mr. Dog?"

Dawson looked at the young boy, his godson, who now stood beside him, admiring the shine, an ice cream running down his hand, all the way to his elbow. Dawson grimaced. "Umm, maybe later, Bryson. After you've cleaned up." The boy appeared disappointed, but then took a lick of the ice cream off his hand and walked away. Dawson leaned against the door and watched him meander over to his father, Red.

It was an amazing fall afternoon. Sunday, sunny, on the base with the families, all the guys shining their true loves. New cars, classic cars, motorcycles. No matter what year or price, no matter mint or beater, everyone was there, taking part. It was the camaraderie of the Unit that made everything they went through worthwhile. This perfect example of Americana, nuclear families, husbands, wives, sons, daughters. All friends, all partners, all comrades. There wasn't a man here he wouldn't die for, and there wasn't a man here who wouldn't die for him.

"Hey, BD." Dawson looked over at his friend, Red, as he approached. "Ready to fire up the grill?"

"You bet!" Dawson smacked his hands together and pushed off the car, heading for the large oil drum BBQ behind the Unit.

"Grill Master Sergeant Dawson's up!" yelled Red to the crowd. A cheer rang out from the gathered families. Dawson smiled and got to work lighting the charcoal grill. It would take a while to heat up.

Not if I had an M21A flamethrower.

He chuckled and watched as the families slowly made their way to the grass behind the Unit. The kids threw beach balls and Frisbees around, while the men and women split into their usual two groups. Dawson looked at the long picnic table with the men of his unit sitting at it, and flashed back to last year when his team had sat at that very table.

So many good men dead.

He shook his head.

Honor the dead. Don't pity them.

His phone vibrated on his hip.

Shit.

Pretty much everyone he knew or cared about in the world was here with him. It had to be business. He flipped it open.

"Mr. White, you're needed."

"I'll be right there."

As usual, the ever-watchful Red was already approaching to take over the grill. "You gotta go?"

Dawson nodded. "Don't wait for me, I'll be gone as long as I can."

Red chuckled and gave the coals a poke as Dawson walked to his car. He sat behind the wheel and fired up the engine, the rumble it made drawing the attention of his men and their families. He turned the car around and glanced in the rearview mirror, his men watching him leave, their expressions letting him know they knew something was about to happen.

He arrived at HQ a few minutes later and headed to Colonel Thomas Clancy's office. His Commanding Officer's secretary smiled. "Go right in, Sergeant Major, he's expecting you."

"Thanks, Maggie."

"Is that BD?" yelled a voice from the office.

"Yes, sir!" said Dawson as he strode through the doorway.

"Take a seat, Sergeant Major." Clancy waved toward the straight back chair in front of his desk, sinking back into his own plush leather one as he took a puff from a cigar that appeared started moments before.

"What's up, sir?" asked Dawson as he took a seat and crossed his leg, his Bermuda shorts riding up, revealing a deep, six-inch scar from last year's excitement. Clancy had long ago made it clear he wanted things casual inside his office unless others were present, which at first had been difficult for Dawson, a career grunt, but he was now comfortable with it.

Clancy pushed a folder toward him. "Urgent op. Need your team in the Red Sea tomorrow."

Dawson took the file and flipped it open. His eyebrows shot up as he read the briefing notes.

"Possible rogue nuke?"

"Yup. Delivered right into the hands of white supremacists, or so the spooks think."

"Who's Control?"

"We are."

Dawson nodded, pleased that for this mission he'd be able to trust who his orders came from. "Our mission?"

"Just get your assets in the area," said Clancy, puffing on his cigar. "The intel is developing rapidly, so be prepared for anything."

"Will the Rooskies have a team in there?"

"No intel on that, but don't be surprised. With that ex-KGB puppet master they've got over there running things, he might be in on it for all we know, so be careful."

"Always am, sir."

"Uh huh." Clancy didn't sound convinced, but Dawson knew if his CO had any doubts in his abilities, he would have been drummed from the Unit long ago. "Well, at least this time you'll be in the Middle East. What possible harm could you do there?"

Dawson smiled. "I'm sure I don't know what you mean."

Clancy chuckled and waved him out of his office. "Go, get, there's a plane waiting to take your team as soon as you're ready."

Dawson stood and headed to the door. "See you when I get back, sir."

"Good hunting, Sergeant Major."

Dawson nodded to Maggie as he headed out, a knowing smile returned, a smile that conveyed her prayers for his and his men's safe return. He headed back to the barbecue, his foot barely on the accelerator, wanting to give his men as much precious time as he could with their families, for he knew the moment he pulled up, the day's festivities would end, and some of his men may never see their loved ones again.

University College London Dig Site
Lower Nubia, Egypt

Laura Palmer leaned over a table, poring over satellite images of her new dig site. She had arrived the night before after five hours of relative luxury in first class on an airliner, then as many hours in the cab of an expedition vehicle that had seen better days, days that had never included an air conditioner. At least here, in the comfort of her tent, she had a portable air conditioner hooked to a solar generator that took the edge off. Anything more was a waste.

The Velcro flap to the tent's outer entrance ripped open. Through the semi-transparent plastic of the inner entrance, she saw someone fumbling with the seal, trying to close the outer flap before entering into the cool interior.

"Bloody hell!"

She smiled, already figuring it was Terrence Mitchell, a brilliant yet painfully awkward grad student of hers from University College London. The outer flap mastered, he pushed aside the inner entrance flap and stumbled inside. He took a deep breath and smiled.

"Lovely," he sighed. He turned to Laura. "I know it's only a couple of degrees cooler in here, but my word, it feels like a heavenly icebox compared to that godawful heat outside."

She motioned to the fridge standing in a corner. "Help yourself to something cold." She sat down as he headed over and poked his head inside the solar-powered fridge that had arrived with her on the transport. He snagged a Diet Pepsi and closed the door, momentarily enjoying the cool air that rolled out and onto his sweat soaked legs. He ran the ice cold can over his face and neck before snapping back the tab, the hiss of carbon dioxide as it rushed from the top made Laura feel as if she had witnessed a real life television commercial.

She reached for her water bottle sitting on the table in front of her and took a sip. Mitchell took a long drag from the can, his Adam's apple bobbing up and down. The satisfied "aaah" after he had drained half it caused her to return the water bottle to where she found it, unsatisfied. She wanted a Diet Pepsi.

Mitchell turned to face her. "Thanks, mum, I needed that." He stepped to the table and glanced at the images splayed over its surface. "Are these the latest?"

Laura nodded. "Yes, the university sent them by courier to Cairo. They were waiting for me at the airport when I arrived."

"Good timing."

"Indeed." She pointed at a grid pattern she had traced out. "I've laid out the grid for us to do our work on. See here"—she leaned in and traced her finger along several darker impressions along the image— "these darker areas appear to be too well laid out to be natural."

"Ancient walls, perhaps?"

"Perhaps. I'm more inclined to believe streets, but there's one way to find out."

Mitchell smiled. "Dig!"

Laura laughed, pleased to hear her prize grad student had forgotten the oppressive heat outside.

He looked at the image. "Where are we on this?"

She pointed at a spot several grid blocks south. Mitchell frowned. "What?"

"Well, there's an NGO that arrived here yesterday and they set up camp right where we're going to be digging."

"An NGO? On my site? What are they doing here?"

Mitchell shrugged. "I don't know. I spotted them as they arrived and went over to explain that we had the entire area assigned to us for a dig, and they said they had permission to be there and that it would only be for a few days."

Laura shook her head. "That won't do. They could be contaminating the site." She grabbed her satchel containing their government authorization forms and headed from the tent. "Take me to them."

Mitchel nodded, polishing off his Diet Pepsi in one final assault before following her outside. She climbed in a jeep parked at the camp's edge, beckoning to Mitchell to get in the passenger seat. He hesitated.

"What?"

"Forgive me, Professor." Mitchell stared at his feet for a moment then spurted, "Well, mum, your driving is, shall we say, legendary?"

Laura laughed. "Get in, I promise I'll go slow."

Mitchell didn't look convinced but climbed into the passenger seat and reached for his seatbelt as Laura started the engine, shoved it in gear, then floored it, kicking up sand and a cloud of dust as the jeep leaped forward. She glanced over at Mitchell and laughed as she eased off the gas. "I'll need you to open your eyes so you can tell me how to get to their camp."

"Of course, mum," stuttered Mitchell as he opened his eyes a crack. A look of relief spread across his face as she drove at what he considered a reasonable speed. He pointed at a dirt road to the right. "Take that, it will lead directly to their camp."

Laura followed the road, or rather indentation in the sand, as it climbed a long, gradual rise. As they crested the top, the jeep tilted forward and began a rapid descent down the much steeper hillside. Below them stood half a dozen tents, and several trucks parked together, facing away from the camp. Several men stood near them, appearing, in her mind, too nervous. In the center of the circle of tents, a UN flag fluttered in the slight breeze.

UN? Here?

As they approached, several men exited the tents and walked toward them. She stopped several feet away and turned off the engine.

"Hi there! How are you?" asked a man as he walked up, a broad smile on display. Laura and Mitchell climbed out, Laura rounding the front of the vehicle, taking the hand extended to her, shaking it firmly.

"I'm Professor Laura Palmer, University College London. And you are?"

"Jack Russell, UNICEF."

Laura looked around. "May I ask why UNICEF is *here* of all places?"

Russell laughed. "You got me! After your boy here"—he motioned to Mitchell—"asked us the same thing yesterday, we started looking at our maps and realized we were in the wrong place. Somebody"—he jacked his thumb at one of his companions who immediately stared at the ground—"programmed the wrong coordinates into the GPS. We've been trying to get a line to our HQ but our satphone isn't working. As a matter of fact, I was about to come over and see if we could borrow yours."

Laura smiled, relieved there might not be a confrontation after all. "Of course, why don't you jump in with us and we'll head back to our camp. Terrence can bring you back."

"Why, that'd be mighty nice of you ma'am." He turned to the others milling about. "I'll be back in half, hopefully with proper coordinates."

The three climbed in the jeep, this time with Mitchell relegated to the back seat. As Laura turned the jeep around, she glanced in her rearview mirror and saw the door on the back of one of the trucks open, revealing at least half a dozen computer screens, all lit, with two men sitting inside. The truck snapped from view as the jeep began its steep ascent. She glanced over at Russell who was staring at her, the same smile still chiseled on his face. Her heart pounded.

If they have that kind of equipment, why would they have only one satphone? And wrong coordinates? Are you kidding me?

She forced a smile. "So, when you finally get to where you're going, what will you be doing there?"

Russell glanced back at the road as they crested the top of the hill. "Digging wells for a remote village. It's amazing how much of a difference a ready supply of clean water can make to the lives of these people."

Laura agreed. "Indeed."

"That sounds like more of an Ethiopian thing rather than an Egyptian thing," piped Mitchell from the back seat.

Laura glanced in her rearview mirror but resisted the urge to glare at her grad student. "Be polite, Mitchell. We're archaeologists. What do we know about wells?" Before Mitchell could reply, she glanced at Russell. "So how long will you be in the village?"

"Only a few days I suspect. We'll need to find a good location, quite often the first few tries end up dry. Hopefully not too long, we have several villages we're visiting on this trip."

They made the turn into the camp and Laura brought the jeep to a stop near her tent. "Come with me, I'll get you the phone."

Russell followed Laura into the tent with Mitchell bringing up the rear. Russell stopped in the entranceway, enjoying the cool air inside. "This is sweet!" He took a deep breath and pulled at his shirt, separating it from his sweat-soaked chest. "Quite the set-up you've got here."

"Thanks." Laura grabbed the satellite phone off her table and handed it to him. "Here you go, hopefully you can get through."

Russell nodded and rapidly dialed a number. After a few seconds he gave a thumbs up. "Tim, it's Jack Russell. Look, no time for small talk, I'm on someone else's satphone here and these things are expensive! I need you to give me the GPS coordinates we were supposed to go to, we've got the wrong ones." He turned to Laura and circled his hand in the air, motioning for something to write with. Laura handed him a pad and pencil and Russell jotted down a set of numbers. "Thanks, Tim, gotta go!" He hung up and returned the phone to Laura, ripping off the top sheet from the pad. He shook the paper in the air. "Now we can get to where we're supposed to be!" he said, laughing as he folded the paper and placed it in his pocket. "Now, I'd best be getting out of your way." He turned to Mitchell. "Can you give me a lift back to my camp?"

"Absolutely."

Laura rounded the table and extended her hand. Russell shook it. "Thanks again for your help, ma'am. It's mighty appreciated."

"No problem at all," smiled Laura. "Have a safe journey."

"Will do, will do." He followed Mitchell out to the jeep, leaving Laura in the tent alone. She sat down at the table, and when she heard them pull away, picked up the pad Russell had written on and grabbed the pencil. Lying it on its edge, she gently rubbed the lead across the pad, slowly revealing the numbers he had written. They were indeed a set of coordinates. She flipped open her laptop and typed them into Google Earth.

And gasped.

They were in the middle of the Atlantic Ocean.

Alamut, Persia
December 16, 1256 AD

Faisal pressed against the wall, the reassuring hand of Hasni gently holding him back as he and the others strained to look. The cave entrance they occupied concealed a tunnel, carved centuries before by some unknown combination of the elements and previous tenants of Alamut. It was an escape route used over the years to clandestinely smuggle operatives in and out of the oft-watched fortress to stage sneak attacks upon their enemies who may have tried to raid their stronghold in the past, and today, a means of preserving the Order.

Hasni turned to face the group of two dozen men gathered in the cave and whispered, "I see four horses, one hundred paces from the entrance. We must be quick and quiet."

Faisal and the others drew their daggers. Hasni and several more experienced warriors led the way, creeping from the entrance, searching about for their foes. After five paces, Hasni crouched and raised his fist, signaling the others to stop. He pointed to the top of a nearby boulder upon which two men stood, their backs to them as they stared up at the fort. Hasni slowly unfurled his bola, signaling another to do the same. Unsheathed, they began swinging them over their heads then, as if reading each other's minds, unleashed them at their targets. The bolas found their marks, the heavy balls at each end propelling the ropes around their victims' necks, cutting off their windpipes and silencing them. The men clutched at the ropes but it was no use. Hasni and the other warrior yanked on the cords attached to their Hassassin designed bolas, pulling the men over the edge of the boulder and onto the hard rock-strewn surface below. They rushed the men, finishing them off with their daggers, then retrieved their bolas from around their victims' lifeless throats.

Faisal's heart pounded with a combination of fear and excitement when he heard a noise to his left. No one else reacted. He slowly walked toward where he had heard the sound and found himself face to face with two Mongols who appeared as surprised to see him as he was them. They both opened their mouths to shout as they reached for their swords. Faisal pulled two short knives from his belt, one with each hand, and threw them, each blade burying deep in the throats of his opponents. They collapsed to the ground in a gurgling heap as he watched them struggle to pull out the blades, the life slowly draining from them.

He heard the sound of rocks shifting on the ground behind him. He spun, his hand reaching for his scimitar, but breathed a sigh of relief as he saw Master Hasni approach him, a slight smile of approval evident. He patted Faisal on the back, nodding as he surveyed the handiwork of his star pupil.

They split into two groups and slowly rounded the large boulder from both sides, carefully searching for companions to the four they had already slain, and found none. From the mountain top above, they heard cheers as the Mongol colors rose above the lookout tower once housing the central chamber of the mighty Hassassin.

Tears flowed freely on the steppes that day, freely from some of the toughest warriors to have walked the earth, and none felt any shame. Faisal was one of them. His heart tightened, his stomach ached as if cleaved hollow. He looked at his master and saw that he too wept.

After a few minutes, Master Hasni cleared his throat and the two dozen warriors that remained turned to face him, leaving the tears they had wept upon their cheeks.

"Today is indeed a sad day," began Hasni. "As I look upon our home and see the fires set by the hordes who would corrupt Islam, I weep. My heart is heavy with the loss. We have lost thousands of our brothers today, but we have survived. And there are more of us out there. It is now our duty to rebuild. We must find our brothers who do not know what has occurred here today. We must find our brethren, and rebuild. For if we do not, Islam as the Prophet Mohammad, peace be upon him, envisioned it, is lost, and so too is the balance between Islam and Christianity."

126

BRASS MONKEY

University College London Dig Site
Lower Nubia, Egypt
Present Day

Laura tossed in her cot then glanced at the clock.

Two minutes later than the last time you looked at it!

James had returned once again from the dig in Peru to attend a fundraiser for the school, and his flight would have arrived about an hour ago, so he wasn't late in calling her. Yet. Knowing him, he might just head directly over to the Miltons, an old habit of his, Sandra delighting in pampering her husband's best friend.

She checked the satellite phone again.

Yes, it's on. Yes, it's charged. Yes, you're getting impatient.

She returned it to the small table serving as her nightstand and turned her head away, closing her eyes. She forced a yawn in an effort to make herself tired. It didn't work.

She started as the phone vibrated. She flipped over in the cot, snatched the phone and swung her legs over the side. She twisted the antenna up and hit *Talk*. "Hello, James, is that you?"

"Hi, babe! Yeah, it's me, how are you?"

Laura sighed as she ran her fingers through her hair in an effort to look presentable, even though he couldn't see her. "I'm fine, darling, just so happy to hear your voice. How was your flight?"

"About what you'd expect from the Lima Express."

"I remember it well!" Her heart leaped as she pictured him tossing his head back as he laughed. She still felt like a schoolgirl. It had been a year since the events in London, the events that had led her to help a man she had never met fight for his life, and to prove once and for all her life's work had not been in vain. It had nearly killed them both, it had killed dozens around them, but through it all, they had survived, a passion kindled between them that had yet to show any signs of burning out.

Only one week before she had suffered the same torture when she left Peru for Egypt to set up this new site for her university. They had been almost inseparable for a year, and the past week was difficult, but they were both independent, strong minded people, top in their chosen profession, and it was their duty to set up dig sites such as those in Peru and Egypt so their students could learn and become the archaeologists of tomorrow. And with her considerable wealth, both knew they were merely a quick flight away from each other.

Well, maybe not quick.

She already wanted to book a flight to Maryland right now to see him.

She sat down in front of her maps and the smile left her face. "James, something has happened."

There was a moment's pause before he answered. "What's wrong?"

She knew from the tone he was concerned. "An NGO set up next to us just before I arrived. They're in the middle of our dig site. I went over and they claimed to be lost. Said they had the wrong GPS coordinates."

"What?" She knew from his voice he found it as unbelievable as her. "Who travels to the middle of the desert of a third-world country without double-checking their GPS coordinates?"

"I'm glad you think it sounded as ridiculous as I did." Laura looked at the pad of paper she had lifted the coordinates from. "I let the head of their expedition use my satellite phone and he wrote down a set of coordinates. I managed to lift them off the pad with a pencil—"

"That's my girl!"

"—and they're in the middle of the Atlantic Ocean!"

"So they're BS."

"Yes, and that's not all, when we were leaving their site, one of their trucks opened and I caught a glimpse of some very advanced computer equipment inside, all functioning, and I thought I saw one of them carrying a gun."

She waited for him to respond and was about to open her mouth when he at last spoke. "Do they know you saw this?"

129

"I don't think so, but I can't be sure."

"What did he say after he used your phone?"

"He said he'd be leaving in the morning."

"Okay, don't do anything. Stay where you are, keep the phone on you, and call me if they haven't left in the morning. Chances are it's innocent, but you can't be too careful these days."

"Really, James, if it weren't for what happened last year, I'd probably never have given it a second thought, but now I find I take another look at everything." She paused and took a deep breath, leaning forward, her elbows on her knees. She lowered her voice. "I wish you were here."

"So do I, babe, so do I. I can be on the next flight out if you want."

She straightened up. "No, no, don't do that, I'm simply being foolish." She yawned. She heard him yawn on the other end. "You must be so tired."

"Empathy, babe, empathy. You know I yawn every time you do."

She smiled. She knew the day he stopped would be the day he no longer loved her. Goose bumps spread across her arms as she pictured him. "I love you, darling."

"I love you too, babe. You get some rest now, I'm going to have dinner with Greg and Sandra then hit the sack."

"Okay, give them my love."

"Will do."

"Love you, miss you, bye!"

"Love you too, bye."

She waited to hear him hang up the phone then returned to her cot, exhaustion sweeping over her. Within minutes she was sound asleep.

CIA Headquarters
Langley, Virginia

Morrison glanced up to see Leroux's head poking into his office, as if the start of a comedy sketch. He looked down, half expecting two more of his analysts' heads to appear with a chorus of "hellos". Morrison waved him in, holding up a finger then pointing at a chair in front of his desk as he read a status update on his display. He pushed the laptop away and turned to Leroux.

"What've you got for me?"

"This is interesting, sir. I've tasked Echelon with as many keywords as I can think of, and flagged them highest priority." He handed Morrison a file. "This conversation took place last night."

Morrison opened the file and scanned the conversation apparently between two lovers. His right eyebrow shot up as he read about the lost NGO. Leroux obviously noticed.

"Are you at the part about the lost NGO that's supposed to be in the middle of the Atlantic?"

Morrison leaned back in his chair. "Sounds like BS to me. Did you check on them?"

"Yes, sir, and there aren't any NGOs in the area. These could be our guys, sir."

Morrison nodded. "Okay, I think we have our starting point. What can you give me on the subjects?"

"Professors Laura Palmer and James Acton. They were the two caught up in that mess in London last year, remember?"

"Aaaahhh." Morrison did indeed remember. The sensation created had taken months to die down. And he never believed their story that they knew nothing about why they were targeted. He jabbed the file. "If these two are innocent, then they are the two unluckiest bastards on the planet."

And whether they know it or not, they're knee deep in it again.

University College London Dig Site
Lower Nubia, Egypt

Laura woke with a start. She looked about the tent, its insulated lining designed to keep the sun's heat out, also kept most of its light out as well, making it hard to determine the time of day. She listened for what may have woken her.

I could have sworn I heard a helicopter.

But she heard nothing. The camp was silent. Too silent for the start of the day. And she still didn't feel rested. She reached for her watch.

4:33am.

Far too early to get up.

She tossed the watch on the table and tried to fall back to sleep. Her mind wandered to the UN group. Something wasn't right. She knew it. There was simply no way an experienced group of aid workers would leave without double-checking their GPS coordinates. And the coordinates he supposedly wrote down were either fake, or another example of complete and utter ineptitude at the other end of the line, that for a moment, made the story of having the wrong coordinates seem plausible.

No, that couldn't be it. And even if it were, wouldn't he have returned to call again as soon as he entered the new coordinates and they showed his destination as somewhere off the Azores? No, something was off. And the computer equipment? Why would digging wells require so much of it? And she was sure she had seen a gun. She reached under her pillow and fingered the 9mm pistol she kept there.

Well, perhaps the gun was justifiable.

She rolled on her back and stared at the tent ceiling. There was no way she was getting back to sleep. He said they would be leaving first thing in the morning. If they were, then they should be getting prepped to leave shortly.

Don't be an idiot!

133

Her inner voice knew before she did what she was about to do.

I have to know.

She climbed from the cot, dressed and pushed aside the inner flap when she paused. She glanced back at the bed for a moment, then quickly walked over and retrieved the gun from under her pillow, stuffing it behind her back in her belt. She exited the tent, looked around to see if anyone else was awake yet, and finding no one, began the walk to the other camp.

It took about fifteen minutes for her to near the top of the hill overlooking the UN site. She crawled on her stomach the final few feet so she wouldn't be seen silhouetted against the dawn sky, then cresting the hill, she gasped at the sight below.

Bloody hell!

Her heart leaped at the unmistakable sound of a round chambering in a weapon directly behind her. She flipped over and before she could reach for her gun, the butt of a rifle smacked her in the face, knocking her out cold.

UNICEF Camp
Lower Nubia, Egypt

Russell, or rather Cole, stood, his arms crossed over his chest, his face revealing none of the excitement surging through him as he watched the helicopter's rotors slowly wind down. Four men, probably mercenaries, had taken up position around the chopper, keeping a wary eye out for anything that might disturb the meeting. Another four unloaded a crate, supervised by, from the sounds of the way he was yelling at the men, an old army sergeant. Another, far more calm, strode confidently toward Cole. The short, stocky man stretched out his hand in greeting. Cole took it, surprised at the strength of the grip. A look at the veiny forearm told him that, regardless of the man's age, which he estimated at over fifty, he wasn't to be messed with.

"Grigori Andreievich Trubitsin," said the man in a thick Russian accent, releasing Cole's grip and bowing his head slightly. "And you must be Mr. Edison Herbert Cole."

Cole's expressionless face flashed in surprise, but only for a moment.

Trubitsin appeared pleased by this. "You wonder how I know your name."

Cole regained his composure. "It had crossed my mind. I thought we'd agreed to no names."

"Mr. Cole, it is my business to know everything about everybody," said Trubitsin, turning to the now approaching crate and extending an arm toward it. "When one is selling one of these, one must exercise utmost caution." He turned back to Cole, staring him directly in the eyes. "And I make it my business to know who I might be, how do you Americans say it, *double-crossed*, by."

The cold tone in which the implied threat was delivered struck a rare chord of fear in Cole, something he hadn't felt in years, in fact, something he couldn't recall ever feeling. "I'm sure we're all friends here."

"Nyet!" said Trubitsin sharply. He softened his tone with a slight smile. "No, Mr. Cole, there are no friends here. But that does not mean there are enemies here either. We are businessmen, you and I. I have something you want, you have something I want."

Cole nodded. "Businessmen. Agreed. You received my deposit?"

"Would I be here if I had not?"

"No, I suppose not."

"Nyet, I should think not." His manner led Cole to believe this man was used to being listened to, without question, and didn't tolerate stupid questions. He resolved to keep them to a minimum. "Shall we inspect the item?"

Cole nodded, his heart pounding faster as the crate neared. The four men carrying it placed it gently in front of their commander and stood back, snapping their heels together. Trubitsin bent over and entered a code on an electronic keypad. A beeping sound preceded a hiss as the crate's locks released. The older "sergeant" flipped open the lid, revealing what was inside. Cole couldn't help but smile this time. Several of his men inched forward, trying to get a look.

It didn't look like much, its old casing had clearly seen better days, the paint chipped, even faded slightly. But none of that mattered. If this was what Trubitsin claimed, it marked a moment in history, a moment, he knew, that would go down as the turning point in the battle with Islam. His heart thudded as one of his men hooked a diagnostic terminal to the device inside the crate and hit a few keys. He smiled at Cole.

Trubitsin reached into his pocket and removed a piece of paper, handing it over. "Arming code."

Cole didn't bother asking how Trubitsin managed to get it, to get the arming code for a tactical nuclear missile from the Cold War, an American tactical nuclear missile no less. Some questions were better left unasked. He handed the paper to his man who took it and quickly entered the code into the terminal. After a moment, he turned to Cole with a bigger smile.

"It's good, sir!"

"Of course it's good!" said Trubitsin in about as cheery a voice as Cole had heard from him so far. "Now, to conclude our business."

Cole turned toward their communications truck and gave the thumbs up to the man hanging out the door. He stepped back inside then a moment later reappeared.

"It's done."

Trubitsin looked over his shoulder at a man who had remained behind in the chopper, staring at a laptop screen. After a few moments, he snapped the screen shut and nodded to Trubitsin.

The Russian smiled and turned back to Cole, extending his hand one last time. "I wish you well in your endeavors, Mr. Cole. Dosvidanija."

Cole shook the man's hand. "And to you."

Trubitsin turned on his heel, marching toward the helicopter, his men falling neatly in behind. The pilot had already powered up the rotors as soon as the transaction was completed, and they lifted off into the night sky, out of sight within seconds.

"Okay, let them out!"

Two of his men standing near one of the trucks opened the rear doors. Cole watched his two al Qaeda "observers" jump to the ground and walk toward him and the crate. "What is the meaning of this?" demanded his counterpart, his muscle standing behind him, equally angry.

"What do you mean?" Cole disguised his delight in what was about to happen. "I could hardly let you be seen by the Russians. They would never have sold us the weapon knowing it was going into Muslim hands."

"I understand that completely. But why are they two hours early?"

Cole glanced at his watch. "Are they?"

The man glared at him. "You know very well they are."

Cole stared straight at him, dropping all pretenses. "Yes, I suppose I do."

"And your explanation?"

"Well, if your men were here, then I couldn't do this."

He reached behind his back and pulled his Glock from his belt, placing a bullet in the man's chest. A surprised expression spread across his face as his mouth opened wide, his eyes then squeezing shut in pain as his mouth narrowed into a grimace from the shock that seared through his system. Cole smiled. His partner turned to run but Cole aimed and fired, hitting the man in the shoulder, dropping him to the ground.

He stepped over his first victim and straddled the man, staring down at his gasping form.

"You didn't really think I was going to give some damned camel jockey a nuclear weapon to use against Americans, did you?" he snarled.

The man muttered something.

"What was that?" Cole dropped to one knee, the other leg still straddling the man's chest. He leaned in.

"The Hassassins will find you," the man whispered hoarsely, blood gurgling in his throat.

"Hassassins?" Cole stood and fired two more bullets into the man's chest. "Who the hell are they?"

He walked over to the muscle who had now struggled to his feet.

"Who are these Hassassins?" demanded Cole.

"I-I do not know," stammered the man as he winced in pain.

Cole raised his Glock then pressed it into the man's wound, twisting the weapon as he pushed harder. The man cried out and dropped to his knees.

"Who. Are. The. Hassassins?" growled Cole, punctuating each word with another twist of his weapon.

The man dropped his head to the ground and extended his arms, muttering something in Arabic.

"Are you praying to your Allah?" yelled Cole in disgust. He kicked sand in the man's face then pointed at the back of his head. "Screw a virgin for me." He squeezed the trigger twice, spraying the man's brains across the desert sand.

"Hassassins? Sounds like a Stallone movie to me!" he said to his men now surrounding him. They laughed, kicking more dirt on the dead men.

"The French version!" yelled another.

Even Cole roared with laughter as the tension of the entire exchange blew off. After a few moments of joking with his men, he clapped his hands together, changing the mood entirely.

"Okay, clean this mess up, we can't leave any evidence we were here. We'll get rid of the bodies at sea."

Cole stepped over to the crate that housed Christianity's deliverance from the tyranny of Islam, and stared at the weapon. Excitement coursed through his veins as the power it represented surged through his body, the hairs on his arms stood up, goose bumps covering his flesh as he read the markings for the first time.

He stepped back then motioned to his men. "Put it in the truck." He turned around and started for the communications vehicle when he noticed one of his men stare and point behind him. Cole turned to see what he was looking at.

"What the hell?"

Somewhere over the Red Sea

Agent Dymovsky stood in the cargo area, his legs spread apart, his arms held out to the sides, shoulder high. Major Koslov was tugging on his gear, making sure everything was secure, then dropped a helmet over his head, attaching it to the black pressure suit he now wore. As soon as the seal was complete, a light flicked on in his visor and his altitude and GPS location appeared in a display at the bottom. Koslov snapped his own helmet on and activated the comm by pressing a button on the control pad on his left wrist.

"Can you hear me?"

Dymovsky gave him the thumbs up and activated his comm. "Da."

Koslov turned to Lt. Colonel Chernov who was already at the back of the plane. "Da, da, I can hear you," he said before Koslov could ask. "Leave your comms activated for the entire jump so we can communicate."

Both Dymovsky and Koslov nodded.

A crewmember stood at the control panel, an oxygen mask covering his face and ears to protect him from the depressurization he was about to initiate. He turned and shouted, holding up two fingers. "Two minutes!" He hooked his flight suit to the fuselage and pressed a button, depressurizing the hold. An indicator flashed, and he pressed another button to lower the ramp.

Chernov led the way down the descending ramp, Dymovsky behind him, Koslov taking up the rear. Dymovsky heard Koslov's voice over the comm.

"Remember what I told you, just follow the Colonel out, arch your back, and extend your arms and legs, just like in your training. This will just last a lot longer than you're used to."

"No problem." Dymovsky's voice didn't betray his fear. He had never liked his parachute training, but to do this from cruising altitude was insane. He hadn't even known it was possible and was stunned to find out Chernov had all the equipment as part of their standard gear. His explanation?

"Most people don't let Russian transports get too low, if they even let them cross their territory. We do this all the time to get where we need to go."

They had lost precious time due to that very reason, trying to obtain clearance to cross Egyptian airspace to get to the Red Sea. That had proven fruitless, so favors were called in by the Foreign Ministry and they landed in Libya to refuel, then crossed the Sudan, Eritrea, and were now over the Red Sea. Luckily the intel had proven correct, with the MS Sea Maiden indeed in the Red Sea. If it hadn't, they had likely lost their last lead out the back of the damned transport plane. Dymovsky shook his head, still not believing what Chernov had done.

Goddamned Spetsnaz, they're crazy!

And the fact they were about to jump out of a perfectly good airplane in the middle of the night into the Red Sea, from this altitude, proved it. Though at least there was a purpose. They had a Russian battlecruiser in the area due to the ongoing piracy from Somalia, and they were rendezvousing with them.

If we survive this jump. If we don't get blown off course. If we don't drown first. If we don't get eaten by sharks. If. If! IF!

Dymovsky took a deep breath.

"Now!" he heard the muffled yell of the crewman as he waved a thumbs up toward the door.

Chernov simply walked over the edge and disappeared from view. Dymovsky jerked forward as Koslov shoved him from behind, toward the edge. He stumbled then jumped, ripped away from the aircraft as if the hand of God had thrown him, his body, traveling at almost 400 miles per hour in the aircraft, hitting a wall of air, slowing him dramatically. He gasped at the sensation of having the wind knocked out of him. And totally forgot to arch. He tumbled through the air, completely losing his orientation in the dark. Every other second he thought he saw stars, but then again, they could be spots in front of his eyes.

"Arch!"

He heard Koslov's voice through his comm but wasn't sure what he was saying.

"Arch now or you will pass out and die!"

Dymovsky tried to concentrate.

Arch. What the hell is arch?

Then it clicked. He thrust his chest out and extended his arms and legs. He stopped tumbling almost immediately, then his head slowly stopped spinning as he regained his equilibrium.

"Good! Now look to your left."

Dymovsky carefully turned his head and saw the silhouette of what must by Koslov, giving him the thumbs up. The figure then pointed below them.

"Do you see the Colonel?"

Dymovsky looked down and for a moment saw nothing, but as his eyes adjusted, he spotted the dark figure below, spread out like a starfish on the ocean floor. "Yes, yes, I see him!"

"Keep him in sight. As long as you can see him, you're on target. If he starts to go behind you, raise your arms slightly, and you will go back. If he gets too far ahead, bring your arms to your sides and lean forward for no more than two seconds, then extend your arms again. Lower your left arm slightly to go left, your right arm slightly to go right. Keep doing small adjustments. Up here at this speed that's all you need."

Dymovsky nodded then realized Koslov couldn't see that. "Acknowledged."

As he relaxed, his eyes glued to the figure below, he started to enjoy the sensation. The pressure against the front of his body as he cut through the air was tremendous, but after a few minutes of getting used to it, not that uncomfortable. His pressure suit rustled against his body, the fabric snapping against him like thousands of gentle, and occasionally not so gentle, whips. And it was oddly quiet. All he heard was his own breathing and that of the others over the comm.

"Check your altimeters," said Chernov over the comm.

He glanced down.

6042 meters.

"At one thousand meters, pull your ripcord. Acknowledged?"

Koslov didn't say anything, and Dymovsky realized these instructions were for his benefit. "Yes, acknowledged."

"Pull the ripcord on the right. You will feel one hell of a snap. Stay calm then check for a good chute. If there's a problem, stay calm, and pull the release cord, count to two, then pull the emergency reserve ripcord on the left."

"Acknowledged."

The indicator had already dropped to 3413 meters during the instructions.

"Pull when I do!" yelled Koslov.

Dymovsky glanced over to his left and saw him less than fifty meters away at the same altitude.

"Deploying chute!" yelled Chernov. Dymovsky glanced down and saw a chute open below him. The differential in speed sent him hurtling toward it, and for a moment he thought he would hit him, when Koslov yelled.

"Deploying chute!"

Dymovsky looked down at his chest and with both hands, gripped the ripcord, and pulled. He heard a fluttering behind him then felt a tremendous yank as his chute opened, it as if a long rope still attached to the plane had reached the end, pulling him back toward it.

"Check your chute!" ordered Koslov.

Dymovsky looked up and saw all four corners fluttering in a perfect rectangle, his lines apparently untangled. "It looks good!"

"Now grab your toggles!"

Dymovsky searched but couldn't see them.

Where the hell are they!

His heart thumped as panic set in.

There's something wrong with the chute! There's no toggles, I won't be able to steer!

He reached for his release and gripped it.

Wait!

He took a deep breath. He glanced at his altimeter and saw he was falling slowly now.

You've got time. Look again.

He looked up. Where the toggles should be, was nothing, just the risers attaching him to the chute mechanism above. Then he saw them— neatly velcroed to the risers. He took a deep breath and reached up, detaching them and gripping them tightly in his hands. He let out a long sigh of relief.

"Are you okay?" asked Koslov. Dymovsky glanced over and saw Koslov floating nearby, expertly guiding his chute with the toggles Dymovsky had just managed to find. He nodded to himself. "Yes, yes, I'm okay."

"Follow the Colonel in. When you see him flare his chute, get ready to pull down as hard as you can on your toggles when I tell you."

"Acknowledged."

Dymovsky could now make out the water below. The only light was still provided solely by the stars and a quarter moon, but his now adjusted eyes made out the wave caps below and then something else, a dark mass with a dull red glow coming off of it from several points. Then it snapped into focus, a flashing red light on a masthead or communications tower now clear, then other telltale lights.

"Get ready!" yelled Koslov.

Dymovsky saw Chernov's chute had flared, the two ends drawn in toward each other.

"Get ready to flare, then when you feel yourself begin to fall, pull the release, then tread the water."

"Acknowledged."

"Get ready...!" Koslov's voice was drawn out. "Flare! Flare! Flare!" Dymovsky yanked on the two chords and looked up. His chute collapsed, the air pulled out as the shape changed. His stomach was suddenly light, as if a thousand butterflies were attempting to keep it in place as the rest of his body dropped, his chute's lift gone.

"Release! Release! Release!"

144

Dymovsky let go of the toggles and looked down at his chest for the release. He grasped it with both hands and yanked. He was weightless for a moment, as if floating in place, but it was merely his imagination, he dropping even faster, the drag his chute had provided, removed. He plummeted to the water far below then hit it a second later, long before he thought he would, it much closer than it appeared. The smack as he hit the water was jarring, and he sank below the surface. His heart raced, panic setting in again as he took a deep breath and held it.

Koslov laughed over the comm. "Breathe, Dymovsky, you're in a pressure suit. That means waterproof!"

He took a deep breath, realizing he wasn't drowning. But he was still sinking.

"Better start kicking those feet of yours or we'll never find you," said Koslov.

He began kicking frantically then calmed himself and slowly kicked. He saw lights playing over the water that appeared impossibly far above his head. As he kicked toward them, his head broke the surface, again sooner than expected. Nearby he saw his two fellow jumpers floating.

"Welcome to the party!" Koslov laughed as he swam toward Dymovsky. Chernov was waving, but not at him. Dymovsky followed his gaze and saw a small boat with a search light, apparently what he had followed up to the surface moments before, the light now trained on them as it rapidly approached.

The engine cut as it neared Chernov. He and Koslov swam for the boat as Chernov was hauled on board. As Dymovsky neared the edge, a hand reached over the side of the rubber dinghy and pulled him inside. He rolled unceremoniously into the bottom of the boat. Koslov followed a moment later, falling on top of him. He laughed over the comm as he rolled off Dymovsky and moved to the side of the dinghy. Another set of hands seized Dymovsky and hauled him to a sitting position against the side. It was Chernov. He had his helmet off, tucked neatly under his arm beside him. Koslov removed his helmet and handed it to a crewmember manning the boat, then leaned forward and, disconnecting the seal, removed the helmet from Dymovsky's head.

He gasped at the pressure change and the roar of the sea and boat engine around them. The salt air smelled wonderful, a smell he hadn't experienced in years.

"Congratulations, Agent Dymovsky. You've joined the Ten Kilometer High Club!" said Chernov.

Koslov smiled. "So, what'd you think?"

"I think I need to change my shorts!"

Both Chernov and Koslov roared in laughter.

"The real question is, would you do it again?" asked Koslov.

Dymovsky couldn't believe the words coming from his mouth.

"I'd do it again, right now!"

UNICEF Camp
Lower Nubia, Egypt

Cole couldn't believe what he was seeing. One of his men, whom until this moment he had thought fairly bright, was carrying someone over his left shoulder, his MP5 grasped by the barrel in his right hand as he sported a shit-eating grin.

"Lookey what we've got here!" He proudly dropped his human cargo unceremoniously on the desert sand. As the torso flopped onto the ground, the face was revealed, along with a spray of crimson from a bloodied nose, cascading on the arid surface that thirstily consumed it.

Cole's anger was forgotten. "Professor Palmer!"

His man smiled, resting his weapon on his shoulder, finger on the trigger guard. "Found the nosey bitch up on the hill, watchin' the goings on."

Cole shook his head, smiling down at the woman. "Interesting turn of events. Saves me a lot of trouble." He tapped her with his boot.

Nothing.

"Christ, how hard did you hit her?"

"Dunno. Glass jaw?"

"She's a woman. You better hope she comes to. I want her to know why she's dying, that it was her meddling boyfriend that cost her her life." He pointed to the ridge. "I want two men up there, now. Make sure no one from her camp is on their way, looking for her. Let's pack up and get the hell out of here, now!"

The camp burst into a flurry of activity as Cole stood, staring down at the woman he had met only yesterday. It had been his intention to eliminate her after their business had been completed, having left enough time for it to still be dark.

But she had saved him the trouble.

Looks like you're just as nosey as your boyfriend.

147

Nuclear Battlecruiser RFS Pyotr Velikiy
Red Sea

"We've found the ship," said Captain Baranski of the Pyotr Velikiy, Russia's pride and joy of the Black Sea Fleet, a nuclear-powered battlecruiser nearly three football fields long, with enough armament to start—and finish—a small war. Agent Dymovsky and Lt. Colonel Chernov sat with him and the commander in charge of the Russian Naval Infantry detachment on board, Captain of the Third Rank Rakov. They sat in a briefing room with no windows, buried in the ship's bowels to protect against electronic eavesdropping. On the wall in front, a map of the area was projected with several flashing dots. "We are here," said Baranski, using a laser pointer to indicate a flashing dot just east of the northern Sudanese border. "And the MS Sea Maiden is here"—he moved the pointer to the north—"about one hundred nautical miles from us."

"Any communication, anything unusual?" asked Dymovsky.

"Depends on what you mean by unusual. I personally think it is unusual that a merchant vessel is sitting stationary near some of the most dangerous waters in the world, under radio silence, with no running lights."

"We've had a drone monitoring the ship since we found her yesterday," explained Rakov.

"I also find it unusual that a chopper left its deck and headed into Egyptian airspace sixty minutes ago," finished Baranski.

Dymovsky leaned forward. "A chopper left that ship?"

"Affirmative."

"Do we know exactly where they went?"

"No. The only reason we know about the chopper is the UAV happened to be over the target. They had it in a storage container. They dropped the walls and had the thing powered up and in the air in less than five minutes. We lost them as they crossed into Egyptian territory.

Their trajectory was pretty straight, however." Baranski hit a key on the notebook in front of him and a near perfect west-by-north-west line was drawn ending in Egypt. "We couldn't send our drone in after it without risking an international incident."

"You said she's one-hundred miles away?" asked Chernov.

Baranski nodded. "Yes."

"Are you heading for her?"

"We'll be within firing range in three hours."

"We need to get there sooner. If the package was on that chopper, it may already be too late," said Dymovsky.

Baranski grunted and crossed his arms. "Perhaps if I knew what the *package* was, I could get us there quicker."

Dymovsky looked at Chernov, who shrugged. "Why not?"

Yes, why not?

Dymovsky sighed and leaned forward, lowering his voice. "What I am about to tell you does not leave this room, understood?"

Baranski and Rakov nodded, the slight rolling of their eyes giving Dymovsky the idea they weren't sufficiently impressed with his warning. Everything nowadays was a state secret.

"The package is an American tactical nuclear missile, with compromised arming codes."

"Bozhe moy!" exclaimed Rakov.

Captain Baranski leaped from his seat and hit the comm button on the wall. "Bridge, this is the Captain. Give me flank speed, now!"

"Acknowledged, Captain, flank speed."

An alarm sounded throughout the ship and Dymovsky instinctively reached for the table edge when a slight surge pushed him forward as the 160,000 shaft horsepower engines spun up to full power.

"You damned bureaucrats!" muttered Baranski as he sat back down. "If you had told us we were after a nuclear bomb, we could have been there by now."

"How much time will it take now?"

"Still over two hours."

"We need to get there quicker," said Dymovsky.

"The only alternative is the choppers," said Rakov. "We can send in a team, be there in thirty minutes from lift-off."

"Won't a chopper tip them off?"

"No more than a battlecruiser pulling alongside."

Chernov chuckled. "Let's take the choppers within a few klicks, drop two inflatables, use the engines then switch to oars and paddle the rest of the way in. As long as we can get there before dawn, we'll take them by surprise."

Rakov agreed. "It can be done, but we need to leave immediately."

Baranski nodded. "Make it happen, Captain."

Dymovsky turned to Chernov. "Coordinate with Captain Rakov. I want you, Koslov and myself to accompany them, plus however many of your team you feel is necessary."

Chernov nodded and rose to join Captain Rakov who was already at the door. As they opened it, the comm on the nearby wall wailed for attention then a voice came from the tiny speaker. "Captain Baranski, please contact the bridge, over."

Rakov hit the button to activate the comm as Baranski rose.

"This is the Captain, go ahead."

"Captain, we're monitoring an Egyptian Air Force intercept of an unidentified chopper. Thought you might like to know, over."

Baranski jabbed the button. "I'm on my way." He opened the door to the briefing room and motioned for the others to follow. "Captain Rakov, you and the Colonel prep for the assault, Mr. Dymovsky and I will be on the bridge."

Egyptian Airspace

"Falcon One, this is AWACS Command Echo, come in, over."

Captain Azim switched his comm to the Command frequency. "Command Echo, this is Falcon One, over."

"Falcon One, prepare for re-tasking, this is not a drill, over."

Azim checked his Heads-Up-Display as new orders fed into his flight computer. "Command Echo, Falcon One. New target coordinates received, over."

"Falcon One, proceed full burn to intercept unidentified target. Identify target, do not engage, confirm, over."

Azim pushed his throttle fully forward then hit the afterburners, shoving him into the back of his seat as his F-16 accelerated toward Mach 2.1. He glanced to his right and saw his wingman not far behind. "Command Echo, Falcon One. Proceeding at full burn to intercept unidentified target. Am to identify and not engage, over."

The ground rushed by as he angled his aircraft to slowly descend as he approached his target. At this speed, he would be there in less than five minutes. He eyed the HUD. His target was at three hundred feet, traveling at two hundred miles per hour.

Small prop? Helicopter?

He switched his comm over to talk to his wingman. "Do you have the target?"

"Confirmed, two miles off the coast at three hundred feet?"

"That's it. What do you think? Helicopter?"

"Certainly fits the profile. HUD should be able to tell us when we get in range."

"I think he'll be pretty close to international waters."

"Affirmative. Probably just a private plane or helicopter that didn't file a flight plan. Tourists probably."

"Or it could be Israeli, Jordanian."

"Saudi maybe?"

Azim eyed the range indicator quickly counting down as they neared the target. They would be there in less than two minutes. "Come on, come on!"

"Falcon One, Command Echo. Do you have eyes on the target, over?"

Azim scanned the horizon, searching for running lights, beacons, anything in the dark sky that might indicate a civilian aircraft. As he searched, the coastline rapidly approached then ripped by as if never there, the water a black mass blending with the horizon. They were now at less than five hundred feet, approaching the altitude of their target.

"Command Echo, negative, I have no visual, over."

"I see it!" yelled his wingman. "Eleven o'clock."

Azim looked over and at first didn't see anything, then he noticed the black outline as it moved in front of the stars. "Command Echo, Falcon One. I have it, over."

"Falcon One, can you identify the target, over."

Azim turned slightly to the left, quickly overtaking the target. He rolled and banked around the shadow, getting a clearer view. "Command Echo, it's a helicopter, repeat, a helicopter, over!"

"Falcon One, can you identify it, over?"

"Negative, Command Echo, there are no running lights, I can't make out its registration, over."

"Falcon One, try to signal it, over."

Azim switched his comm to broadcast on the standard civilian frequency. "Unidentified helicopter, unidentified helicopter. You are in Egyptian airspace. Identify yourself, over."

Nothing.

"Unidentified helicopter, if you are unable to transmit, signal visually, over."

Again, nothing.

"Captain, we're about to hit international waters."

"Command Echo, Falcon One. They do not acknowledge our signals, there's no way they missed us, request permission to engage, over."

There was a pause. "Falcon One, Command Echo. Permission to fire warning shots."

"Falcon One firing warning shots, over."

He flipped the weapons selector on his stick to his cannons and lined up his sights to fire ahead of the helicopter. He squeezed, sending several dozen rounds, including tracers, past the helicopter's nose, lighting up the fuselage briefly.

What was that?

Azim eyed the tail as the helicopter swerved to the left then resumed course. He swung around for another pass, firing another salvo, this time training his eyes on the tail section. The flash lit it up and this time he was certain.

"Command Echo, Falcon One. They took evasive maneuvers then resumed course, but, I saw something..." He trailed off, second-guessing whether he should report it.

It was too late.

"Falcon One, did not receive your last transmission, over."

"Command Echo, I ah, I saw the tail. It was Soviet, over."

There was a pause as he pictured the crew in the AWACS processing this new information. The Soviet empire had been defunct for over twenty years. Who would use their hardware now with the old insignia still intact? Several possibilities popped to mind. Israeli's, they'd do anything. Eritreans, Somalis. He couldn't see the Jordanians or Saudi's doing it.

Mercenaries?

"Command Echo, Falcon One. Should I engage, over?"

"Falcon One, negative, you are now in international waters, disengage, repeat, disengage, over."

Azim cursed under his breath as he slowly banked his aircraft back to Egyptian soil. "Command Echo, Falcon One disengaging, over."

He glanced back at the target and cursed as all its running lights blazed on, the red hammer and sickle in clear view against the black of the helicopter.

Now that you know you're safe you show yourself. Bastards!

Nuclear Battlecruiser RFS Pyotr Velikiy
Red Sea

Agent Dymovsky listened to the chatter between the pilots and their command, his heart pounding as he silently urged the helicopter into international waters. Though they were ultimately his target, and his enemy, he needed them alive. He had little doubt now the missile had been sold. Why else would they have clandestinely entered Egyptian territory? His, and the free world's, worst fears were about to be realized. A terrorist organization likely had a fully operational nuclear bomb. Who would they target? New York, Washington, London, Moscow? He shuddered at the thought and made a mental note to call his mother and have her visit her sister in the country as soon as he had the chance.

"Okay, they're in international waters and should arrive at the MS Sea Maiden in thirty minutes. Dawn breaks in forty minutes so you better hurry." Captain Baranski snapped his fingers at a seaman standing at the starboard bridge entrance. "Take Agent Dymovsky to the helipad."

The crewman snapped his heels, nodding. "Follow me, sir."

Dymovsky followed the crewman through a maze of corridors, gangways, ladders, and hatches. Up and down, left and right. He could find no pattern, no rhyme or reason to the path the crewman followed. The only thing that kept him going without asking questions was the look of complete confidence on the crewman's face as he urged him toward where he hoped would be the correct final location.

They burst through a hatch and he saw Lt. Colonel Chernov and Major Koslov there, geared up with half a dozen of the Spetsnaz team, along with Rakov and about half a dozen of his own men. All eyes were on Dymovsky as he emerged from the hatch. "Here you are, sir," said the crewman. "Good luck."

"Thanks." Dymovsky hurried toward the assault team. Koslov grabbed some gear and tossed it to him. "Get dressed, we leave in two minutes."

Dymovsky stripped off his shirt and pants, pulled on the wetsuit, and followed Koslov onto one of the two choppers on the platform. As they completed the loading, an alarm sounded and several warning lights spun around them. A jolt shook them all before the platform they occupied moved. He saw a large set of doors overhead open up and out, revealing the night sky and more of the ship as they rose. A final jolt signaled the end of their rise, the pilots firing up the engines.

Koslov slapped Dymovsky on the knee. "When we get within range, we'll drop the boats. They'll inflate on impact with the water. We'll drop from the chopper. You'll jump after the Colonel." He pointed at Dymovsky's neck. "Before you jump, put your goggles on." Dymovsky fingered them without looking, making sure they were indeed there, as he had no recollection of putting them on in all the excitement. "Take a deep breath then jump. When you hit the water, don't forget to kick to get to the surface."

Chernov laughed and punched Dymovsky on the shoulder, a little too hard. "Not like last time, eh!"

Dymovsky managed a smile through the pain.

"It won't be as bad as last time," said Koslov. "You're jumping from about five meters. Nothing to worry about."

Dymovsky nodded.

"When you surface, get your ass into my boat and keep your head down. I'll give you further instructions as we approach."

"Understood," said Dymovsky as the helicopter lifted off. Within seconds they were racing across the water, barely clearing the chop as they rushed toward their target thirty minutes away.

Skydive from ten thousand meters into an ocean, and now assault a ship in the dark. What next?

International Waters, Over the Red Sea

Trubitsin looked at Yakovski with a grin as the Egyptian fighters peeled off. He and his sergeant were the only two left of the original six who had discovered the weapon over twenty-five years ago. It had taken a long time, years of planning, years of waiting for the right opportunity, and years of waiting for the right buyer. Trubitsin wasn't insane. He was greedy, but not insane. He wasn't about to sell the missile to Chechens who would turn around and use it on his homeland. He had no intention of living in Russia, and may never set foot there again, but it was still his home. He loved his country but couldn't stand it at the same time. The corruption and violence were out of control, and now with that ex-KGB bastard running things, it was slowly turning back into the Soviet Union, something he now realized should never be allowed to happen.

Maybe I did sell it to the wrong people?

The fleeting thought was dismissed. He had always assumed it would be sold to terrorists hell-bent on destroying some city in America. Never in a million years would he have thought Americans would want to buy it themselves. He knew the target and didn't care. As long as it wasn't used on Mother Russia, or where he happened to be spending his millions, he didn't give a shit. Anywhere else was fair game.

He frowned as it occurred to him that he couldn't trust what he had been told. He turned to Yakovski. "I think we should rent a yacht."

Yakovski raised his eyebrows. "Why?"

"What if they were lying about the target?"

Yakovski's eyebrows shot up even further. "Never thought of that."

"Or we could go back home, wait it out there."

"Something tells me we're not very popular there."

Trubitsin nodded. "Yacht it is." He turned to the rest of the hired crew. "When we get to the ship, your shares will be wired to your accounts, then I suggest you all go on a long vacation at sea."

There were smiles and American style fist-bumps passed around by the young group of freelancers. He was giving them each a quarter of a million Euros for a few days' work. Not bad.

The co-pilot turned around and shouted to him, "We're clear now, sir!"

Trubitsin peered out the window at the inky blackness below. Tomorrow they would never find him. Not with the amount of freedom tens of millions buys you.

Over the Red Sea

Agent Dymovsky stood in the open door of the helicopter as it hovered low above the water. Lt. Colonel Chernov hit the surface and disappeared for a moment, then reappeared, giving a thumbs up. Dymovsky braced. Major Koslov slapped him on the back and he jumped, taking a deep breath. He hit the water and found himself completely submerged for the second time in one night, but this time was indeed different. He was calm. Relatively calm. His heart still pounded, but not in the near panic he had experienced less than two hours before. Which he thought was odd considering this time he was about to go on an armed assault where he could very well get killed. He kicked gently and waved his arms, pushing against the water and propelling toward the surface. He broke through and gasped, taking in a deep breath of fresh, salty air.

"You okay?" yelled Chernov as Koslov hit the water beside them.

Dymovsky gave a thumbs up.

Chernov pointed at the nearby dingy that had finished inflating. "Get in!"

Dymovsky swam for the boat and grabbed a rope-hold ringing the outside. He paused to catch his breath as Chernov swam up beside him and grasped him by the back of his wetsuit, and without a word, half pulled-half pushed him into the raft. He tumbled in, the raft rocking violently from the waves and the sudden addition of an occupant. Koslov's hand appeared over the side and Dymovsky clasped it, pulling him in.

"Thanks," said Koslov as he positioned himself to help the others. Dymovsky looked to the right and saw the second raft quickly filling with members of the assault team from the second chopper.

Chernov tumbled in beside him and shuffled to the back, firing up the motor. Dymovsky was surprised at how quiet it was. Chernov appeared to read his mind and looked at him with a wry smile.

"A design we *borrowed* from the American Navy SEALS. *Very* quiet."

Dymovsky grunted as one of the assault team landed on him.

"Sorry, sir," said the man as he rolled off and into a spot beside him, against the side. "She's going to be cramped, I think!"

Dymovsky nodded and searched for the MS Sea Maiden. At first he didn't see her, but then Chernov gunned the engine and turned the boat to the right. After a few minutes, he saw what he thought might be the outline of a ship on the horizon. He pointed. "Is that it?"

Koslov looked at where he was pointing. "Da, must be. No lights."

They continued in silence for another five minutes, the boat bouncing on the waves. The engine was quiet, but not that quiet. Dymovsky wondered when Chernov would cut the motor and switch to oars.

It must be soon!

The MS Sea Maiden was now large on the horizon.

He gasped as the entire ship lit up as if someone had thrown the switch on the Christmas tree at the Rockefeller Center. Almost every square inch of the ship was lit, and so was the surrounding water. Chernov cut the engine, as did the other boat.

"Do you think they spotted us?" whispered Dymovsky.

Koslov raised his eyebrows and scrunched his mouth. "Possibly. I doubt it, though. Something else must be going on."

They sat in silence for a minute, all eyes on the ship. Koslov had a set of binoculars trained on her then handed them over to Chernov. "Doesn't look like they've spotted us."

Chernov grabbed the binoculars and brought them to his eyes when everyone heard it—the roar of an engine in the distance getting steadily louder. They all looked up to try and spot the source of the unmistakable sound of helicopter rotors.

"Everybody down!" yelled Chernov in a hoarse whisper.

Dymovsky ducked and turned his head, looking toward where Chernov was searching. From the corner of his eye, he saw the helicopter race by, just above the water, so close he could feel the wind from the propellers as its running lights blazed against the dark night sky, a Soviet hammer and sickle proudly lit on the side.

Dymovsky noticed he was holding his breath and let it out slowly, gasping for another. Everybody remained low, creating as minimal a profile against the choppy sea as they could. The lights from the ship worked to their advantage now. Anyone on the ship would have difficulty picking them out on the dark ocean with the lights blazing around them.

Chernov appeared aware of this and fired up the engine, racing for the ship, the roar of the chopper far louder than the small engine on the boats, providing them with excellent cover. Even Dymovsky knew the helicopter would prove an excellent diversion, with all eyes on board probably directed at the new arrival. Chernov angled the boat to approach from the rear, and within minutes both boats pulled alongside, their engines cut.

The MS Sea Maiden, her rusted hull in desperate need of a paint job, towered above, its curved hull slowly arcing over their heads. They tied themselves to a ladder, its metal rungs extending up the side of the ship and out of sight. Chernov grabbed on and began the long climb, the rest of the team following him. Koslov slapped Dymovsky on the back and motioned him toward the ladder. He crawled for the nearest rung as the boat rocked and swayed with his movements. He fell forward and flailed for the ladder. His hand made contact and he gripped it, pulling himself upright. He grasped the next rung and pulled himself up and out of the boat, Koslov already directly below him. He looked up and gulped. He could see several of the team already well above him, with one disappearing from view as he passed the curve of the hull.

He felt a tap on his boot. He glanced down at Koslov, whose eyes urged him forward. Dymovsky nodded and began the climb as the second boat took position near the ladder.

Within minutes, the entire assault team was on board, hiding behind a large cargo container that provided them with perfect cover. Farther forward, they heard the chopper engines winding down and the yelling

162

of crewmembers, their voices too indistinct to make out what they were saying.

Chernov turned to Captain Rakov and whispered, "You take your team up the starboard side, I'll take port."

Rakov nodded.

Dymovsky leaned toward both men. "Remember, we need prisoners."

Both men nodded then positioned themselves on either side of the cargo container. Chernov raised his hand over his head then pointed forward with two fingers, signaling the start of the assault. Rakov slowly rounded the container, his team heading out of sight as Chernov led his Spetsnaz unit around the port side. Dymovsky remained behind Koslov and was second from the rear, which was fine by him. He glanced down the deck, realizing they were now exposed if any watchful eye looked this way.

That was when the lights flickered out, the entire ship immersed again in darkness, leaving them all momentarily blind. They froze, their eyes adjusting, then, with no indication of activity, moved forward, this time more rapidly.

A shout rang out from the other side of the ship, then gunfire.

"Damn!" muttered Chernov as he bolted forward. The lights blazed on again and gunfire erupted all around them.

Koslov turned and shoved Dymovsky to the ground. "Stay here!"

Dymovsky didn't have to be asked twice. He crouched behind a crate as the rest of the assault team raced forward, shots ringing out from all directions. He heard shouting, some of it sounding like it was coming from the assault team, but most of it sounding disorganized, panicked, not the types of shouts he would expect to hear from trained soldiers.

But there was entirely too much gunfire.

Prisoners! We need prisoners!

University College London Dig Site
Lower Nubia, Egypt

Mitchell finished relieving himself in the latrine, thankful no one had seen the morning wood he had been sporting, and looked around for Professor Palmer. A few other students moved about the camp, the early birds eager to avoid the hot sun, starting their day just before sunup. But the professor, usually the earliest of them all, was nowhere to be seen. "That's odd," he said aloud as he walked to her tent. He neared the entrance, and rather than walk in as he normally would, he paused outside in case she was still asleep. "Professor Palmer! Are you in there?"

No answer.

She couldn't still be asleep!

He raised his voice slightly louder this time. "Professor? Can I come in?" Again nothing. Several other students had taken notice and approached the tent. "Has anyone seen the professor this morning?" A few headshakes later, he pointed at one of the female students. "Jenny, you go in and see if she's okay."

"Why me?"

"Well, you're a girl, she's a girl," explained Mitchell feebly. "What if she's not, you know, decent?"

"Honestly, Terrence," she said, shaking her head as she flipped the flap aside. "You'll never get laid if you keep calling us girls."

Mitchell's face flushed as several of those gathered, laughed. Jenny disappeared inside then quickly poked her head out again. "She's not here."

"What?" Mitchell followed Jenny back into the tent and looked around. The bed was slept in, but the professor was definitely gone.

"She must have gone somewhere, her boots are missing."

Mitchell frowned then exited the tent. The full dig site complement had gathered while they searched inside, murmuring to each other.

164

They became silent as Mitchell and Jenny appeared. "Listen everyone, the professor is not in her tent. Her boots are gone, so she must have gone off somewhere." Mitchell took another look around, hoping to spot her walking toward the camp. "I've been on a dig before with her, she would never wander off, not without telling someone." He lowered his voice. "Let's search the camp. Inside every tent, behind every box, she may be hurt somewhere." Nobody moved. Mitchell smacked his hands together. "Now, people!" They scattered as he headed for the jeep.

"Where are you going?" asked Jenny, jogging after him.

"Just a hunch."

A hunch I hope I'm wrong about.

MS Sea Maiden
Red Sea

Trubitsin and Yakovski crouched on either side of the hatch, each spraying alternating gunfire in the general direction of the assailants on the deck. They were trapped in a crossfire, with no hope of escape.

"What the hell are we going to do?" yelled Yakovski as he reloaded.

Trubitsin held his AKS-74 out and squeezed the trigger, sending a spray of 7.62mm shells in an arc across the deck, the ricochets bouncing harmlessly away, his enemy impossibly hidden.

Yakovski leaned in and fired a volley at the other side of the deck. Both bursts of gunfire were met with a steady wall of lead from their attackers, the bullets pelting the metal wall surrounding the hatch, but none making it into the room they had holed up in. "They're not trying to hit us!" yelled Trubitsin. "They must want prisoners."

Yakovski agreed. "Da, interrogation!" He leaned out and fired another volley, apparently bolder now that he realized Trubitsin was right.

Trubitsin looked about the room, his eyes drawn to a sealed hatch at the back. "Keep them busy!" He scrambled over and spun the wheel to open it, pulling down the handle then pushing the hatch aside slowly. He poked his head out to look and saw no one. It led to a corridor he recognized as leading toward the crew quarters and then out again to the deck. He looked back at his sergeant—his friend—of over twenty-five years.

Yakovski fired a volley then glanced over his shoulder at him. "Go! I'll keep them busy. Just promise me one thing!" He fired another volley.

"Anything."

"If I make it out of this alive, find me."

"You have my word."

Yakovski fired another burst. "And if I don't, say goodbye to all the hookers on Tverskaya Street!" He laughed and fired again, then looked back at Trubitsin. "Are you still here?"

Trubitsin gave him a quick salute, then ducked through the hatch, closing it behind him, knowing he wouldn't see his comrade again.

He ran down the corridor, ducked through the crew quarters, then reaching the end, cautiously opened the hatch and peered out. He saw no one. He stepped out onto the deck and slowly made his way toward the prow. As he rounded a crate he saw one of the crew hunched over, his back to him, as he sought cover from the gunfire at the other end of the ship.

Trubitsin stepped toward the man, reaching out to let him know he was there. His foot hit something. His eyes darted to the deck and he saw a small pipe roll away from his foot, the distinct hollow sound of metal on metal clearly heard in the tight confines of the stacked crates. The man whipped around and Trubitsin opened his mouth to warn him off, raising his hands in a gesture of friendship, but the look of panic in the man's eyes let Trubitsin know it was too late, the glint of a weapon held tightly against the man's stomach confirming it. Trubitsin's hands were now almost up, his assault rifle still gripped tightly, his muscles twitching as time slowed. The signals firing toward his limbs seemed lost in his old age, his weapon aiming far too gradually as he pushed his body to the right to avoid the shot he knew was coming. He stared at the other man as he yelled, "No!"

The man squeezed his eyes shut and Trubitsin knew it was no use. As if in slow motion, his eyes moved down the terrified, squinted features of the man's face, to his chest and ultimately the weapon, a weapon that now belched lead at Trubitsin, the muzzle flash unmistakable. He didn't feel the first few rounds hit, but as his leap sent him flying off his feet, he hit the ground hard, his right hand now extended across the deck plating, his weapon pointed directly at the man who continued to fire where Trubitsin had just been. He squeezed the trigger, emptying what remained of the mag into the man, his body shaking as each bullet hit, his eyes opening in shock, his gaze now fixed on Trubitsin.

Trubitsin squeezed the trigger of the now spent weapon as he watched the life fade from the man's eyes, his pupils dilating, the muscles once holding them in place having lost their strength as his blood spilled on the deck, rushing toward Trubitsin. He followed the path of the blood and pushed up to try and avoid it, when he noticed it had merged with another pool. He looked down and saw it was coming from his stomach, his fatigues matted with the dark liquid, several wounds oozing onto the deck through holes ripped in his shirt.

He dropped his weapon and rolled onto his back, grabbing at his stomach with both hands as he tried to stop the rush of blood escaping his body. He gasped as a jolt of searing pain raced through him, tensing his muscles and forcing him to arch his back, leaving only his shoulders and feet momentarily touching the deck. His feet then slipped out from under him as his body collapsed back on the unforgiving metal deck, the pain slowly fading. He looked up, searching for the stars, but couldn't find them, the night sky giving way to the breaking dawn, leaving his last memory one of disappointment, as visions of his youth spent staring through a telescope with his father played out in his mind.

What a waste.

UNICEF Camp
Lower Nubia, Egypt

Mitchell pulled the jeep to the crest of the hill then hit the gas, pushing it over and down the other side as dawn broke. His heart sank. The camp from the day before was gone, the only evidence they had ever been there, footprints and tire tracks, which the desert wind would make quick work of over the coming hours. He jammed the brakes on and skidded to a halt near the edge of the camp then jumped out, followed by a hesitant Jenny.

"What're we looking for?"

"Anything," muttered Mitchell. "Anything that might suggest she was here this morning."

They wandered the former campsite for several minutes but found nothing. Mitchell scanned the surrounding dunes and spotted indentations coming down the rise they had crested. He ran over to the hill and climbed, following the trail.

"What is it?" asked a breathless Jenny as she followed.

"I think they're footprints."

He reached the top and turned around to pull Jenny up. They stood, examining the surroundings.

"Look!" Jenny pointed at a set of indentations in the sand resembling a jumble of footprints. Mitchell walked over, careful not to step on them. A trail of smaller indentations lead back to their camp, another, deeper set, approached across the hilltop, and then a third, even deeper set, lead away, turning into the indentations they had just followed.

"What do you make of this?" he asked aloud, not expecting an answer.

"Seems pretty obvious to me," said a clearly excited Jenny. "Professor Palmer came up the hill, a man jumped her, then carried her down the hill to their camp."

169

Mitchell was skeptical. "How do you figure?"

"Grad student, eh?" Jenny pointed at the smaller steps then at the deeper steps. "The deeper steps mean the person is heavier, so obviously a man." She pointed at the even deeper set leading into the camp. "There's two sets of prints leading here, but only one leading away, and they appear to be even deeper, which suggests that he's carrying something heavy."

Mitchell nodded, impressed. "Good theory. Or"—he smiled slightly— "the smaller steps could be older, so the wind has filled them in more than the others."

Jenny frowned. "Hadn't thought of that."

Mitchell pulled his cellphone out and started taking pictures of everything.

"What are you doing?"

"Documenting the evidence before it blows away."

"I thought you didn't like my theory?"

"That's not what I said, I merely proposed another. To be honest, I think you may be right."

Jenny growled. "Bloody hell, you grad students are so frustrating sometimes!"

Mitchell ignored her and scampered down the hill and back into the camp, taking photos of what remained of the tire tracks and several odd indentations in the sand. Finished, he waved to Jenny, also taking photos. "Let's go back to the dig."

Jenny climbed in the passenger seat as Mitchell put the jeep in gear. "Maybe she'll be there?"

"Maybe," said Mitchell, unconvinced.

She's been taken, I'm sure of it.

"If she's not at the camp, I'm going to call Professor Acton. He'll know what to do."

Milton Residence
St. Paul, Maryland

Acton sat at the kitchen table, laughing as Sandra Milton flipped pancakes with her daughter, Niskha. He turned to his friend. "I can't believe how much she's grown in just the past six months."

Milton agreed. "It's crazy. I don't notice it as much, seeing it every day, but every birthday when I make that tick on the door frame, I'm amazed."

Acton looked over at the door that Milton had indicated and saw the marks with the year scratched beside each one. Acton shook his head. "Hard to believe she was ever that small." He watched as she helped her mother carry the plates to the table, barely clearing the height of the counter.

"Jim, is that your phone?"

"Huh?" He looked up at Sandra as Niskha placed a plate, filled with pancakes, bacon, and eggs, in front of him.

"I hear a phone ringing and it doesn't sound like one of ours."

Acton cocked his ear and listened to the faint ring. "Sounds like it." He got up and quickly mounted the stairs, two at a time, to the spare bedroom where he had left the phone after calling Laura last evening. He had spent the night as he often did when the conversation dragged into the late hours, his home now lonely since he was used to Laura being with him.

As he entered the room, the phone stopped ringing. "Damn!" He grabbed it and pulled up the last caller's number. Unknown. And they had apparently called at least ten times through the night.

I must have been really tired.

He stuffed it in his pocket, returning to the kitchen.

"Who was it?" asked Milton.

"Don't know, call display says unknown and they didn't leave a message, but there's about ten missed calls through the night. I must have slept like a log."

Milton laughed. "You certainly sawed at one."

Acton feigned a punch.

Sandra sat down at the table and clasped her hands in a moment of silent thanks then opened her eyes and smiled. "I'm sure they'll call back if—"

As if on cue, the phone rang again. Acton fished it from his jeans and flipped it open. "Hello?"

"Is this Professor Acton?"

Acton frowned, not recognizing the voice, but, having spoken to people on a satellite phone before, he knew he was doing so again. "Yes. Who's speaking?"

"Oh thank God I finally reached you! This is Terrence Mitchell." A pit formed in Acton's stomach as he recognized the name.

Something's wrong.

"I'm one of Professor Palmer's grad students on the dig in Egypt."

"Yes, yes, I remember her mentioning you." He took a breath. "Has something happened to Laura?"

This brought the activity at the table to a stop with the exception of Niskha, who continue to cut her pancakes deliberately with the edge of her fork, a look of concentration on her face as she diced the moist wedges of dough into near perfect squares. Milton and Sandra both looked at him with concerned expressions.

"Yes, ummm, I'm not quite sure how to say this, but the professor is missing."

Acton's stomach flipped and his heart pounded like a drum. "What? Did you say she's missing?"

Sandra's hand darted to her mouth. Milton's eyes flew open for a moment then he leaned over to Sandra and tapped her on the arm to get her attention. She looked at her husband, tears filling her eyes. He motioned for her to take Niskha from the room.

"Yes, she's missing."

172

"Since when?" asked Acton as Sandra picked up Niskha.

"But, Mommy, I'm not finished yet!"

"Shhh, honey, Uncle Jim has a very important phone call. I'll make you fresh pancakes. Right now I need you to go play in your room for a few minutes."

"Okay," she said as her mother put her down in the hallway.

Acton hit the speaker button so they could all hear, then placed the phone on the kitchen table.

"We think since this morning," said Mitchell.

Milton signaled for Sandra to get a pen and paper, which she grabbed off the counter. He began to take notes.

Acton leaned toward the phone. "Have you searched the camp?"

"Yes, everywhere, and she's nowhere to be found." There was a pause then Mitchell lowered his voice. "We're really quite concerned."

Acton kept his voice calm.

There's no need to panic the kid.

"Who have you notified?"

"Well, you're the first, sir. I wasn't sure what to do. They didn't exactly train us for this."

Acton sensed the fear in the kid's voice. "That's okay, you did the right thing."

"Professor Acton, there's something you should know."

A sense of foreboding filled Acton as he waited for what must be worse news. "What's that?" he asked with trepidation.

"There was a UN NGO here yesterday, claiming to be lost. I didn't have a good feeling about them."

He experienced a momentary sense of relief as his mind had reeled thinking the worst. "Yes, she mentioned them to me last night. She thought there was something odd about them as well."

"Well, we went over to their camp this morning to see if she was there, and it looks like they broke camp only a couple of hours before we got there."

"Do you think she went there?"

173

"Perhaps. There were what looked like a woman's footprints climbing the hill, then a man's approaching the same spot, then only one set of heavier prints leaving."

Acton looked at Milton who shrugged.

"Are you sure?"

"No, it's just a theory. I took photos of all the prints and the campsite, I'm having them emailed to you as we speak."

Milton pointed at a netbook sitting on the kitchen counter. Sandra grabbed it and placed it in front of him. Milton typed furiously for a few seconds then flipped it around to face Acton.

"Okay." Acton typed his password into the university's webmail then pushed the computer back to his friend.

"But that's not all. A couple of the students swear they heard a helicopter during the night."

"What?" exclaimed Milton.

Acton shuddered, his last experience with a helicopter anything but pleasant. "A helicopter?"

"Yes."

"Strange for a helicopter to be in that area."

"What should we do?"

Milton cleared his throat. "This is Dean Milton from Saint Paul's University."

"Oh, hello, sir, Terrence Mitchell."

"Listen, Terrence. Call your university as soon as you end this call and tell them everything you've told us. They'll have people that will contact your embassy in Cairo and send out some people. We're going to make some calls from our end as well."

"Okay, thanks." Mitchell's voice sounded relieved.

Acton leaned into the phone. "Listen, Terrence. Everything is going to be alright. We'll get somebody out to you as soon as possible. For now, just keep everybody in the camp, let everybody know what's going on and that help is on the way."

"Yes, Professor."

"And keep in touch with your university, and with me. You're on the dig's satellite phone?"

"Yes, sir."

"Okay, I'll call you in a few hours, so make sure you keep close to this phone and keep it charged."

"Yes, Professor. I'll do that."

"Okay, goodbye, Terrence, I'll call you soon."

"Goodbye."

Acton flipped the phone shut then leaned back in his chair and tossed his head back, staring at the ceiling for a moment as what he had just heard sank in.

"Look at this." Milton spun the netbook to face him, the screen showing the photos Mitchell had taken in Egypt. Acton flipped through them, his heart sinking with each one.

"They definitely look like footprints."

"Yes," agreed Milton. "And the heavier set could be someone carrying another person."

Acton stood abruptly. "I've got to get out there. Now."

Unknown Location, Egypt

Laura was jolted awake. Her head pounded with a throbbing, pulsing pain that radiated from her face all the way to the back of her head, the sound of rushing blood filling her ears. And the sound of a truck changing gears. She opened her eyes slightly then blinked several times, trying to moisten them, the dry air having turned her eyeballs into arid orbs. She reached to rub them when she discovered her hands couldn't move, and in a moment of panic, it all came rushing back to her. Crawling up the hill. The sound behind her. The man hitting her in the face with something. And now this, tied up in a vehicle heading to who knows where for who knows what purpose. The truck bucked forward again, the gnashing of gears roaring in protest, the driver having trouble shifting.

Laura was lying down on the cool, metal floor of some sort of truck, the side that filled her vision piled high with boxes and canvas bags, most of which appeared military issue, their distinctive green with black stencil lettering a dead giveaway. She rolled onto her back and examined her surroundings.

She was alone.

She breathed a sigh of relief, lifted her back off the ground, then pushed with one leg to swing around so she could lean up against the equipment she had surveyed. She gasped against the gag she just realized she had in her mouth. She pushed against it with her tongue to no avail. It was there to stay unless she freed her hands. She turned and rolled onto her back again, this time kicking her legs in the air and pushing down with her hands, extending her arms as far as she could. She lifted them up as she tucked her legs into her chest and then bent one leg to the side. With a push and what she thought would soon be a dislocated shoulder, she freed one leg, then the other. She lay back down, catching her breath, her gasps against the gag ragged.

A few more breaths then she reached up, pulling the gag from her mouth and gulped deeply. She looked at her hands and discovered them bound by a plastic tie, the tough plastic something she wasn't chewing through with ease—she needed something to cut it with. She rolled onto her stomach and pushed to her knees, and was about to lift her head when she saw a bolt in the truck floor. She dropped to her elbows then positioned the plastic tie over the rough edge, and rubbed.

Milton Residence
St. Paul, Maryland

"I've booked you on a flight for Cairo leaving in six hours," said Milton as Acton carried his bag down the stairs and deposited it near the front door.

"Okay, thanks."

"I know I can't talk you out of going, hell, I'd go too if it wasn't for this"— Milton waved his hands at his wheelchair—"but have you thought this through?"

"What do you mean?"

"I mean, what're you going to do when you get there?" Milton motioned for his friend to sit down. Acton, pacing near the kitchen counter, eyed the chair then sat down reluctantly and sighed. "You're going into a violent, third world country, with no support network."

"I know, but what choice do I have?"

Milton leaned back in his chair. "Well, I've been thinking about that."

"And?"

"Reading."

Acton smiled. "Of course! I hadn't even thought of him! He's perfect!"

Milton agreed. "With that new Interpol job he took after London last year, he might be able to help you."

Acton grabbed his phone, found the number, then dialed.

"Sir!"

Morrison looked up to see an excited Leroux rushing into his office, waving a file. "Reports of a Soviet helicopter over the Red Sea!"

This piqued Morrison's interest. "Did you say Soviet? From where?"

"As near as our guys can tell, it launched from a Russian cargo ship, entered Egyptian airspace, landed for thirteen minutes, then returned to the ship. The Egyptian Air Force sent planes to challenge it, but it was in international waters before they could engage. We intercepted the communication."

Morrison leaned back in his chair, rubbing his chin.

"Okay, so we have a *Soviet* chopper in Egypt, illegally. We have the Russians pulling in favors to apparently do a flyby at thirty thousand feet in the same area. We have a Russian battlecruiser re-tasked into the same area. We have a white supremacist group, claiming something big is going to happen and they are going to Egypt as part of a UN NGO. And we have a British archaeology professor who may have stumbled upon them, in Egypt. Go on."

"Well, as soon as I found out about the chopper, I found the coordinates for where they think it landed."

"And let me guess—"

Leroux cut him off, apparently too excited to let his boss finish his sentence. "Right next door to Professor Palmer's dig site!"

Morrison let out a thin whistle.

Unbe-freakin'-lievable!

"Chris, I don't know how you pull these things out of your ass, but that is something."

Leroux grinned. "So, what do we do?"

"*We* do nothing. *You* keep doing that brilliant thing you do and keep me posted on anything to do with Acton, Palmer, New Slate, Egypt, Russians, etcetera, etcetera. I'm going to let our assets in the area know."

MS Sea Maiden
Red Sea

The gunfire had stopped. Agent Dymovsky cautiously stepped out from the crates he was hiding behind and saw Major Koslov farther down the deck leaning over the rail, looking in his direction. Koslov waved for him to come forward, but also waved his hand at the deck, indicating he should keep his head down. As he approached, he saw that most of the assault unit had their weapons pointed at a single open hatch, the metal surrounding the compartment scarred from hundreds of hits.

"Come out slowly, with your hands up!" ordered Lt. Colonel Chernov.

Koslov snapped his fingers at him and pointed at a nearby crate. Dymovsky ducked behind it, watching through the slats as the action unfolded. A pair of hands emerged holding a TEC-9 machine pistol, raised in front of the still shadowy figure.

"Toss your weapon out first."

The man's hands withdrew slightly into the darkness then thrust out again, the weapon sailing through the air, clattering on the rusted deck several paces away.

"Now come out with your hands up, slowly."

The shadow solidified as it emerged from the hatchway. Dymovsky smiled.

Sergeant Yakovski.

Yakovski took several more steps into the light, his hands held high as the assault team inched toward him.

Dymovsky rose from behind the crate.

Yakovski looked at him, a sly grin creeping across his face. "Agent Dymovsky."

Dymovsky stepped toward him. "Sergeant Yakovski."

181

"Get on your knees and put your hands behind your head!" ordered Chernov.

Yakovski complied, gripping the back of his head with his hands as Koslov moved in with another Spetsnaz commando covering him. Koslov grasped Yakovski's hands then pushed a knee into his back, sending him sprawling, face first, into the deck. Yakovski grunted with the impact. Koslov gripped Yakovski's left hand and bent the arm behind the prisoner's back, then brought the other hand down, gripping both in one hand while he fished a plastic tie from his utility belt. He expertly bound Yakovski's hands then searched him for weapons, running his hands up and down Yakovski's arms, back and legs, then flipped him over and searched his front. He gave Chernov the thumbs up.

"Get him up," ordered Chernov. Koslov hauled Yakovski to his feet and marched him to Chernov as Dymovsky walked over to join them.

Yakovski ignored Chernov, focusing instead on Dymovsky. "First Red Square and now the Red Sea." Yakovski laughed at his own joke. "You get around, Agent."

Dymovsky didn't react, instead keeping his face as impassive as he could. He stared directly into Yakovski's eyes, letting him know there was no room for amusement this time. "You know why we're here." His voice was firm, monotone.

Yakovski met his gaze. "I do?"

"Where's the weapon?" snapped Dymovsky

"Over there on the deck," Yakovski shot back, indicating his TEC-9.

"You know what I'm talking about. Don't make me turn you over to him." Dymovsky tossed his head at Chernov, catching a glance at his blank stare.

Cold.

The expression, or lack thereof, on Chernov's face even made Dymovsky's heart shudder. He pictured the last two prisoners and the fate they had met under his care.

"Who's he?" Yakovski sneered in contempt, giving Chernov a glance up and down.

"Spetsnaz."

The single word wiped the look off Yakovski's face, and for a moment a flash of fear filled his eyes. He quickly regained his composure, returning his stare to Dymovsky, but it was too late. Dymovsky knew he had him. With Yakovski ex-military, he would definitely know how crazy Chernov very well could be.

Dymovsky pressed the advantage and stepped to within a few inches of Yakovski, his face so close he felt Yakovski's slightly quickened breath on his cheek. He leaned in closer, toward Yakovski's left ear, opposite where Chernov stood, and whispered, "I follow the rules. He doesn't. Tell me what I want to know now, or you will die, and still have told me everything I need to know." He straightened and took a step back. "Where is the weapon?" he repeated, this time louder for everyone to hear.

Yakovski glanced at Chernov from the corner of his eye, as if weighing his options. "You're too late," he muttered, his shoulders sagging with the decision he had just made.

"What do you mean?" But Dymovsky knew what he meant.

"It's gone. Sold."

A pit formed in Dymovsky's stomach. "To who? Chechens?"

Yakovski laughed. "Nyet."

"Who then?"

Yakovski shook his head then stared directly at Dymovsky. "You'd never believe me if I told you."

"Who were they?"

Yakovski, still staring at Dymovsky, looked from eye to eye, as if taking a baseline to measure the surprise of his next statement.

"Americans."

Simmons Army Airfield

Fort Bragg, North Carolina

"Bravo Zero-One, Control Actual, come in, over."

Dawson grabbed the comm off the table in front of him, recognizing Colonel Clancy's voice. All around him his team and the ground crew kept busy loading a C-17 Globemaster III with any and all equipment they might possibly need. Dawson activated his comm. "Control Actual, Zero-One, go ahead, over."

"Zero-One, what's your status?"

"Wheels up in fifteen minutes."

"Check your secure email. I have a pickup for you to make, out."

Dawson looked at Red who had a laptop in front of him, checking off the inventory as it was loaded on board. He flipped over to the secure email server and pushed the laptop to Dawson who logged in and brought up the message.

"Are you kidding me?" Dawson read the message, not sure if Clancy was playing some sort of sick joke on him.

"What is it?" asked Red.

Dawson finished reading the email then spun the laptop toward Red. "You're not going to believe this."

Red scanned the email then laughed. "He is *not* going to be happy to see us."

Dawson wasn't as amused. "No shit. Get me a chopper. I'll take Mickey, Niner and Spock with me, you take command until I join you in Egypt."

Red nodded and headed for the Wing Ops Officer to arrange the chopper.

Dawson re-read the email.

This is not *going to be pretty.*

CIA Headquarters
Langley, Virginia

"Send him in." Morrison leaned back in his chair and smiled as Leroux rushed in, waving a folder in his hand. His hair was matted down on one side, his five o'clock shadow had long since expired, and his clothes appeared suspiciously like the ones Morrison had seen him in yesterday.

"Sir, you gotta see this!"

"Did you sleep here last night?"

Leroux stopped in his tracks, his cheeks taking on a slight reddish hue. "Sir?"

"Nothing." Morrison decided not to test his underling's sense of humor. "What have you got?"

"Intercept from the Russians." Leroux handed the folder over then started spewing its contents before Morrison had a chance to open it. He tossed it on the desk in front of him, deciding to get the human version instead.

"From what I've been able to piece together, a Spetsnaz team from the re-tasked battlecruiser led an assault on a hijacked freighter off the Somali coast. The same freighter that we suspect the helicopter might have landed on."

Morrison frowned. "And?"

"They report no survivors. They claim the pirates killed the crew then they themselves were killed during the assault."

Morrison slammed his fist on his desk. "Effin' Russians."

"Sir?"

"This was a cleanup job from the get go."

"What do you mean?"

"There were no pirates—"

"Of course."

185

"—and the crew they refer to were obviously those involved in the nuke exchange."

"Do you think they made the exchange?"

"If they didn't, the Russians will make a bunch of noise then eventually hand it over as part of the START agreement, but if they did, we won't hear a peep." Morrison tapped his fingers on his desk. "Has there been any more chatter from that area?"

"Nothing, sir."

"And if they'd recovered the weapon—"

"They'd probably be lighting up the airwaves between them and Moscow."

Morrison nodded. "Agreed. So the weapon is definitely still in play."

Former Detective Chief Inspector Hugh Reading tossed his watch on his nightstand and climbed into bed, throwing the duvet over his legs for a quick afternoon nap. He yawned then reached over to turn off the light.

You know you're getting old when an afternoon nap has more appeal than a nooner.

His cellphone vibrated, demanding his attention. "Bloody hell," he muttered, knowing a call at this hour couldn't be good news—only work and his few friends had this number, and his friends knew not to call at this hour. This was one of the reasons he had retired from regular police work and joined Interpol. Regular hours, and less chance of recognition by the general public on the street after last year's fiasco. He grabbed the phone, looked at the call display and raised his eyebrows.

Jim?

He flipped the phone open for a man he now considered a friend, despite the fact he had pursued him a year ago as a multiple murder suspect. After those frantic hours, they had kept in touch, a special bond having formed only events like that could cause. "Jimmy, old boy, do you have any idea what hour it is? It's this old man's nap time!"

"Hi, Hugh, I'm sorry about that, but I need your help."

Reading swung his legs out from under the duvet and over the bedside, sitting upright. He knew from the sound of Acton's voice something was indeed wrong. "What is it?"

"Laura's missing. I think she's been kidnapped."

Reading's mind flashed back to the firebrand woman who had challenged him last year in his pursuit of Acton. He had been there for their first kiss and had seen her a few days ago when she had made a brief stop in London before heading to Egypt.

Egypt! Bloody hell!

"Tell me everything you know."

Acton filled Reading in with the details, details entirely too sparse for his liking. When he had finished scribbling down notes, he glanced at his watch.

"I'm going to make some calls on this end then I'll join you in Egypt."

"Really?"

"If Laura's missing, I'm going to do whatever I can to help you find her." He smiled. "Hell, I practically got you two together."

Acton laughed. "Not exactly how I remember it."

"Meh, you have your version of events, I have mine," said Reading, shrugging. "Let me know what flight you're coming in on and we'll arrange to meet."

Unknown Location, Egypt

Laura tugged at the plastic tie, now worn almost through from an unknown number of minutes of painstaking scraping at the bolt in the floor. Her shoulders and neck screamed in agony, burning from the strain of bending over for so long. The plastic tie holding her wrists together stretched, but the thin band that remained, tantalizingly close to snapping, held on. She opened her wrists as much as she could and brought them to her mouth. Like a dog hanging onto a rope pulled by its master, she clamped down on the tie with her molars and pulled with all her might, finally feeling a snap. Her head jerked back and her hands flew away from her and each other, at last freed from their bonds.

She sat against a soft canvas bag nearby and gently rubbed her raw wrists. They tingled as the circulation returned, and within minutes, besides a ravenous thirst, she felt herself again. She turned her attentions to her surroundings. She was definitely in a truck, likely one she had seen earlier at the camp. It was loaded with supplies that filled the two sides and back, the only empty space the small sliver down the middle she occupied. The door to the outside and potential freedom was at the back. She pulled herself up and stumbled toward it, her legs still not quite under her as she struggled to regain her balance. She reached for the door handle and grasped it.

The truck lurched to a halt, sending her sailing backward. She landed on her back, hard, and her head smacked the metal floor, a searing pain overwhelming all the others before the interior of the truck slowly faded away.

Milton Residence
St. Paul, Maryland

Acton snapped the phone shut, feeling slightly better now that Reading was on the case. He sat at the kitchen table with Milton and Sandra, impatient to leave for the airport, but realizing there was no point since the flight wasn't leaving for hours. He stared at his coffee cup that remained untouched. The silence in the room was broken only by the humming of Niskha as she colored in the next room on the floor.

As he stared at the coffee cup, ripples appeared on the surface.

That's odd.

Then he sensed the vibrations through his chair. He looked up to see if anyone else had noticed.

"What the hell is that?" asked Milton.

"I don't know," said Sandra. The entire house vibrated, a noise that had remained unnoticed in the distance growing louder.

"Look, Mommy!" shouted Niskha, excitement, rather than fear, in her voice.

Acton turned to where she was playing and saw her run to the window. The noise was now so loud they had to shout to be heard.

"That sounds like a helicopter!" yelled Milton as he wheeled his chair toward the window where Niskha was pointing.

Acton strode quickly to the window, his heart hammering as he recognized the distinctive sound of chopper blades slicing through the air. When he reached the window he gasped. A large black helicopter was setting down on the front lawn, four armed men, all dressed in black, jumping out. Two ran toward the back of the house, one remained at the chopper, and the fourth strode for the main entrance.

Acton searched for somewhere to hide, anywhere, the sound of rushing blood filling his ears. He felt dizzy.

Get a grip!

He looked at Milton who was yelling at him but Acton couldn't process anything in his panic.

I can't go through this again!

Something gripped his arm, squeezing tight. The pain snapped him back to reality as he yanked his arm away, spinning toward the person who had grabbed him. He saw Milton looking at him, fear in his eyes. As reality rushed back, he heard the noise from the chopper dying down as the rotors slowed, Niskha, who saw the fear on her parents' faces had begun to cry, and Milton was yelling at him.

"Wh-what?" asked Acton, now back in control.

"Who are they?"

"I don't know," replied Acton, realizing Milton couldn't see over the sill and therefore had missed most of what had played out. "Four men, armed, uniformed, just came out of a military chopper."

Milton's face paled. "You don't think—"

He didn't get a chance to finish his sentence as the doorbell rang.

Everyone in the room stopped and turned toward the door.

The doorbell rang again, followed by a firm, yet not too firm, knock.

"What do we do?" whispered Sandra as she held Niskha against her leg.

Acton took a deep breath. "I don't think we have a choice."

Milton gripped the wheels of his chair. "This is my house. I'll get it."

Sandra reached to grab the chair, but Acton placed a hand on his friend's shoulder.

"No," he said gently. "They must be here for me. I'll try to keep you out of it."

Milton turned to Sandra. "You two go hide upstairs, don't come down until you hear from me."

Sandra nodded and picked up Niskha, rushing up the stairs.

The doorbell rang a third time, the knocking more insistent.

Acton walked to the door. Spotting a baseball bat sitting in the umbrella stand, he grabbed it and held it behind his back. He gripped the door handle and turned, pulling the door open. His entire body numbed, and if he had had anything in his bladder, it would have released.

Before him stood the man who had tried to kill him in London a year ago.

"Hello, Professor Acton. We meet at last."

Dawson was of mixed feelings. He stood, staring through his sunglasses, at Professor James Acton, the man responsible for the deaths of so many of his men, at least one by Acton's own hand, yet he knew that in the same situation he would have done the same thing. Ultimately, it hadn't been Acton's fault—he was innocent, which was the only reason Dawson didn't kill him where he stood.

He had to give the professor credit. He had balls. Dawson could tell Acton was scared, but he stood his ground, a look of determination creased his face as he fought the instinct to flee. Dawson knew very well he was dealing with somebody who had faced incredible odds before and come out on top, and wasn't about to underestimate him.

That was why, when the bat swung from behind Acton's back, he was ready, stepping into the swing and grabbing the top of the bat, breaking the momentum before it had time to build. He gripped Acton's shoulder by the shirt and pushed him over his leg, sending him toppling to the side, controlling the fall. Acton let go of the weapon as he reached out to grab onto something. Now on the floor, Dawson let him go, spun the bat he now possessed, appreciating the well-worn wood, then tossed it behind him into the yard.

"Professor Acton, I'm not here to hurt you."

Acton glared at him as he scurried back a couple of steps. Dawson stepped toward him and extended his hand to help him up.

Acton didn't take it.

Dawson removed his sunglasses and stared directly into Acton's eyes. "Trust me, Professor Acton, if I wanted you dead, you would be already." Dawson watched as Acton processed the information, then reluctantly reached forward and clasped Dawson's hand. Dawson leaned back and pulled him to his feet.

192

"Why are you here?" asked Acton, his voice surprisingly steady.

"We have a national security situation that we believe your partner, Laura Palmer, may have stumbled upon."

This struck a chord as Acton's face turned red, anger flaring in his eyes. "What did you do with Laura!" he growled, stepping toward Dawson.

Dawson didn't move. "What do you mean?"

"What did you do with her?" repeated Acton.

"Nothing," said Dawson as he tried to figure out the reaction. "Why? Has something happened?"

"You tell me. You said she stumbled upon your national security situation and now she's missing." Acton sneered, surrounding 'national security situation' with air quotes. "What have you done with her?"

She's missing?

"Professor, I can assure you this is the first I've heard of this. You said she's missing, when did this happen?"

Acton clearly didn't believe him. "This morning."

Dawson took a step back to deflate the situation. "Professor Acton, my men left for Egypt just a few hours ago."

"What? What does that mean?" Acton sounded confused.

"It means, Professor, that we don't have Professor Palmer. We aren't even there yet."

Acton's rush of adrenaline wore off as the reality of the situation sank in. The man who had tried to kill him and Laura, and had possibly paralyzed his best friend for life, was now telling him he had nothing to do with Laura's disappearance. He wasn't sure what to believe.

"Professor, we don't have much time. Perhaps if I explained the situation to you, you might better understand what is going on." The man extended his hand toward the kitchen table.

Acton held his ground. "After you."

The man smiled. "Of course." He entered the kitchen, all the while keeping an eye on Acton. Acton followed him to the table where they found Milton in his wheelchair, the phone in one hand, a kitchen knife in the other. "Dean Milton," said the man, nodding. "I know it won't mean much if anything, but I am sorry about that." He motioned at the wheelchair. "We were told you were a terrorist and were just following orders."

"'I was just following orders' is an excuse used far too often throughout history."

The man sat down. "True, but let's not get carried away. It's not like we were indiscriminately killing civilians, we were hitting specific targets, under orders, who were supposedly threats to national security. The fact that I am still here, working for the government, should indicate that the new administration agrees we did nothing wrong."

Milton glared at him. Acton sat down at the table and turned to Milton. "I think you can put the knife down."

Milton looked at Acton for a moment then at the knife, as if he had forgotten he was holding it. He let out a sigh and his shoulders sagged as he realized the futility of it all. He placed the knife and phone on the counter then rolled up to the kitchen table.

The man turned to Acton. "We don't have much time, so I'll be brief."

Acton raised his fingers off the table to stop him. "What's your name?"

The man smiled. "Sorry, I guess you never did get that. I'm Mr. White."

Acton gave a single chuckle. "Riiight."

White smiled. "No, that's not my real name, but if it were to come out, the lives of my family and friends could be put in jeopardy."

"What about *my* family and friends?" Acton glanced at Milton.

"I'm not here to debate procedure. I'm here to deal with a national security issue that your girlfriend now seems to be knee deep in."

Acton nodded, realizing the man was right. If Laura was kidnapped, having this man on his side might save her.

White fished two folded sheaves of paper from a pouch on his vest. "Non-disclosure agreements. I need you both to sign them."

Acton was about to tell him to go eff himself when Milton leaned forward and signed the bottom. He looked at Acton. "For Laura," he whispered.

Acton's chest tightened.

Choose your battles.

He frowned, took the pen Milton was holding out, and signed the paper in front of him.

White took the pages, folded them up and returned them to his pouch. "Thank you." He leaned forward and lowered his voice. "I've been authorized to give you the following information. We have been ordered to attempt to intercept and retrieve a black market nuclear missile that we believe is being sold to a group posing as a United Nations Non-Governmental Organization in Egypt. We believe the UN NGO Professor Palmer spoke to you about last night is this group."

Acton's eyebrows shot up as he processed this information.

A nuclear bomb?

His eyes narrowed.

He listened to my phone call?

"How did you know about our phone call?"

White smiled but ignored the question.

"Why are you here?" asked Milton.

Acton's eyes narrowed. "Yeah, why *are* you here?"

"Because, Professor Acton, you have a knack for sticking your nose where it doesn't belong, and with your girlfriend involved, it was decided that you would start asking questions which would raise too many red flags internationally. This, Professor, is a containment situation."

Acton didn't like the sound of that. "What do you mean, containment?"

"I've been sent here to take you, and if necessary, everyone in this household, into protective custody."

Somewhere over Continental Europe

Reading hadn't been to Egypt in years. He hated flying, preferring to take the train wherever he could, but there was no train to Egypt. It wasn't that he was scared of flying. On the contrary, after flying in God knows how many military transports, especially during the Falklands War, flying was nothing to him. What he objected to was the way airlines now treated, or more accurately, mistreated, their passengers. He was not a small man. He was tall, which meant his knees were usually pressed against the back of the seat in front of him when the inconsiderate bastard pushed it back, and since he had a frame that wasn't designed for ballet, he actually filled his seat, meaning the battle of the armrest must be won by him. Hence his preference for trains. The one blessing on this flight was that he had managed to secure an aisle seat, meaning he could at least stretch one leg out and lean into the aisle, giving himself more room. He just had to guard against the flight attendant rocketing down the aisle with a cart. Having taken one in the shoulder years ago, it was an experience he'd prefer not to repeat.

Normally he would have slept, but with Laura likely kidnapped, he couldn't. He was going crazy, his police-trained mind imagining every horrible scenario he had seen a thousand times before. Ransom, white slavery, terrorism. There were too many possibilities. His mind wouldn't let him rest. And if that damned baby three rows ahead of him didn't stop crying, he wouldn't be responsible for what he'd do. Who the hell brings a baby on a five-hour flight? What kind of mental midget thinks this is a good idea? "Hey honey, let's go to Egypt, a violent, Western-hating country, with terrorists who'll kill you just because you're Christian." – "Great idea sweetheart, but only if we can take our poor defenseless child!" – "But of course!"

Reading turned up the music on his headset as loud as it would go, drowning out the rage. He closed his eyes and took a deep breath in through his nose, and slowly exhaled through his mouth. He imagined a small white ball on the back of his eyelids, and focused, trying to make the image coalesce, concentrating his entire mind, his entire being, on turning that one mental image into a visual reality. The whirring pinks and blacks of his eyelids at first refused to cooperate, but as he calmed himself, blocking out the noises around him, he could almost picture the white ball dancing in front of him. He sighed and opened his eyes, feeling about as relaxed as he had all flight. He glanced up at the display showing how much time remained in the flight.

Too long.

He closed his eyes again and quickly fell asleep.

Unknown Location, Egypt

A stinging pain seared through Laura's cheek. And another, this time accompanied by a slapping sound. She opened her eyes and saw someone leaning over her, hand raised, preparing to slap her again. She instinctively raised her arms and closed her eyes.

"She's awake."

Her wake-up call gripped her shirt and pulled her to her feet. She opened her eyes and squinted as sun poured in the now open back of the truck. She heard a roaring sound from nearby, almost rhythmic.

Is that the ocean?

The man, still holding her shirt, pulled her toward the truck door then jumped down, letting go of her shirt as he did so. He motioned for her to follow, beckoning with his hand.

"Come on," he urged as she stood, looking about. The trucks of the convoy were now parked, their backs facing what she assumed was the Red Sea, the waves gently rolling to the sandy beach stretching as far as the eye could see in either direction, unmarred by tourists' umbrellas or beach towels. She took a deep breath of the salty air then gripped one side of the truck door and jumped to the ground. The man gripped her by the upper arm, leading her to a throng of men nearby, staring out at the water. As they approached, one of them pointed to the horizon.

"There!"

One, who she recognized as Jack Russell, the leader of this supposed UN aid group, raised a pair of binoculars and scanned the horizon. He handed them off to another man, nodding. "That's them."

"Look to be about fifteen minutes out," said the man who now held the binoculars.

"Let's get everything unloaded!" Russell ordered, clapping his hands together several times, loudly. "I want everything off these trucks and ready to be loaded on the boat before it gets here. Move!"

The men split into groups, each racing for a truck, and within seconds, crates, bags, guns, and more, were being unloaded.

"Mr. Cole, here she is."

So it's Cole, not Russell.

Cole turned toward her, glancing at her unbound wrists now hanging at her sides. "Professor, so good to see you again."

"Likewise, I'm sure." Laura's heart pounded as she struggled to remain calm on the outside. "I thought your name was Jack Russell?"

Cole smiled at her, motioning with his eyes for the man who still gripped her arm to let go. "I guess it won't matter soon. Edison Cole." He bowed slightly, a condescending smile smeared across his face.

Laura rubbed her arm where the iron grip had been. "Why have you kidnapped me?"

"Your boyfriend is Professor James Acton?"

Her eyes widened.

How could he possibly know that?

"I see he is," smiled Cole, her reaction providing the answer.

"H-how do you know that?"

Cole stepped closer. "Your asshole of a boyfriend interfered in our affairs a few weeks ago. Now he pays the price." His smile broadened. "Or more accurately, *you* pay the price."

Laura's chest tightened and her jaw dropped as she realized who these people were. "You're New Slate!"

"And you're already dead."

Milton Residence
St. Paul, Maryland

Acton wasn't sure who shouted first, but he did know that Milton actually stood up. For a moment the anger was frozen in time as both he and White stared at Milton, and then Milton, realizing what had happened, stared down at his legs. He collapsed back into his chair, the effort exhausting him, but Acton couldn't help but react to the excitement on his friend's face. He was about to say something when White spoke.

"The situation has evidently changed, however."

Acton turned his attention back to the armed man at the kitchen table.

"How?"

"You tell me. What's happened to Professor Palmer?"

Acton took a deep breath, steeling himself. He did not want to show any weakness in front of this man. "We received a call from the dig site saying she's gone missing, and there's evidence that she may have been taken by this UN NGO you were talking about."

"Don't forget the helicopter," said Milton, still staring at his legs.

"Helicopter?" White's eyebrows jumped, his interest apparently piqued.

"The students think they heard a helicopter during the night."

White frowned and activated some type of communications device. "Bravo One-One, please join us in the kitchen, Zero-Five and Zero-Six, stand down."

"Can I tell my wife that everything is okay?" asked Milton.

White nodded and Milton wheeled into the foyer, yelling up the stairs. "Hon, everything's alright!"

There was no answer at first, then the creaking of floorboards overhead, followed by a timid voice. "Are you sure?"

"Yes, dear, everything is going to be fine. Just stay with Niskha in her room."

Sandra said something, likely to Niskha, then he heard her start down the stairs. "If it's supposedly safe, then why can't I come—"

Acton heard the front door open as he caught sight of Sandra. She screamed. Milton spun his chair toward the door.

"It's okay," he said to Sandra, not sounding entirely convinced. Sandra for her part had frozen on the steps, one foot in midair, both hands gripping the rail as if about to turn and run back upstairs.

Acton heard footsteps, then a man appeared in the foyer where they could all see him. Dressed the same as White, Bravo Eleven also sported some sort of machine gun that he had his hands resting on, using the straps as support. He splayed his fingers out, as if to indicate he meant no harm, showing his fingers nowhere near the trigger.

"Good morning, ma'am."

White turned to the new arrival. "Get on a secure channel and find out about any helicopter activity in the target zone, and tell Control we're going to need another bird on standby."

Bravo Eleven nodded, did a two-fingered salute at the still frozen Sandra, then turned on his heel and walked back out.

White turned to Acton. "You're going to have to come with us."

Acton shook his head. "No damned way are we going with you."

White held up his hand. "I think you misunderstand me. *You* need to come with us, to Egypt."

Acton's eyes shot open in surprise. "But—" He wasn't sure what to say.

"But he's already got a flight leaving in a few hours," said Sandra, still on the stairs, leg still suspended in midair.

"Come on, honey," whispered Milton as he urged her forward with his hands. She took a tentative step then joined her husband in the foyer.

White smiled.

"Trust me, I can get you there far faster than any airline can."

J. ROBERT KENNEDY

Red Sea Coast, Egypt

Laura watched as her captors hurriedly loaded a large yacht she estimated at over two hundred feet long, anchored offshore, several small boats ferrying men and supplies, mostly weapons from the looks of things, to the ship. Her hands bound again, along with her ankles this time, she sat in the sand, thankfully in the shade of one of the vehicles. Nobody could be spared to guard her, which for her made no difference, hopping away simply not an option.

Oh, James, I wish you were here!

She knew they planned on killing her, and the fact they hadn't yet meant they had something special in mind. If she were to survive, she would need to escape before getting on board that boat, or convince them not to kill her once there. She glanced again at the ties. There was no way she was escaping.

What can you offer them in return for your life?

She made the mental tally. Men like this always wanted one thing according to the movies. Sex. She'd rather die than offer herself up like a piece of meat. Money? This operation appeared well funded. But she was rich. Very rich. *Money talks*, she had heard James say on many occasions when dealing with suppliers in the third world. Would it talk with these men? What was their agenda? Was it even compatible with money?

It's your only hope. Try to play the ransom game.

One of the men approached her and reached down, seizing her by the tie holding her wrists together, then yanked her to her feet. Her wrists screamed in agony, the plastic cutting through the already raw skin, but she forced herself to keep her face emotionless, meeting his stare with as little reaction as she could muster, his smirk and sadistic eyes revealing disappointment at not receiving the response he had hoped for.

He leaned into her, burying his head in her breasts, sniffing deeply. She shut her eyes and turned away, closing off her mind for what she feared was about to come. His nose pushed into her flesh, his hot breath scorched her navel then her thighs. She heard the sound of a knife unsheathing and she opened her eyes, looking down to see what was happening. He was staring up at her with a leering grin, the glint of a large Bowie knife filling her vision as he pulled it from the sheath on his belt. She returned her attention to him, trying to read what he would do next. He licked his lips then turned his head toward the ground. The knife disappeared from view, then a tugging sensation at her feet led to the sudden release of pressure as the tie binding her ankles was cut. She watched as he sheathed his knife then repeated his journey with his nose and mouth up her body, finishing again at her breasts. He stared at her as he cupped a breast in one hand then slowly turned his face toward it, his mouth opening like the sucker on a leach.

"Quit fooling around and bring her already!" yelled a voice in the distance. She looked and saw a man in one of the dinghies waving.

The letch straightened up and pulled her waist tight against his crotch. His erection pressed against her, through her pants, and a slight dizziness overcame her as she realized she had just avoided rape.

"Come along, princess." He shoved her toward the shoreline. "Time for your swim."

She chose not to say anything. Her plan to buy time with a ransom offer was forgotten as the panic of the situation took over. But as she neared the boat, her mind returned to the task at hand. There was no point in talking to the help. She would wait until she saw the man whom she assumed was the leader, Edison Cole. And he was already on the boat. Her feet, still shod in her hiking boots, splashed through the water on shore as she was herded toward the dinghy. Reaching it, the man already sitting in the rear held out a hand. She stretched for it as she raised her foot to step into the boat. A shove on her back sent her flailing forward and into the boat, her head landing in the lone occupant's lap.

Her wrangler roared in laughter behind her as she struggled to her knees. "Perhaps we can get a little somethin' somethin' out of this bitch before we toss her to the sharks?" he said to his companion as he climbed on board.

"You're a pig, Gabe," said the man as he helped Laura upright.

The letch, Gabe, shrugged and lit a cigarette as the other man powered up the boat's small engine and turned them toward the yacht. They bounced along the waves as the nose of the dinghy skipped across the water, the pig at the prow, his arms spread wide across the rubber shell, all the while eying Laura like a starving fat man who stumbled upon an all you can eat Chinese buffet. Laura was determined not to give him the satisfaction of knowing how uncomfortable he was making her feel, not to mention how terrified. Would she become this man's next conquest before she died? She shuddered at the thought.

He smiled.

Damn!

Somewhere over the Atlantic

"How are you doing back there?"

Acton wasn't sure. He was giddy. He was perfectly *fine*, but he was also more excited than he could remember. A good excited. Not the kind of excited where you're afraid you're going to get your head blown off, but the kind of excited you get on a rollercoaster. And this was one hell of a rollercoaster.

"Fine!" he said, the roar of the twin General Electric F414-GE-400 turbofan engines of the F/A-18F Super Hornet he was occupying the rear seat of, surprisingly unobtrusive.

I guess when you're going faster than the speed of sound…

He would never have dreamed he'd get to fly in a fighter jet, going Mach 1.8 over the Atlantic Ocean then the Mediterranean Sea. When White, whom he had later heard his men call BD, had said he had a faster way of getting to Egypt, he had assumed he meant skipping customs. With Laura missing he shouldn't be having this much fun, but he couldn't help it. He was like a little boy getting to ride in the fire truck. A fifty-five million dollar fire truck with a Vulcan cannon, 22,000 pounds of thrust and half a dozen missiles.

Greg is never going to believe this!

His mind flashed back to his friend and he made a mental note to get in touch when they landed in Egypt to let him know he was okay.

"We're going to be refueling in about five minutes," said the pilot, pointing to his two o'clock position above them.

Acton looked up and saw a large refueller above them. To the right of his aircraft he saw four Super Hornets, flying in formation, each containing part of what he assumed was a special ops team, perhaps Delta Force. Apparently at the speeds they were traveling they would reach Egypt just after the rest of the team arrived. To do what, Acton didn't know. He didn't care about the nuke. Well, he did care, but his primary concern was Laura.

I wonder if Reading has found out anything.

Cairo International Airport
Cairo, Egypt

Reading awoke as the person sitting beside him moved. He opened his eyes, still groggy. It took him a moment to remember he was on an airplane, and then another moment to realize they had landed and already arrived at the gate.

How the blazes did I sleep through the landing?

He wiped his eyes with his knuckles then bent over to put his shoes back on, removing them at the beginning of the flight a trick Acton had mentioned, and he now had a chance to try. As he stood waiting, he noticed how much better his feet felt. They weren't tired or sore from being cramped for hours in footwear never designed for sitting in a pressurized aircraft without moving.

It works!

He patiently waited for the cattle to move, then joined the crowd inching their way toward the exit. Fifteen minutes later he was at the baggage carousel, and another half hour later, he had his bag and was heading for customs. After making it through the snaking lineup, it was, at last, his turn.

"Passport, please."

Reading presented his passport and waited while the man flipped through it.

"What is the purpose of your visit?"

"I'm an off-duty police officer, joining a friend on an archaeological dig site in Lower Nubia."

The man frowned. "You are not here perhaps to steal Egypt's treasures?"

Reading knew he was being baited, and remained calm. "Of course not. This is a sanctioned dig, authorized by your government."

The man scanned Reading's passport and frowned at what he saw on the computer screen. He waved at another agent standing nearby.

The man approached, and judging from his accouterments, was definitely a superior. They spoke in hushed tones for a moment then the new arrival took the passport and looked at Reading.

"Please come with me, Mr. Reading." The man held out his arm, indicating he should walk in the direction he was pointing.

Reading didn't move. "Is there a problem?"

"No, sir, but I need you to come with me."

Reading again didn't move.

"I must insist." Two armed guards walked toward them. Reading picked up his bag and they walked to a side room with no windows.

And no witnesses.

The man held the door open and Reading walked in, not sure what to expect, the horror stories of third world countries flashing through his mind.

"I would be searching his luggage very thoroughly if I were in your position."

Reading recognized the voice and smiled at the man sitting at the table, feet up, sipping a cup of tea. "Rahim!" Reading dropped his bag and rounded the table as his friend stood. "So good to see you! I thought we were meeting at the hotel?"

Rahim shook Reading's hand then motioned to another chair. Reading sat down as his friend poured him a cup of tea and the other officers closed the door, leaving them alone. Reading had met Rahim years before on a case that had brought him to Egypt with Scotland Yard, and with them both now in Interpol, he was an obvious phone call. Reading took the cuppa, and a sip, pleased Rahim had remembered his penchant for tea.

"Yes, that was indeed the original planning, but something of the unexpecting kind has happened."

"What?"

"Your friend from America, your Professor Acton, he never did the boarding of his flight."

Reading's heart thudded, his tea forgotten. "He never boarded? Are you sure?"

Rahim nodded. "I have done the pulling of the passenger manifest. He is not on the flight."

Reading pulled his cellphone out and tried Acton's number, but it went immediately to voicemail.

If he's not on his flight, where could he be where he'd be out of reach?

Red Sea Coast, Egypt

As the dinghy pulled alongside the yacht, the letch she had heard the other man call Gabe, grasped the ladder running down its hull and steadied the craft alongside. He motioned for her to climb the ladder as a doorman at a posh hotel might. She crawled forward and gripped the rung with her bound hands then pulled herself to her feet, steadying herself by leaning forward against the ladder. She let go and quickly moved her hands up, grasping at a rung at shoulder height as the boat swayed under her feet. She fell forward and her hands slid down until she managed to grab the bottom rung once again.

"For Christ's sake!" yelled Gabe before she felt a hand on her behind as she was shoved up and over the side of the boat. She spilled onto the deck, her face smacking the polished wood, sending a jolt of excruciating pain through her cheekbone. She heard the clang of boots on the metal ladder and looked around to see Gabe step on board. He reached down and hauled her to her feet, again by the plastic tie, tearing her skin open. She winced, but immediately looked for the leader of her captors.

She was pushed toward a doorway farther along the boat, past several crew and men from the shore party stowing equipment. She searched behind her, past the letch who shoved her shoulder to get her moving faster, but again didn't spot Cole. She turned her gaze upward and saw him standing on the upper deck, talking to what might be the ship captain.

"I need to talk to you!" she yelled.

He looked down at her and tilted his head, indicating to Gabe to get her moving.

As she neared the doorframe, her heart pounded and the world closed in on her. She had moments before she may be out of his sight forever. She reached out with her bound hands and grabbed onto a handhold, grasping it as hard as she could.

211

"I'm worth a lot of money!" she yelled.

This got his attention. He smiled at her. She almost heard him thinking, "Sure you are!"

"I'm worth millions!" Gabe was now pulling at her wrists and she wouldn't be able to hold on much longer as he gripped her raw wrists and twisted. Her eyes teared from the pain.

"You expect me to believe an archaeology professor is worth millions?" she heard Cole say through the pain. "Nice try, lady, but it won't work."

Her hands jerked away from the handhold, her grip at last broken. Gabe pushed her toward the door.

"I'm worth over one hundred million pounds! Google me!" she yelled as she was shoved through the door frame. She grabbed onto the edge and pulled herself out. "Laura Palmer! Google my brother!"

Gabe tore her from the doorframe and tossed her down the hallway, opening a door and pushing her inside. She tumbled forward and landed on a small, narrow bed occupying one of the walls. He gripped her feet and bound them again, then rolled her onto her back, straddling her waist. He leaned forward and kissed her, his open mouth smearing over her clenched lips, his tongue flicking at her like a massive slug, the saliva and heat from his breath making her gag in disgust. She felt herself shutting down as her mind protected her from the horror. His mouth continued its assault on her face as he manhandled her breasts. Her heart pounded and adrenaline rushed through her veins, fueling the panic. The world closed in on her, darker and darker, her focus narrowing, ignoring the room around her. His mouth moved down her neck, and his ear touched her lips.

She opened her mouth and clamped down hard. He screamed in agonizing pain and pulled away. She tightened her grip, refusing to let go, her hold like a pit bull with its favorite bone. Her teeth sunk further as the skin and cartilage tore, the salty taste of blood filling her mouth.

"Let go you bitch!" he yelled, punching her ribs as he struggled to break free. She twisted her head with a sudden jerk and tore away the flesh she was biting. He cried out again as she opened her eyes and glared, spitting the chunk of flesh at him as he gripped what remained of his ear, blood pouring down his face and hands.

"You bit my ear off!" he cried as he reached for the earlobe that lay in a bloody mess on the floor.

"Be thankful that's all I bit off!" The entire cabin abruptly returned to focus, her fight instinct now winning out over her flight.

Gabe reached for his gun and pulled it from its holster.

Laura met his gaze with defiance. She didn't care anymore. If she was going to die, she was going to die. On her own terms. No way was she letting this rancid piece of meat touch her. Not without a fight. And if that meant dying today, right here, right now, then so be it. She watched as the finger squeezed the trigger, the hammer slowly raising. She refused to close her eyes, determined to make him remember them for the rest of his life.

She stared deep into his eyes. She could see the hesitation, then the commitment.

Goodbye, James.

The door to the cabin swung open and hit Gabe on the back. The trigger squeezed and the shot fired. She heard the splintering of wood behind her, but no pain.

"What the hell is going on in here?"

It was Cole.

My savior?

The letch was shocked. "That bitch bit my ear off!"

Cole looked at the man's ear then at her bloody mouth. "Did this man try to rape you?"

Strange question.

She nodded.

Cole turned to Gabe and held out his hand. "Weapon."

Gabe handed it over with a look of confusion.

Cole readied the weapon, pointing it directly at Gabe's chest. "We are not rapists." He squeezed the trigger. Laura yelped in shock as Gabe's eyes shot wide open in surprise. He grunted as the bullet exploded through his chest, his shoulders rolling forward as his torso

213

was forced back. Laura spun away then slowly returned her gaze to the body that now lay crumpled in the corner.

"Thank you," she whispered.

Cole turned to her. "We are *not* animals."

Laura nodded.

Cole held up his cellphone, an image of her on it. "I took your advice and Googled your brother."

"And?"

Cole sat down on the bed beside her, bending his knee up, his left foot on the thin mattress, the hand holding the gun resting on his kneecap. He stared at her then at last replied.

"I think we can do business."

242nd Tactical Fighter Wing
AFB Beni Suef, Egypt

Red and Atlas, having arrived with the rest of the Bravo Team less than an hour earlier on the C-17, stood at the edge of the airstrip, the last of the F-18s touching down, their nose gear hitting the concrete runway with a puff of smoke as the rubber raced from zero to 140 knots in an instant. The first of the five planes had taxied to a stop near the end of the airfield where their Egyptian hosts had sequestered them. The timing had worked out, the unplanned pickup having only cost them an hour thanks to their high-speed transport arranged by Colonel Clancy. With the night sky about to break into dawn, the Egyptian ground crew, not wanting anybody to see American-flagged aircraft touching down, hurried to refuel the jets, their turbines barely having stopped spinning down.

Atlas elbowed Red and pointed at the first plane as the canopy popped open and the pilot and the rear seat passenger stepped out, waving at them.

Atlas returned the wave. "That's BD!"

Red smiled as he saw his friend jump down from the last of the handholds and approach them, removing his helmet. Red walked up to him and shook his hand. "Good flight?"

Dawson laughed. "The best. We should use them flyboys every time we need to get somewhere. Much quicker."

Atlas jogged over to greet Spock, Mickey and Niner as Dawson leaned in so Red could hear him.

"Status?"

"All our gear has been unloaded and we're ready to go. I received a set of coordinates from Control. They're about an hour from here by chopper. They think the deal went down there, and get this—"

He stopped as the man from the fifth plane walked toward them. The other men stared, the expressions on their faces making it clear they were shocked to see him.

Dawson waved at them and the men jogged over, the last plane's engines now quiet. "Did you not tell them he was coming?" whispered Dawson to Red.

"No, figured I'd leave that pleasure to you."

Dawson grunted. "Gentlemen, this, as most of you know, is Professor James Acton."

Red stuck out his hand and Acton appeared at first reluctant to take it, but then, at last, did, returning a firm handshake and a flash of a smile. "I'm Red, nice to meet you, Professor."

Acton nodded. "Red? Is that another Mr. White?"

Red chuckled. "Nope, just my nickname."

"What's he doing here?" Atlas looked Acton up and down. He had been extremely close with Spaz, their comrade Acton had killed the year before.

"Professor Acton will be assisting us. His partner, who some of you know as well, Professor Laura Palmer, is missing, and we believe may have been taken by the very men we are after."

"No shit?" exclaimed Atlas. "Sorry to hear that." He leaned in and slapped Acton on the back. "Sorry about all that, you know, trying to kill you stuff, last year."

Niner roared in laughter. "Good thing we didn't succeed, huh!" He leaned in and shook Acton's hand. "Your girlfriend, is she the one that was driving that Porsche?"

Acton nodded.

"Damn, that chick can drive."

Acton smiled. "I'll let her know you said so." A cloud of gloom covered his face. "If we can find her."

"Don't worry. If she's with them, we'll find her," said Mickey.

"Okay, enough of the family reunion," said Dawson. The men stood more upright, facing him. "Get the chopper ready, wheels up in fifteen."

"Yes, Sergeant Major!" they yelled in unison and ran toward the nearby hangar housing the Black Hawk helicopter they had brought with them.

Dawson turned to Red and Acton. "Let's check out those coordinates and see what we find."

Al Kosair-Safaga Highway, Egypt

The drive to the camp was long, bumpy, and made all the worse by Reading's growing worry over what might have happened to his friend. Faisal, he now remembered, was a chatterbox, as his ex-partner Chaney would have called him, pointing out everything they drove by, including sand, full of facts about anything that cast a shadow, that every once in a while even Reading knew not to be entirely accurate. He could just imagine what Acton would have said. He was thankful he was sitting in the back seat of the van, the front passenger seat apparently stolen years ago. It allowed him to relax, arms spread across the seatback, legs splayed out, desperate to catch the wind blowing in through the windows, the air conditioner probably not even invented when the beast they traveled in was manufactured.

"Are you okay back there?" Rahim asked, his head turned around as they continued their breakneck drive down what passed as a highway.

Reading grunted. "I'll live."

"I am begging your forgiveness again, but my car, I am not trusting it to make this long distance, so I borrow my cousin's van. Very reliable. But very hot." He laughed, still looking squarely at Reading, whose eyes opened wider and wider as he watched the road in front, Rahim apparently not concerned about the ox cart they hurtled toward.

"Ah, Rahim?"

Rahim continued to look at Reading. "Oh, not to be worrying, Rahim will get you there, not you worry."

"Rahim, watch the road!"

Rahim jerked his head and deftly swerved around the ox cart, its operator gently waving a whip over the two animals pulling the load. Reading looked back at the man they had almost hit. He gave no indication he knew anything had happened.

Rahim stared at Reading through the cracked rearview mirror. "See, I very good driver, you are in good hands, my friend."

218

Reading nodded and closed his eyes, feigning sleep. It only took a few minutes before it turned into the real thing.

"Rising and shining, my friend!"

Reading opened his eyes and saw Rahim looking back at him. "Are we there?" The bouncing of the van indicated they hadn't yet arrived, but the fact they were driving in the pitch dark, the only light from the stars above, the dim headlights on the front of the van, and the GPS perched on the dash, suggested they were much closer than when he had nodded off.

"Almost, GPS is saying five kilometers."

Reading stretched. "Jesus, how long was I out?"

"Long enough to be getting your rest, I am trusting, my friend. I am thinking it will be a busy day."

Reading sat up and grabbed a canteen sitting beside him. He unscrewed the cap and took a long drink. He glanced at the GPS that had them nowhere near any road.

Reading frowned. "We're not lost, are we?"

Rahim laughed. "We were, the GPS map has not been updated for many times, so there was a bit of flying by the seating of Rahim's pants, but we are now back on the track. No worrying, my friend."

"Uh huh."

Rahim looked back at Reading. "Don't worry, old friend, we are almost there!"

"Rahim, watch the road!" yelled Reading, the headlights revealing a sharp turn ahead.

Rahim spun his head forward. "Sorry, my friend!" he said cheerfully as he dropped into a lower gear, jammed on the brakes and spun the wheel. Miraculously they kept on the now dirt road. At the bottom of a short hill, they could see lights.

"That must be the dig." Reading leaned forward. Rahim honked his horn as they barreled into the encampment. Reading checked his watch. "Well, if they weren't awake, they are now."

Rahim skidded to a halt in front of the latrines, one of the camp's few lit areas, much of the rest still smothered in darkness. Reading slowly pried his fingers from the back of Rahim's seat, muttering under his breath, "I'm driving next time."

"Oh no, Hasni, my cousin, he would not be permitting of this."

"What your cousin doesn't know…" Reading began but gave up at the look of horror on Rahim's face at the thought of lying. Reading looked around the camp. Considering the amount of noise Rahim had made as they entered, he was surprised to see no one coming to investigate their arrival. Rahim turned the engine off as Reading slid open the van's side door and stepped out onto the desert sand. It appeared abandoned, the only sounds the flapping of the tents in the gentle breeze and an odd knocking sound from the van that erupted in a huge explosion from the tailpipe.

"Jesus Christ, Rahim!"

Almost filled my trousers on that one.

"Sorry, my friend!"

A scream from a nearby tent let Reading know they had not gone unnoticed. He stepped forward and held up his hands. "My name is Agent Reading. I am with Interpol and a friend of Professors Laura Palmer and James Acton. You should have been informed that I was coming!"

A nearby tent flap opened and a young man, about twenty-five, stepped out, shining a flashlight at Reading and Rahim. He took a few tentative steps from the tent, then stopped.

"Did you say Reading?"

Reading took a few steps toward him, slowly lowering his hands. "Yes. Are you Terrence Mitchell?"

"Yes, yes I am!" exclaimed the young man, the sound of relief in his voice so obvious Reading felt sorry for him, the past couple of days' pressure clearly having taken its toll. "Oh, thank God you're here!" He stepped toward Reading, his hands out. Reading half expected him to drop to the ground and hug his knees, but he instead fell into Reading's arms and hugged him. Reading returned the hug, awkwardly, patting the young man's back.

"It's okay, lad, we're here now."

Mitchell let go and stood, wiping his eyes. "I-I'm sorry. It's just been so crazy. Professor Palmer's missing and we just didn't know what to do. Everybody has been hiding in the central tent." He pointed to the large tent he had exited. "We've been too scared to come out. When we heard you coming, we didn't know what to think."

Reading smiled, conveying as much reassurance to the boy as he could. "How about we go in the tent and talk to everybody?"

Mitchell's head bobbed. "Yes, yes, that's a good idea. I think everyone will be relieved now that the police are here," said Mitchell as he led Reading and Rahim to the tent, "and they aren't Egyptian." He looked at Rahim. "Sorry, I didn't mean anything by that, I just mean that it's someone from home that we can trust." Mitchell shook his head again. "Sorry, I didn't mean trust—"

Rahim cut him off. "It is okay, my friend, I am understanding what you are meaning." He extended his hand to Mitchell. "I am Agent Rahim al-Massri, also of Interpol."

This brightened Mitchell's mood. "Interpol? Really, well, that's…" Mitchell paused for a moment, apparently searching for a politically correct word.

"Wonderful?" suggested Reading.

"Wonderful? It's bloody brilliant!" exclaimed Mitchell, shaking Rahim's hand furiously. "Come, I'll introduce you to everyone!" He opened the tent flap. "It's okay, they're police, Interpol!"

Reading heard the murmurings of relief from several bodies inside and lights flicked on as they entered the tent. He stepped through after Mitchell, and as he cleared the entrance and raised his head, he was charged by a nearby girl, screaming. He didn't have time to react to defend himself, but when she hit him, full force, she wrapped her arms around him and bawled.

I think I arrived in the nick of time.

Karakoram, Capital City of the Mongolian Empire
August 13, 1257 AD

Grand Headmaster Hasni held Faisal back. "No, my son," he said in a harsh whisper. "I understand your desire, but this must be allowed to happen. It is our Master's wish."

Faisal relaxed slightly and Master Hasni removed his hand from Faisal's chest. It had been a year, a year of hiding in shadows, of gathering lost followers, of trying to maintain the Order, while publicly, those that had survived the siege of Alamut were paraded about and humiliated, and now were about to be ultimately betrayed.

Under the guise of clemency, the remaining members of the Order were allowed to travel to Karakoram, the capital city of the Mongolian horde, to publicly beg forgiveness and to pledge their allegiance to the Mongol emperor, Mongke Khan. Faisal knew this was a ruse, they all knew it, including their former Grand Headmaster Khurshah, who Master Hasni had spoken to only days before while disguised as a camel herder. Khurshah had told Hasni to under no circumstances attempt a rescue. Their final sacrifice would allow those that remained to continue on, as the world would think the Order was no more.

Master Hasni and several others, including Faisal, who had proven himself time and again in battle and in covert reconnaissance over the past year, now hid among the rocks strewn across the plain about to become the forgotten graveyard of the final members of the original Hassassins.

Faisal held his breath, a lump forming in his throat as the Mongol chief yelled something unintelligible to his ears and raise his arm, then abruptly lower it. Dozens of curved blades descended as one, severing the heads of their victims, and publicly eliminating the Order of the Assassins once and for all from the whispers of men.

Former UNICEF Camp
Lower Nubia, Egypt
Present Day

Reading quickly determined the students had seen nothing on the night of Laura's disappearance, but several were certain they had heard a helicopter early in the morning, before sunrise. He, Rahim and Mitchell now bounced along the road toward the site where the UN NGO had been and where Mitchell was convinced they had kidnapped her. Reading gripped the dash as the boy crested the dune and hit the gas, sending them tipping down the other side. He glanced back at a smiling Rahim in the back seat, his arms outstretched as he took in the sparse landscape.

Mitchell brought the jeep to a halt at the bottom of the hill and turned off the engine. "This is it."

Reading climbed out and quickly scanned the area, Mitchell and Rahim joining him.

Mitchell pointed at the hilltop they had descended. "Up there is where we found the footprints."

Reading nodded. "I saw the photos."

"So, do you think our theory is right?" Mitchell sounded eager to have validation from an expert.

"It's definitely one possible theory, and if the professor wasn't missing, I would tend to dismiss it. However…" He trailed off as he raised his finger.

"What is it, my friend?" asked Rahim.

"Shhh!" Reading cocked his ear. "Do you hear that?"

"I hear nothing, my friend."

"Listen."

Reading barely heard it, it sounded like an engine, or something, approaching.

"I hear it!" exclaimed Mitchell.

The sound got louder and louder, filling the entire area. Reading couldn't determine where it was coming from, the number of small hills in the area concealing everything.

"Look!" Mitchell pointed at the hill they had crested.

Reading's eyes first fell upon Mitchell's face, a look of terror etched across it, then followed the finger to where he was pointing. He gasped. The blades of a helicopter appeared above the hill then the entire machine revealed itself. Reading's heart raced as he had flashbacks of the last time he had seen a helicopter this close. He instinctively placed himself between Mitchell and the new arrival, reaching for his weapon, but not drawing it.

The chopper pulled its nose up and slowed to a stop, landing less than a hundred feet away, forcing them to cover their faces as the sand was whipped around by the now slowing blades. The door to the chopper slid open and four men dressed head to toe in black jumped out, their weapons drawn. They quickly spread out, taking covering positions, their weapons curiously not pointed at Reading and his companions. Two more men climbed out and walked toward them as the blades died down. He squinted as the sand settled, and through the dust, he thought he recognized one of the men.

It can't be!

"Jim?"

Acton strode toward his friend with a huge grin. He had known Reading would probably eventually come to Egypt, but he had never imagined his friend would get here so soon. He noticed Reading's hand behind his back. And apparently so had the Bravo Team Commander who muttered to him, "Better get your friend to calm down." Acton strode ahead, placing himself between Reading and the Delta operator he now knew as BD.

"Hugh, how the hell are you?" Acton grabbed Reading in a hug and whispered in his ear. "Don't worry, they're okay."

Reading returned the hug then stepped back and looked at the soldier standing before him. He extended his hand. "Agent Reading,

Interpol, and this"—he turned to his friend—"is Agent al-Massri, also Interpol."

BD accepted the handshake, removing his sunglasses. "Didn't it used to be Detective Chief Inspector Reading of Scotland Yard?"

Reading was taken aback for a moment and studied the man, a look of recognition springing on his face as he made the connection. His hand reached for his back when BD raised his hands, palms out. "We're all friends here, isn't that right, Professor?"

Acton nodded and again placed himself between the two. "That's right. The past is the past, they're after the same people we might be after."

Reading's hand stopped its movement to his weapon and he stared BD in the eyes. "Why?"

"Can I tell him?" asked Acton.

BD nodded. "You will the first chance you get anyway, so you might as well." BD walked away, yelling orders to his men to sweep the area.

Reading lowered his voice so only Acton and Rahim could hear. "What in blazes is going on? Why are you with them?" He checked his watch. "And how did you get here so bloody quick? I thought you missed your flight?"

Acton took a deep breath, and began. "Shortly after we talked, they showed up at Greg's house to take me, and them, into custody."

"Why?"

"Because they apparently intercepted the phone call from Laura about the NGO. They had them under surveillance or something and were worried I'd start asking questions because of what happened last year."

"Well, they were right there," said Reading with a wry grin.

Acton chuckled. "Yeah, well, you're probably right. But what they didn't know was that Laura had gone missing, which was why they decided to take me with them. I guess to deal with the students and not start an international uproar."

"You said they were watching the NGO. Why?"

"Because…" Acton leaned in and lowered his voice further, glancing around as if worried someone might be listening. "Because they think they might have a nuclear missile."

Reading bristled, his chest expanding as he took in a deep breath at the news, his shoulders squaring as he held it. He slowly let it out through pursed lips. "This changes everything."

"It most certainly does." Rahim pulled out a satellite phone and hit the speed-dial. "Yallah!"

A dull roar came from behind them. They all turned but saw nothing.

"Look!" Acton pointed at a cloud of dust that appeared about half a mile away, the source hidden by one of the dunes. "What the hell is that?"

The Bravo Team Commander walked over to them. "It's just some Bedouins, we saw them as we passed over."

"They seem to be coming this way." Reading turned to his friend. "Who did you call?"

Rahim smiled. "Do not do any worrying, my friend, all will be well."

Acton glanced at Rahim then back at the dust cloud. The roar, like the sound of hundreds of rugs beaten with as many shoes, continued to get louder, the cloud now filling their entire field of vision to the north.

BD stepped backward, toward the chopper, motioning his men to fan out. The roar surrounded them when, over the crest of the hill, a lone horse appeared, its rider dressed all in black, his face covered with a keffiyeh headscarf. He stopped then stood in his saddle, waving his right hand in a circle, yelling something in Arabic Acton couldn't understand.

More horses and riders appeared, fanning out to either side of the lead man, and within less than a minute, at least fifty men surrounded them.

"Prepare to repel!" Acton heard BD yell. Acton spun around and saw the Delta team drop to one knee, aiming their weapons at the men on the surrounding hills. The lead man yelled something else in Arabic and in unison, each of the men flipped part of his robe aside, revealing an AK-47.

But they didn't remove them from their chests. They left them in place, as if to merely show they were armed, and that Acton and his companions were vastly outnumbered.

Rahim raised his hands and turned to BD. "I am suggesting to you that you put down your weapons, they mean you no harm."

BD kept his eyes on the new arrivals. "That'll be the day."

As if on cue, the surrounding men placed their right hand on their weapons, still not pointing them at the party below, but the sound from dozens of hands smacking metal sent a chill through Acton's spine as he realized if the situation was not defused soon, they could be cut down in seconds.

"Mr. White, please!" yelled Acton.

BD looked at him then raised a hand, slowly nodding as he holstered the Glock he had drawn. "Stand down!" His men lowered their weapons, pointing them at the ground, then climbed to their feet.

The lead horseman urged his steed forward and descended the hill with two of his men in tow. They approached the small cluster of men formed by Acton, Reading, Rahim and now BD.

"Who are you?" asked Reading.

"I am Abdullah bin Saqr, Grand Headmaster of the Order of the Assassins. And you are all my prisoners."

Dawson's jaw clenched tightly.

Like hell we are.

He surveyed the situation through his shades. About fifty men, all on horseback, all on the top of the ridge surrounding the small depression they occupied. He clasped his hands behind his back and made a small circular motion with his index finger. From the corner of his eye he saw his men react, inching back toward the helicopter. Dawson knew the key was whether these men were trained. Fifty amateurs panic after the first half-dozen go down, and so do horses. His men would eliminate a dozen before the enemy got their first shot

228

off. But if they stood their ground, his men would face scores of AK-47s from all directions and would be quickly overwhelmed.

Negotiation first.

Dawson stepped closer to Acton.

"Who did he say they were?" he whispered.

The man on horseback was old but apparently had young ears. "We are the Hassassins," he repeated. "Perhaps Professor Acton could explain who we are?"

Acton's eyebrows shot up for a moment. "How do you know who I am?"

The man smiled, leaning forward in his saddle as he made the rounds. "Agent Reading of Interpol, Professor Acton of Saint Paul's University, and you"—he looked directly at Dawson—"are Mr. *White*, from the United States Delta Force." He sat up in his saddle with a pleased expression as no one reacted. "Of course, Mr. White is not your real name, but we need not ruin your cover."

Dawson kept his face emotionless. The man had good intel.

Too good.

Clearly this fellow with Reading was a traitor, or at least a double-agent. That would explain how they knew who Reading was. Reading was here because of Acton and his girlfriend, so the traitor would explain him knowing that as well.

But how the hell does he know who I am?

"You are wondering how I know who you are?" The man had a bemused smile.

Dawson nodded.

"Unfortunately, I cannot tell you that. But to illustrate how well informed I am, I will state your mission. You are here to prevent the sale of a tactical nuclear missile to a group posing as a United Nations Non-Governmental Organization, who potentially kidnapped Professor Laura Palmer, the partner of Professor Acton."

Dawson knew there was no point in denying any of it. There was clearly a security breach, a breach he would worry about later. For now, he needed to keep the situation calm until he figured a way out of it.

"You are extremely well informed, sir."

Abdullah clapped his hands twice in apparent delight. He swung his leg over the back of his horse and jumped to the ground. The two accompanying him remained on their horses as they kept wary eyes on Dawson and his men.

Abdullah approached Rahim who bowed his head. "As-salam alaykum."

"Wa alaykum e-salam," replied Abdullah who then extended his arms and embraced Rahim. Dawson noticed the old man was missing his middle finger on his right hand.

Curious.

He glanced at the two men on horseback and noticed they too were missing their right middle fingers.

Very curious.

"It is good to see you, my son," Abdullah said as he freed Rahim from the embrace.

"You as well, master." Rahim motioned to Reading. "May I present Agent Hugh Reading, formerly of Scotland Yard, now of Interpol. A trusted colleague and old friend."

The expression on Reading's face made it clear to Dawson that he didn't feel the same way about Rahim anymore. The glare he gave him could have bored a hole if it had continued. Rahim averted his gaze, suggesting to Dawson at least a feeling of guilt at what he had done.

Abdullah clearly had chosen to ignore it and approached Reading with a smile and arms extended. "It is a pleasure to make your acquaintance, Agent Hugh Reading of Interpol. I am Abdullah bin Saqr." Reading extended his hand.

"All mine, I'm sure."

Abdullah grasped Reading's hand with both of his and shook it vigorously before letting go. Reading turned his head to face Rahim. "Your English suddenly got a lot better."

Again Rahim couldn't make eye-contact. "I am sorry, my friend, but I have what you might say is a higher calling."

"And what would that be?" The derision in Reading's voice notched him up a spot in Dawson's mind, the fact the man was maintaining this much control after being betrayed by somebody he had apparently known for years, was more than Dawson was certain he could do.

I might have broken his neck by now.

"Which brings me back to my original question," said Abdullah as he now faced Acton, standing within what Dawson would characterize as the kill zone, and what civilians might call their "personal space". Abdullah brushed his right hand across his forehead, tucking some stray locks of hair under his keffiyeh, revealing the missing finger for all to see. Dawson watched Acton for his reaction.

Acton stepped forward and seized the man's right hand, shoved it high into the air, then yanked his robe, exposing his arm. The surrounding horsemen aimed their weapons at the professor.

Wasn't expecting that.

Acton stared the Sheik in the eyes as he gripped his wrist. The man was grinning, and not struggling against him. The fact he was still alive at this point amazed even him. Why he had tested his theory in this fashion, he didn't know. He'd leave that for when the adrenaline wore off. He turned his attention to the man's now exposed arm that was covered in an ornate metal sheath, running from the wrist to the elbow. With his free hand, he reached over and bent Abdullah's wrist forward.

The sound of metal scraping on metal momentarily startled him even though he was expecting it. A blade shot forward from the sheath, through the empty space Abdullah's finger would have occupied, and when fully extended, its foot long length glinted in the sunlight.

Acton heard BD whistle and Reading use an American style curse for the first time Acton could remember since knowing him. He released the man's arm and stepped back. Thankfully, Abdullah waved his men off and they sat back in their saddles. Acton noticed the Delta team lower their weapons as well.

"Well, Professor?" asked Abdullah as he slid a clasp on the sheath from the wrist toward the elbow, retracting the blade, a click indicating it had returned to its locked position. "Are we who I say we are?"

Acton nodded, not quite believing it. He turned to the others. "*If* we are to believe them, they are Hassassins."

Reading shrugged. "Who are?"

"An Islamic sect believed to have been wiped out in the thirteenth century."

"Evidently not." Reading leaned into Acton and whispered in his ear. "Are they friendly?"

Acton shrugged and turned his head slightly to Reading, whispering, "You don't want them as your enemy."

Reading grunted then turned his attention to Abdullah. "We are not your enemy."

Abdullah roared in laughter, prompting the rest of his men surrounding the depression to join in, creating an odd effect that made Acton feel as if he were the cheesy half-time act at a local football game, failing to kick a field goal for a chance to win a car he didn't like.

"Hopefully that's a good sign," muttered Reading.

Abdullah raised his hand, cutting off the laughter. "Our brother, Rahim, has vouched for you, Agent Reading. The word of a brother is all I need." He turned to Acton. "As for you, Professor, we are well aware of what happened last year in London, and know you can be trusted to do the right thing. And with the disappearance of your beloved, Professor Palmer, I believe your motives pure."

Relief washed over Acton at Abdullah's words.

You just might make it out of this alive!

"But you," said Abdullah, stepping toward the Delta operator. "You, I know your mission. But I do not know if I trust you."

"And why is that?" BD removed his sunglasses in an effort, Acton guessed, to convey his honesty.

I think you'll need to do more than let him gaze into your eyes.

Abdullah stepped closer then grabbed BD by both shoulders, staring deep into his eyes. BD, to his credit, didn't even flinch, instead simply meeting his gaze. Abdullah lowered his voice, speaking *at* BD, but not *to* him. "If you knew the true mission of those who now possess the weapon, I wonder how willing you would be to sacrifice your life to stop them?"

"Tell me their mission and judge me not by my words, but my actions." Abdullah leaned in and whispered in his ear, then leaned back to see the reaction. The moment Abdullah's lips had stopped moving with what appeared to be a single word, BD's jaw dropped for a moment then snapped back shut. His eyes narrowed slightly, his jaw set, and the skin over his temples drew thin. "We *cannot* let that happen," he said through clenched teeth.

Abdullah continued to read BD's face then let go of his shoulders and stepped back, nodding. "I believe you."

Acton and Reading both let out audible sighs of relief, Abdullah waving his arm and yelling something in Arabic. The men surrounding the depression turned and disappeared over the crest one by one, the hoof beats the only indication they had been there. Abdullah sat on the sand, cross-legged, and gestured for the others to join him.

BD signaled for his men to stand down, then sat across from Abdullah, with Reading, Acton, and Rahim completing the circle.

"So what's the target?" asked Acton.

Abdullah grimaced. "A target that will result in an unending war, a target that will result in the end of mankind."

Acton glanced at BD, who much to his horror, was nodding in agreement. Acton searched his face for the answer to the question that remained unanswered. It was Reading who at last broke the silence.

"What the bloody hell does that mean? Washington? Jerusalem?"

Abdullah shook his head. "No, much worse, my friend. Their target is Makkat al-Mukarramah, or as you Westerners call it—"

"Mecca," whispered Acton. If the desert they sat on could get any quieter, it just did. Acton's strength left his body as if he were about to pass out. He took a breath then looked at the men sitting around him. Reading was clearly as shocked as he was, and Acton could tell by the look they exchanged that he realized the ramifications. If white

American Christians were to destroy Mecca with a nuclear weapon, it would trigger a Jihad the likes of which the world had never seen, nor likely would again.

"My God, the killing would never stop," gasped Reading. "It *couldn't* stop."

Abdullah looked at BD. "Not without one side eliminating the other. There could be no peace after this. Either all Muslims would be erased from the face of this Earth, or all Christians. There could be no middle ground."

BD grunted. "Clearly these guys think we would win. We need to find this weapon. Now."

Abdullah agreed. "Unfortunately, we were supposed to capture the weapon on this very spot but were thwarted, our agreed upon rendezvous time advanced, our operatives slain, their bodies discovered on the shore not an hour from here." The pounding of hooves interrupted him and a lone horseman appeared over the crest of the hill behind Acton. He twisted to see the man jump off his horse still in mid-gallop, tumble on the ground and recover at a run, something held tightly in his outstretched hand.

Abdullah extended his hand and took the object from the new arrival. Acton was shocked to see it was a satphone. "Marhaba?" Abdullah listened then hung up. "It is as I feared. Our brothers across the sea have confirmed that the Americans and the weapon have arrived. They are only hours away from being in position. And should they succeed, all is lost."

"What sea? Where are they?" asked Reading, clearly impatient.

"The Red Sea," replied Acton. "That means they're already in Saudi Arabia?"

Abdullah nodded. "Yes, and spotted on the shore, most likely preparing to head to Mecca for the Hajj."

Acton closed his eyes for a moment.

The Hajj! As if things couldn't get any worse!

Every year on the eighth day of the last month of the Islamic calendar, millions of Muslims from around the world gathered. The death toll among the devout of Islam would be staggering. It was genius in its simplicity. Start a war you knew you had to win, then rely on your government, with the most powerful arsenal in the world at its disposal, to do just that.

"If they're already there then we have no time to lose," said BD, standing. He whipped his hand in a circle over his head. Acton flinched at the sound of the turbines firing up in the helicopter.

"And where do you think you're going?" asked Reading.

"Mecca."

Red Sea Coast, Saudi Arabia

Cole hid his disgust for the man in front of him, his blackened teeth on full display as he laughed at Cole struggling with the Ihram, a robe he was informed was mandatory for all men attending the Hajj. The long white wrap was at first unwieldy, though rather comfortable once in place, and contained plenty of loose areas to conceal weapons, weapons his men now brought ashore. His wrap secure, he climbed in the back of one of the three trucks now parked on the beach. Inside the cube-shaped interior, stacked from floor to roof, were crates of dates, a popular food during the celebrations.

Disgusting.

"This truck meets your specifications exactly," said the man, his hands clasped, fingers wriggling like the worm he was. "Here, I show you."

Cole jumped to the ground and followed the man. Their contact approached the gas cap located behind the cab of the truck and unscrewed it. He then unscrewed another cap inside and pulled, lengthening the tank inlet severalfold. "See, with this"—he held up the cap—"you can fill it like any other gas tank." He reached in with his hand and pushed something inside. Cole heard a clicking sound and a portion of the truck-bottom directly behind the cab dropped slowly to the ground, a hydraulic hiss the only hint of the mechanism behind it. "Now you climb inside, pull up the ramp, and your cargo is secure, hidden from anyone. No false backs to discover, undetectable."

Cole eyed the ingenious design. It provided a hiding place directly behind where the driver would sit, but integrated seamlessly into the storage area of the truck, accessible only from the hidden door underneath. "You've used this before?"

The worm's head bobbed profusely. "Oh yes, many times, to transport, shall we say, *special*, cargo?"

His leer and suggestive eyes sent Cole's blood boiling.

Most likely human cargo. Most likely white sex slaves for the sheiks. Girls and *boys.*

He pointed at Chip. "Climb in, let me know." Chip nodded and slid up the ramp, disappearing from sight. The ramp pulled up, incorporating into the truck design, leaving no hint it had been there save the crease in the sand. A few moments later the ramp lowered again and Chip slid out, feet first, scrambling crablike onto the beach.

"Looks good, boss." He wiped the sand off his pants and hands. "There's enough room for I'd say three people plus a good chunk of equipment if we uncrate it. It'll be tight, but we'll fit. I'd suggest coming out the way I went in, though—on hands and knees."

"Room for the item?"

Their supplier's eyes shot up for a moment.

Curiosity killed the cat. And the Ay-rab.

Chip nodded. "Uncrated."

"Okay, see to it." Chip ran off toward the men gathered around the growing pile of supplies as Cole approached the truck. He reached inside the tank inlet and searched around the cool, smooth interior. It took a moment to feel the slight indentation in the metal. He pressed against it and his fingers moved forward a couple of inches. A click followed by the sound of a latch freeing itself was followed by the hydraulic hiss of air forced by the pistons controlling the ramp. He turned to the man. "Anything else I need to know?"

He nodded then climbed into the truck. "Look here." He pointed to the back of the cab between the two headrests of the well-worn, threadbare seats. Cole looked and noticed nothing special beyond a scraped and scuffed sheet of metal, at one time painted plain white. The man pressed against the center, a portion of the rear panel receding about an inch, the rivets on either side for show. He slid the panel aside, revealing an opening. "See, you can talk to your men through here." He grasped the sliver of the panel remaining in view and pulled it most of the way across, then placing his fingertips on it, dragged it until it clicked back into place, hiding the opening. "And when you open it,

237

compartment light goes off, then close it, light goes on. Same with ramp. You like?"

Cole nodded.

"Everything okay?"

Cole nodded.

"You have the rest of my money?"

Cole snapped his fingers and Calvin Brannick, his moneyman, ran over with a briefcase. "Pay him."

Brannick flipped the case open and around, revealing stacks of Euros. Greed scrawled across their contact's face, his leathery skin stretched in a crooked smile, exposing his blackened teeth, his tongue darting across dried lips. He took the case in one arm, reached in with another, and grabbed a stack of bills, flipping through them. He checked several more, all the while his head bobbing up and down faster and faster. Finally, he snapped the case shut.

"Thank you, I wish you a good day." He bowed and scurried to a car idling on the road above, the three drivers who had brought the trucks, waiting inside.

Cole watched as the car pulled away then noticed a flash in the distance. He froze, watching the area intently. Another flash.

Binoculars?

A third flash and he was convinced. He waved Charlie Parker over who had supervised the unloading of the weapon.

"We're being watched."

Parker gazed at the horizon. "Are you sure?"

Cole nodded. "Pretty sure. Looked like some sort of lens."

"Who could know we're here?"

"I can think of only one possibility."

"Our Ay-rab friends?"

Cole nodded. "They may be better connected than we thought. Have everybody stay sharp and we'll have to pick up the pace a bit." He glanced at the case. "Let's just hope that thing doesn't set off any alarms before we can get it into position."

"Maybe we should arm it now?"

Cole thought for a moment.

A failsafe?

If they armed it now, and something went wrong, it would still go off and accomplish their goals. It just meant they wouldn't be around to see it.

He could live with that.

"Do it."

Red Sea Coast, Saudi Arabia

Sabir knelt, hands open in front of him, repeating the Salah as he had done five times daily since childhood. His hands opened to Allah and his eyes closed, he bowed down, prostrated on the ground in submission to Allah's will, a joy filling his heart as his prayers fulfilled one more time, put him once again in good standing with the Creator. He rose to his feet and rolled up the carpet laid out minutes before on the desert sands. It had taken ten minutes. Only ten minutes to pay his respects to the one who had created the world he now enjoyed, who had given him life, and who would reward him in the end for being a good Muslim.

Are ten minutes too much to ask?

He thought of the infidel Christians who went to their churches only once a week. He had heard from his Imam that most Christians never even went to church. This hadn't surprised him, their world decadent, filled with blasphemous pleasures he would chastise himself for even trying to imagine, corrupting their souls and their path to their God.

Which was another thing that had surprised him in his youth, that the Christian God and Allah were one and the same. As he had learned more of the Koran, he came to realize the Christian path was a lost one, and that Islam was the true path, the only path that would lead to salvation and an eternity of bliss as reward for following it. Christianity had started off well but was co-opted by the evil Roman Catholic church that had corrupted the original teachings of the Prophet Jesus, peace be upon him, and turned it into the corrupt organization it was today, with its myriads of bastard offspring each trying to correct the deviation of its parent, but with little success.

Islam was the way, and the sooner the world converted, the better the world would be.

His teachings, however, differed from those of many Muslims. His teachers taught pure Islam, the original version, without the political and cultural leanings Imam's preached today. Islam was a religion of peace, that was what he was taught. And if peaceful, forcing Christians and Jews and other misguided believers to convert, was wrong. They must see the path themselves and choose to follow it willingly. With time and patience, and careful guidance, the world would see its way to Islam. It wouldn't be in his lifetime, or even that of his children or grandchildren, but it was inevitable.

As his Imam taught, the corrupt ways of the West, their decadent lifestyles and obsession with self-gratification, had resulted in a birth rate so low, they could no longer sustain themselves. Their insatiable appetites for more than the basic necessities of life had led them to bring in people from around the world to sustain their economies, people who did not share their beliefs, who did not share their obsessions—and who bred. His Imam had taught that within one generation, the Muslim populations in the West would be large enough to sway elections, and within two, enough to win. Within several generations, Islam would win purely through making babies, here, and in the Infidels' backyards.

Without a drop of blood shed.

This was the way of the true Muslim. Peace and self-awareness, contentment within oneself, at the expense of no one, through peace with one's God. By leading their lives as Allah willed, they would win. Not through violent Jihad as those who had corrupted much of Islam taught, but through peaceful coexistence. Demographics, his Imam had said, would win in the end.

That was why today his duty was of extreme importance. He had been told by the Imam of his local chapter of the Hassassin that a group of American Infidels was trying to start a war between Islam and Christianity, and if they succeeded, the bloodshed from all previous conflicts would pale by comparison. And it was something they must all fight to prevent, even if it meant their deaths.

He mounted his steed standing patiently by his side as he prayed, retrieved a set of binoculars from a pouch on the saddle, and scanned the coastline for any activity. The sandy beach flashed past his eyes as he searched for anomalies, the gentle ebb and flow of the waves as they hit the coast, lost in the blur.

He saw something.

He stopped his left to right motion and slowly scanned back until he found it. A boat, betrayed by the sun glinting off the white of the hull, gently bobbed in the water, several smaller boats ferrying men and equipment to the beach, where to his ire, several trucks waited.

Only traitors to Islam would help them here!

With Westerners few and far between in Saudi Arabia, whoever was supplying these Infidels was corrupted by greed. That money was the root of all evil was no doubt true, as was evidenced by this display. His heart pounded in fury, his mind imagining racing his horse into their midst, sword drawn, and separating the heads from the shoulders of those who would betray their beliefs for a few pieces of paper made by man, inscribed with a blasphemous phrase, In God We Trust. To associate money with God, to associate the source of all greed with the source of all that is divine, was an affront to all who truly believed.

Sabir took a deep breath in through his nose and slowly let it out through his mouth, closing his eyes.

Allah, give me strength.

He repeated his mantra several times then opened his eyes again. He reached into his robes and pulled a satphone from an inner pocket. He flipped it open and hit the speed dial. It picked up on the first ring.

"Marhaba?"

"This is Sabir. Please tell the Master that I have spotted them from my location. They have three vehicles here waiting for them, trucks."

"Follow them and report back."

"I will."

He snapped the phone shut and returned it to its previous hiding place, buried deep within the many layers of clothing he wore to keep him cool in the desert heat. He glanced through the binoculars again and saw the trucks leave the beach, the boat heading back to sea. He clicked his tongue, urging his horse into motion with a flick of his reigns. The beast started forward, knowing Sabir's wishes as if they were one, the two together for almost a decade. She was getting old but she was reliable, calm in battle, and one of the few things in his life outside of his brotherhood that he could rely on without question. He patted her neck as they cleared the crest of the small dune he had been perched on, heading down to the road the trucks had turned onto.

Had turned south onto.

So it is *true.*

Sabir leaned forward and urged his horse faster. He needed to get closer to get a better description of the vehicles to pass on to the next lookouts.

Everything depended on it.

Former UNICEF Camp
Lower Nubia, Egypt

Dawson activated his comm. "Control, Zero-One, come in, over."

"Zero-One, Control, go ahead, over."

"Control, we have a possible target for the package." Dawson paused and looked at Acton, who nodded. "We believe the target is Mecca, Saudi Arabia, over."

A pause then a burst of static. "Say again, Zero-One? Did you say Mecca?"

Dawson recognized Clancy's voice taking over, probably having just jacked his headset into the conversation.

"That's correct, sir, Mecca, over."

Again a pause. "How reliable is this intel?"

"High. We have met some"—Dawson paused for a moment, carefully choosing his words as he looked at Abdullah—"friends here, who had someone on the inside of the deal. They confirm the target is Mecca, and they have half a day's head start."

"Options?"

"We'll require stealth insertion at the target."

Abdullah cleared his throat.

"Standby, Control." Dawson turned to Abdullah. "What is it?"

"If I may be permitted to interrupt?" asked Abdullah, not waiting for Dawson's permission. "We can get you in."

"Are you sure?"

"Most assuredly. As we speak our brothers are already gathering in Mecca and arranging transport. We can be there before nightfall."

Dawson nodded, having no doubt this man could deliver. "Control, Zero-One, we've secured transport to the target, will contact you in sixty mikes with an update, out." Dawson deactivated his comm, picturing what the Colonel must be thinking.

And doing.

He imagined his CO was moving as many assets as he could into the area, and briefing the White House on the fact they were about to send troops onto the shores of a country who was a tenuous ally at best, whether that ally liked it or not. He wondered what the President would say, considering he got the job about a year ago after Dawson's unit had wreaked havoc across London.

Above my paygrade. Don't care.

Dawson turned to Abdullah.

"What's your plan?"

Jeddah-Makkah Highway, Saudi Arabia

Cole eyed the flat, jet-black asphalt stretched out before them. The heat from the afternoon sun played tricks on the eyes as shimmers of phantom lakes danced just out of reach. He closed his eyes as he thought of the timer in the container behind him, its inexorable countdown to extinction ticking off the seconds, unless they themselves chose to stop it. His heart beat faster than usual.

Is that fear?

Why would he feel fear? It concerned him. He knew he was doing the right thing. He knew this was the only way to save the way of life he loved. He was doing this for all those in the West who were asleep to the threat Islam posed.

He had read the books. He had studied the demographics himself. Eventually, there would be too many to defeat. They were well over a billion now. They bred at three times the rate of the West. And that included those our own leaders had let in as immigrants. They made up only a few percent of the population now in the US, but in ten years? Who knew? When would it be too late?

He couldn't take that chance. This was the one opportunity to wipe the slate clean. One all-out war, a war the West would have no choice but to win, would end this once and for all.

He had played it out in his head for years but had never dreamed he would get the means to do it. He had thought he would need some sort of chemical or biological weapon to trigger his plan, but when he had heard the rumors shudder through the black market of a nuclear weapon for sale, he had focused all his energies on acquiring it.

And now he had it. And with an American weapon, his plan was now foolproof. With a Russian weapon, which was what he had expected to acquire, the scientists would have traced it back to Russia through identifying the plutonium used. There would still be a war, but not necessarily focused in the right direction. But an American weapon.

246

That would be traced right back to the US, and the anger, the Jihad that would result, would be focused on the West, where he wanted it.

He knew how it would play out. The blast would wipe out Mecca and hundreds of thousands of the devotee lemmings who circled that damned rock day in and day out. The world would react in horror. Aid would pour in, the Saudi government would ask for help in investigating. The UN would send scientists, trace the plutonium's unique signature straight back to the US, and the war would be on.

American and Western embassies would be attacked overnight, their occupants massacred. Western icons such as McDonalds and KFC would be torched. No business from the West would be safe in any Muslim country. Foreigners would swamp the airports, desperate to flee to safety, but the airports would be swarmed, the waiting throngs hacked to pieces while the gore played out across the world's television sets on CNN.

And that would be the first week. At home, the devotees to Islam would begin their own attacks. So-called home-grown terrorists would spring up throughout the West, wreaking havoc for months, until finally the population would have enough and demand their governments put an end to it.

And there was only one way.

They would round up all Muslims, place them into camps, and increase security throughout the nation.

Immigration would stop completely.

That would be the first victory.

The camps would swell with the millions of people the West had let into their countries, let in in good faith. But it would prove too many.

New Slate already had a campaign in place, ready to fill the Internet with viral videos, messages, and emails, along with fliers that would be posted on every lamp post in every city.

Sterilization.

After all, it would be humane. That would be the message. Sterilize them. Those who didn't want sterilization would be sent back to their homelands. Those that remained would slowly be released back into the population, but under close supervision.

And within a generation, the West would be saved from the demographic time bomb threatening to destroy it as assuredly as the nuclear weapon that would soon save it.

The fear of dealing with the Middle East would force the US government to finally exploit its untapped domestic oil supplies. He and many of the inner circle had already positioned themselves to profit from the inevitable boom in shale oil production and bio-fuels. It would be tough for a few decades, but in the end, the West would be saved. Countries like Iran and Pakistan, with their nuclear weapons, would be dealt with swiftly, and eventually, the fundamentalist nutbars would realize their fight was futile and turn on each other as their economies collapsed when no one needed their oil anymore.

The West would be saved and the Middle East destroyed, without the power or money remaining to wage war against the "infidel".

Then they would beg for help.

And the West being the West, would be happy to provide it.

But this time with strings.

You want Western money? Then implement freedom of the press. Freedom of speech. Freedom of religion. Equality of the sexes. Democracy.

Drag your asses out of the twelfth century, and into the twenty-first.

They would resist at first, but their populations, inundated with a constant bombardment of information, would demand the freedoms, and the first cracks would begin. And that would be all it would take. The floodgates would open and the Muslim world would have its renaissance, its age of enlightenment, its own revolution, and would join the rest of society in a modern, free world, led by a strong, free, proud, and indestructible United States.

He sighed.

I hope I live to see it.

But still that nagging sense of fear.

What was it that was bothering him? Was he having second thoughts? He was about to kill hundreds of thousands, and in the end, millions, if not hundreds of millions. He might be remembered as the Hitler or Stalin of his time if the right people didn't write the history books.

Could he go through with it?

He had to.

He turned around and tapped on the window. Charlie Parker, napping against a crate, snapped awake.

"Give me the codes."

"What?"

"Give me the disarming codes."

Parker removed the code key from around his neck and handed it through the partition. "Why?"

Cole rolled down the window and tossed it out.

"Jesus! Without those—"

Cole cut him off. "Now activate the failsafe."

Parker looked at him. "Are you sure? Once we activate that, there's no way in hell we can disable it. That thing was designed so even the experts would take hours."

"Do it."

Parker leaned over the weapon for a few seconds, then sat back down. "It's done," he said, his voice slightly subdued.

Cole turned back to face the road. "Now there's no turning back."

Somewhere over the Red Sea

Abdullah's plan was more twelfth century than Dawson had patience for. Horseback to the coast, boat, albeit modern, across the Red Sea, land in a secluded spot along the coast, then rendezvous with a Hassassin cell on the other side.

Too slow.

Especially with a nuke in play, and however clichéd it sounded to him, the fate of the world in the balance. He had been on enough missions where he had heard similar clichés used and never bought into it, until today. If these nutbars succeeded, it would be a holy war unlike any other, in which only one side would remain in the end.

They must be stopped.

This was exactly why they now screamed thirty feet above the chop, across the Red Sea in their Black Hawk helicopter. Dawson, half his team, Acton, Reading, Abdullah, along with two of his bodyguards, sat in the back. They had left Rahim behind with the students to await the arrival of British Embassy staff.

"Look!" Mickey pointed through the side window.

Dawson looked and saw the dark outline of another chopper, borrowed from the Egyptians, carrying Red and the rest of the team as they caught up. Dawson checked his watch.

Perfect timing.

"Wings, report!" he yelled to their pilot and fellow Bravo Team member.

"Five minutes, BD."

Dawson turned to Abdullah. "You're sure your people will be there?"

Abdullah raised both hands, palms facing Dawson, nodding his head, his eyes closed. "Absolutely, there is nothing to be worried about."

Dawson nodded then turned to his men. "Weapons check, we land in five."

Jeddah-Makkah Highway, Saudi Arabia

"You'll need to get in the back now."

Cole opened his eyes and looked over at Jason Sharpe, one of three drivers who had been preparing for months for this mission.

"What's that?"

"Look." Sharpe jutted his chin at the windshield, the thick, long beard he had grown and tended over the past six months pointing the way. Cole followed the follicles and saw that traffic had picked up since he last looked. It was still sparse, the odd car scattered across the blacktop shimmering into the distance, but even one was too many if they saw the transfer.

"Okay, find us a spot."

Sharpe pointed up ahead where a turnoff led to a smaller road. "We'll drive up a bit, should give us cover."

Cole slid the window to the hidden compartment open and peered inside. "Get ready, I'll be coming in as soon as we stop. Let's make this fast."

Brannick nodded as he and Parker shuffled around to make room. Cole slid the partition closed, hiding it from view as Sharpe turned off the main highway and onto a smaller road. Cole looked at Sharpe, his white Ihram robe contrasting with the dark tan he had developed over the past summer. Daily visits to the tanning booth had given him a full body tan that would meet any inspection up to and including a cavity search, Sharpe having informed everyone of his cheek spreading technique when tanning, and then demonstrating it when doubted. Cole shook his head at the memory.

Nasty!

Sharpe geared down, bringing the truck to a slow stop on the side of the road.

Cole pointed at the beard. "Let's hope that thing works. You've got your papers?"

Sharpe patted the travel documents laying on the dash. "Good to go."

"Don't forget you're deaf."

Sharpe smiled. "What?"

Cole leaped out and took one last look in the cab. "Good luck." He slammed the door shut, unscrewed the gas cap and the outer ring, then reached inside, pressing the switch. The hydraulic hiss was followed by the ramp lowering to the ground. He quickly returned the caps to their former positions then, looking both ways to confirm there were no cars in sight, ducked down and climbed inside.

The first thing he noticed was the smell.

"What the hell have you two been doing in here?" He crawled up the ramp and pushed to his feet.

"Sweating." Brannick yanked the chain attached to the ramp, pulling it up, the clicking of the latch indicating the floor was again secure. He and Parker, who had been holding their feet up off the floor, got comfortable again as Cole took the spot farthest from the ramp's exit. He rapped on the rear of the cab and heard Sharpe shift the truck into gear as Brannick and Parker raised their feet, bracing them against the opposite stack of supplies.

Cole looked at them curiously, Parker opening his mouth to say something when the truck lurched forward, sending Cole to his feet, and splayed over the weapon occupying the bulk of the available cargo space inside the hidden partition. Someone gripped the back of his shirt and pulled him into his seat.

"Sorry, forgot to warn you to brace yourself," said Parker. "Whoever thought having the seats facing backward was a good idea should be shot."

Brannick grunted. "Definitely not designed for comfort."

Cole, seated again, stretched his legs out in front of him and pushed his feet against a case of water lying opposite. "Well, we better get comfortable. With traffic and security, we could be in here for hours."

Brannick farted. "Sorry. Shouldn't have eaten that Ay-rab shit yesterday."

Cole eyeballed Brannick as the odor assaulted his nostrils. He pointed at the nuke. "Do that again and I'll chain you to that thing."

Parker leaned toward Brannick and whispered, intentionally loud, "You think he's kidding, well uh-uh. You're lucky you ain't a raghead, he'd kick you out right now without slowing down."

Cole chuckled as he tried to get comfortable on the hard metal seat, the temperature over one hundred degrees. "Get some rest, we're going to need it. Next stop, Mecca."

Red Sea Coast, Saudi Arabia

"Sixty seconds!" yelled Wings through the comm. "Get out and get clear, the skids are on the ground for no more than thirty seconds!"

Dawson positioned himself at the door. He gripped the latch and yanked it open, sliding the door to the rear of the chopper. He turned to his men. "Take up covering positions as soon as we exit, but don't fire. Remember, we're rendezvousing with friendlies, no matter how much they look like the enemy!"

"Yes, Sergeant Major!" shouted his men who shuffled closer to the now open door. The wind howled through the cabin, the rotors overhead beating down on them, drowning out the sound of Wings as he yelled from the front.

"Hold on, this'll be a little bumpy!"

Dawson gripped a handhold as he took a knee at the exit, looking out over the helicopter edge. He saw Red's chopper landing about ten seconds ahead of them, his men already jumping out and taking up covering positions as Wings hurtled them toward the ground.

Jesus Christ!

"Hang on!" he yelled to the others as he reached forward with his free hand and grabbed onto some nearby cargo netting. His head still out the door, he watched the sand of the beach race toward them, and at the last minute, Wings pulled up, slowing their descent dramatically. A second later they hit the ground, jostling everyone inside.

"Go! Go! Go!" yelled Wings.

Dawson leaped out and searched for Red and his men. The other chopper, fifty yards away, was already leaving the ground, the pilot banking hard toward the water then pushing the stick forward to gain as much speed and as little altitude as he could, in an effort to get into international waters as quickly as possible.

Dawson spotted Red near a berm with Spock and Atlas, peering over the edge. He waved at Dawson then pointed at his eyes then inland. Dawson knew what he meant.

We have company.

Dawson's men leaped from the chopper, racing into position with the rest of the team, and to his surprise, Acton and Reading were already out, helping Abdullah and his compatriots. The last of them jumped to the ground as the chopper powered up then rose. Dawson looked at Wings who gave him the thumbs up then banked away, leaving a cloud of dust as he chased after the other helicopter to safety.

"Get to that ridge!" said Dawson in a hoarse whisper, motioning to the civilians to head for where Red was positioned. Acton and Reading responded, racing hunched over toward the hill.

Abdullah and his men didn't, instead sauntering casually for the ridge.

"Do not worry, Sergeant Major. All is according to plan."

Dawson looked at him in frustration then spun around at the grinding of gears and the unmistakable pounding of horses' hoofs on sand. He took several steps back, placing himself between the oncoming sound and Abdullah, in case he had to use him as a hostage to gain control of whatever situation might arise.

As if they knew what he was thinking, Abdullah's two bodyguards stepped between Dawson and their charge, turning to face him, their fingers on their trigger guards. Dawson nodded, a slight smile of respect allowed.

Not amateurs after all!

Impressed they were well enough trained to infer his plan and neutralize it, he instead headed for his men at a jog. As he reached the ridge, headlights from several vehicles sliced through the darkness, bouncing as they drove across the rough terrain of the Saudi Arabian coastline.

Dawson was within five feet of Red's position when he looked up and saw a pair of hoofs clear the ledge, followed by the rest of a massive horse, its rider obscured by the immense bulk of the beast's frame. Dawson leaped forward and rolled against the ledge, next to Red. He pressed his back against the berm and looked out at the beach as horse after horse jumped over their heads, landing deftly on the soft sand in front of them, encircling Abdullah, their riders cheering "Allahu Akbar" over and over. A tingle raced down Dawson's spine, the other times he had heard chants like that always resulting in gunfire, usually aimed at him.

A vehicle slid to a stop above them, its headlights illuminating the scene before them. It was soon joined by another set.

Red slapped him on the shoulder.

"I sure hope these are the guys we're supposed to meet!"

Dawson agreed. "Let's keep everyone cool until the Sheik gives the all-clear."

As if on cue, Abdullah raised his hands, quieting the crowd, then gestured for Dawson to join him.

Dawson glanced at Red.

Red grinned. "Better you than me."

Dawson punched him in the shoulder, Red feigning injury. "Some friend you are," muttered Dawson as he rose, careful to shoulder his weapon. He looked over at Reading and Acton who huddled nearby, covered by Atlas and Niner. He cocked his head at the group on horseback. "Care to join me?"

Reading looked at him with an, "are you kidding me?" look, then rose as Acton did. The three walked toward Abdullah, the eyes of all the horsemen on them.

Abdullah stepped toward them with both hands outstretched and gripped Dawson by the shoulders, leaning in and kissing him on both cheeks. He repeated this with Acton then Reading, who appeared as if he were about to belt Abdullah if he got fresh.

"Welcome, my friends, to the Kingdom of Saudi Arabia. Someday it will be returned to the people, rid of the tyranny of the House of Saud, a family so arrogant they allow those in the West to call Arabia by their own blasphemous name." He turned, his arm sweeping in a great circle at the men around them, then spoke in Arabic.

Dawson, fluent in Arabic, leaned in and translated. "He is saying, 'Brothers, these men are our friends, and are here to aid us in our most desperate mission, for if we fail, all we have strived for, all our ancestors have fought and died for, will be lost. Tonight, we will do nothing less than save Islam from destruction by the infidel!'"

The men roared, shaking their rifles in the air. "Allahu Akbar!" they chanted, three times in unison.

Abdullah smiled and turned to the trucks on the ledge and yelled something in Arabic. A man, silhouetted in the headlamps, waved back, yelling an acknowledgment. Moments later bundles of something Dawson couldn't identify were tossed onto the beach. Abdullah walked over to the closest one and picked it up. He tossed it to Dawson.

"You and your men will put these on."

Dawson held up the bundle of coarse cloth. He shook it out and the black material fell to the ground, revealing some sort of long robe.

"What the hell is this?"

Acton leaned toward him, chuckling.

"It's a burqa, dear."

Jeddah-Makkah Highway, Saudi Arabia

The rap on the metal his head was resting against jolted Cole awake. Several more raps in quick succession sent adrenaline rushing through his veins. He took a quick look at the others to make sure they were awake then returned the signal, rapping his knuckles against the still sealed secret panel to the cab.

"This is it," he whispered. "Nobody make a sound, no matter what."

The others quickly secured their gear, making sure nothing could shake loose and make a sound. This was the critical phase of the operation. They needed to make it through the ring of security surrounding Mecca. And the keyword was *they*. The other two trucks were expendable, merely their means of escape, however if caught, it would trigger a security alert leading to their discovery, and discovery of the bomb.

But this truck would be first in case something went wrong. They could detonate from here if need be, but they couldn't guarantee the blast would wipe out the Kaaba along with the hundreds of thousands of nutbars tossing little pebbles at it then rejoicing by sacrificing a damned animal.

That's something we should do when we get back. Get PETA onboard.

With over two million animals slaughtered during the Hajj, they should be outraged. Would Pamela have the courage to get out there and say they deserved to die because they were killing the poor, defenseless animals?

Doubt it.

She, like so many others, had a double standard when it came to Muslims, or any minority for that matter. If it's white folk doing it then it's okay to protest, it's okay to force them to change. But if it's Muslims or some other effin' minority, *we* have to change, *we* have to accept *their* ways.

Unless you're an Eskimo.

But the seals are so cuuute!

Screw you, Pamela, they're not killing the cute babies, they're killing the fat old bastards that look like an oversized slug and eat all the damned fish.

Why am I getting worked up for the 'skimos?

Cole took a deep breath to calm himself. He knew the rage that consumed him day in and day out would eventually kill him. Either in some fight, somewhere, or by just having a stroke.

But today, if they could get through this roadblock, there might be hope, there might be a way to bring everything back on track.

If only we succeed.

The truck jolted to a stop. Cole, his feet braced against the now half-empty box of water bottles, was ready for it this time. A loud double-bang, the sound of something hitting metal, rang through the cab and into their hiding place.

Someone slapping the hood of the truck?

The engine cut off as if in response. Cole removed his feet from the case of water and one of the bottles, an empty placed in there earlier, snapped back into shape with a loud crackle that echoed through the tiny area.

Cole's heart stopped. He gripped the edge of the bench he was perched on with both hands, his knuckles turning white as he cursed himself for the moronic mistake. The other two did the same, staring at the outer walls as if in an attempt to see through them, to see if anyone outside heard the sound.

Shouts erupted on the other side of the thin metal wall separating them from the massive security force inches away, a security force that would be only too happy to make sure they never were seen again if caught, torture to fill the remainder of their days, which would probably not be brief enough.

He heard Sharpe in the cab grunt something in Arabic, distorting his voice to suggest he was a deaf mute. Sharpe repeated the sound, something unintelligible to anyone listening. He had practiced on them for weeks. He had practiced on strangers for weeks. Cole was impressed with how the three drivers chosen for the mission had taken their work seriously. They each would need to get through the road blocks in plain sight. There was no hiding from the guards. Their clothes would help, the dark tans and beards they had worked on for months would help, and so would their covers. Sharpe was playing a deaf-mute. Eid "Eddie" Kowalski spoke Arabic, his mother Lebanese Christian, something some of the members of New Slate weren't comfortable with at first, but after getting to know him, realized he was as American as any of them, which was what they wanted. Yes, a pure white America was a great idea to some, but it wasn't realistic, nor was it his. Cole was more concerned with a pure *American* America. White, black, brown or yellow, he didn't care. Were you a true American? Then fine, stick around. Otherwise, piss off and get out of my country.

More grunting erupted from the front then shouting, in clear Arabic, from outside. The click of the door opening in the cab sent Cole's pulse racing. He glanced at Brannick and Parker. Both were as on edge as he was, Brannick bent over, pulling at his hair, Parker sitting, his back straight against the cab wall, his hands gripping the bench as he drew steady breaths in and out. They heard the shouting move its way from the front of the truck, down the side, then to the back where the clanking of metal on metal echoed. The roar of tiny wheels sliding through their runners screeched through the hold as the truck's rear door was thrown open.

This better work!

The truck shook from side to side as the weight shifted, likely as someone climbed into the back. They would be greeted with crate after crate of dates. Heavy to search, easy to stack floor to ceiling. The perfect cover.

As long as no one measured the size of the cargo area.

Cole found himself holding his breath, not daring to make a sound. He had no idea how much soundproofing was built into the walls surrounding them, but every creak from the truck, along with the orders barked at whoever was searching the back, seemed amplified in their confines.

Brannick sneezed.

It was a small sneeze. A stifled sneeze. A sneeze that anywhere else might not be even noticed. But today it was the loudest sneeze Cole had ever been witness to. Both he and Parker stared at Brannick in shock, who returned their gaze, horror written all over his face. All three turned slowly to face the back of the truck where the search was taking place.

Silence.

Or was it Cole's imagination? He focused on the sounds around them, drowned out by the roar of blood rushing through his ears, the panic created by the sneeze, growing. He took several deep, shallow breaths, as quietly as he could manage without them turning into gasps, and closed his eyes.

Calm down and listen!

The roar slowly settled, the sounds outside the truck coming back into focus.

Had they changed?

No, he was certain they hadn't. But then again, it was the same screaming and shouting they had listened to for the past fifteen minutes, all in a language none but Kowalski understood, and he wasn't here to tell them what was going on.

The truck shook, sending his pulse racing again, then he heard the rear door rolling down, the crash as it smashed into the floor of the truck, then the click of the lock engaging, the most satisfying sounds he ever recalled hearing.

He smiled at his companions and gave a thumbs-up. Parker returned the gesture, while Brannick, who had one hand pinching the bridge of his nose as if fighting another sneeze, was too terrified to notice their ordeal was almost over.

The cab door opened and the truck shook again, followed by the door slamming shut. The engine roared to life, the gears ground, and they lurched forward.

This time, Cole let out a deep sigh and looked to the heavens, his eyes closed.

"My God, that was too close."

Jeddah-Makkah Highway, Saudi Arabia

Tarek threw open the door and stepped out onto the scorching pavement, the sunbaked desert finally yielding its trapped heat, the jet-black asphalt, years old but barely used, quickly making the bottom of his feet sweat in his sandals. He looked both up and down the highway, lit only by the moon and stars, spotting no one. He leaned back into the car to grab his satellite phone as the dash gently chimed at him, indicating his door was ajar and his engine was screwed. He grabbed the phone off the passenger seat and stood back up, stretching as he flipped up the antenna. He dialed his brother, ready for the "I told you so" conversation about to occur.

"Hicham? Is that you?"

"Tarek? As-salam alaykum."

"Wa alaykum e-salam. Brother, I need your help."

"What is it?"

Tarek thought he heard something in the distance. He looked down the road and saw something—what, he wasn't sure.

What is that?

"My car broke down. I need you to come get me, and to send a tow truck."

His brother laughed.

Here it comes.

"I told you you shouldn't have bought that piece of junk."

"Yes, yes, I know I should have bought the Mercedes."

His brother laughed again. "Everybody knows Jags are shit. They look good, but a diseased camel is more reliable!"

Tarek smiled slightly.

He's right. I should have listened.

"Yes, yes, I know. I'll never get a Jag again. Piece of dung has spent more time in the garage than on the road." Tarek kicked the tire. "So, are you going to pick me up or what?"

"Where are you?"

The noise was closer now. Tarek looked again and was shocked to see two trucks barreling toward him and a dozen horses racing beside them in the sand. The vehicles whipped by, their drivers eyeballing him, their face coverings hiding their details. He was more surprised by what was in the back. Rows of women, their faces covered by the burqa. One pointed at him as they sped past.

Was that a gun?

It was over in moments, the cloud of dust left behind the only evidence they had been there.

"Tarek? Are you still there? Where are you?"

Tarek had let the phone drop to his shoulder as the procession raced by. The muffled sounds of his brother yelling brought him back to reality. He raised the phone to his ear.

"Where are you?"

"About one hour outside Mecca."

Reading pointed at the broken down car as they sped past and leaned toward Acton. "Notice what kind of car that was?"

Acton shook his head. "No!" he yelled over the sound of the wind and engine in a seeming duel as to which could drown out the creaking of the truck as it rocked along the road, the vehicle having seen far better days.

"Jag!" He elbowed Acton. "Just like I told you in London last year."

Acton laughed, recalling the incident. "No worries, a Jag isn't in my budget anyway."

"You really ought to let Laura treat you to some luxuries. You know she'd do it happily, no expectations." Reading watched his friend's eyes glisten as they stared into the distance as if seeking his missing love through the vast desert expanse. Reading leaned in and lowered his voice so only Acton could hear. "Sorry, mate, shouldn't have said that."

Acton grunted. "Don't worry about it. I just hope we find her."

"As do I, my friend, as do I." Reading decided to take his friend's mind off her. "Tell me about Mecca. What's the big deal with this thing they walk around?"

Acton smiled, likely seeing through Reading's attempt to distract him, but grateful regardless. "It's called the Black Stone. It's actually quite the Russian doll. You have the Al-Masjid al-Haram mosque, that's the huge white building you see on TV, it surrounds the Kaaba, which is the large, black structure they walk around during the Hajj."

"What's this Black Stone?" asked BD, the Delta team now listening.

"Nobody really knows. According to tradition, it's from the time of Abraham. We're pretty sure it was worshiped by pagans, pre-Islam. It forms the eastern cornerstone of the Kaaba, and over time was broken into several fragments. They sealed them in silver, and over the centuries it has been polished smooth by the millions of hands that have touched it during the Hajj."

"So it's just a black rock?"

"Not just any rock. It's the holiest of all rocks. Some say it's a meteorite, others say it's just a rock that was used as the cornerstone of the Kaaba, which the Koran claims was built by Abraham and his son, Ishmael, when they settled in Arabia. What it might mean or not mean to us is irrelevant. If it's destroyed, it would be the ultimate attack on Islam. Unlike the Twin Towers, this is the center of a religion and can't be rebuilt."

Mecca, Saudi Arabia

They had been stewing in their own sweat for several hours, parked in an alley behind the Makkah Hilton Hotel, waiting for one of the other two trucks to pick them up. Parker eyed his watch and looked at Cole then at the weapon, its locked-in countdown persistently ticking. Cole glanced at his watch too.

"Maybe you shouldn't have thrown away the codes," said Parker. Cole knew from his voice he wasn't serious, but he'd be lying if he wasn't having the same thoughts. They had little more than two hours before detonation.

Two hours, eighteen minutes and thirteen seconds to be exact.

Sharpe rapping on the rear panel saved Cole from responding. The hidden window slid open and Sharpe whispered, "Here they come!"

"Thank God!" sighed Parker, leaning back and letting out a deep breath. He slapped Brannick on the leg. "See, nothing to worry about!"

Brannick managed a slight smile, not saying anything. Cole looked at him.

Weak.

He should have followed his gut and left him behind, but after killing Gabe, he needed a replacement. Brannick was too young. Cole had no doubt he believed in the problem, but wasn't as convinced he believed in the solution.

Cole turned his attention to Sharpe. "Both of them?" He peered through the opening though saw nothing but a garbage dumpster in front.

Sharpe shook his head. "No, looks like just one. They're coming up from behind. Let me make sure everything is all clear and I'll let you out."

He slid the panel closed again and they heard him climb out, then a few moments later the hydraulic hiss of freedom sounded, the ramp dropping from under their feet. Brannick was first to scramble out followed more slowly by Parker then Cole.

Sharpe waved his hand in front of his nose. "Holy shit, boss, you guys stink."

"Should fit right in with the locals then," said Parker, chuckling at his own joke.

Cole took a whiff of his pits and his eyes watered. "You might be right, but there's not much we can do about it right now." He searched for prying eyes. It was a deserted back alley, filled with garbage bins from the hotels lining either side, a few dim lights providing the only illumination, the sun having set hours before. He checked his watch again.

Shit!

He raised his hand, snapping his fingers three times, the sound echoing in the alley. His men turned their attention to him rather than their aching muscles. "Listen up. It's in position and armed, with no way to disarm it, so mission accomplished. Now let's get the hell out of here before we're turned extra crispy."

"Sir?"

The hesitant voice came from behind. It was Brannick.

Cole turned to face him. "What?"

Brannick pointed to the end of the alleyway. "Look."

Cole turned to where he was pointing and his pulse raced. Several men stood at the end, abreast of each other, blocking the exit. As he watched, another half-dozen joined them.

This can't be good.

He spun around and saw the other end of the alley filled with men as well, walking toward them.

"Shit, boss, what do we do?"

Cole turned back to see the first group advancing. As they passed under a light he saw all were dressed in black, their faces covered, revealing nothing but their eyes.

Eyes filled with hate.

Outskirts of Mecca, Saudi Arabia

Reading yawned and stretched, then grasped at emptiness as the truck took a sharp turn onto a smaller road, sending them all sprawling in the back. Curses filled the air as he and Acton, along with half the Delta Force team, helped each other back onto the benches lining the sides. Less than a minute later the truck slowed, pulling off the paved road and onto a dirt trail. Reading peered ahead but could barely make out if there were tracks already in place, or if the lead truck was blazing a new trail. He just hoped the drivers knew the road ahead, the dim headlights doing little to light the way.

After another few minutes of bouncing up and down in the back, the road, if it could be called that, had provided a vigorous workout to the suspension and Reading's ass, to the point where he was ready to jump out and walk. Mercifully, the truck slowed then halted. Reading glanced ahead then elbowed Acton. "Look!" He pointed at several dozen men on horseback forming a wall of flesh, blocking the trail.

Another escort?

Along the way they had been joined several times by teams of riders who would keep pace for several minutes, information exchanged between them and the Hassassins accompanying their motley crew, but they had never stopped. This time, their drivers not only stopped, but hopped out and opened the backs.

"Yalla yalla yalla!" they yelled, urging their cargo to disembark. As soon as Reading and the others reached the ground, the truck engines roared to life and they sped off into the night, leaving them in the near pitch black, the only light provided by the stars and moon.

Abdullah walked toward them, seemingly well rested, due no doubt to his privileged seat in the front of the lead truck. He waved at the riderless horses. "We will ride the rest of the way. I trust you all are capable of handling a horse?"

Acton and Reading looked at each other. Reading grimaced at Acton's grin, knowing full well his friend knew he had never ridden a horse in his life. And that Acton was an expert.

"Sure, no worries," said Reading.

Acton laughed and walked to the nearby horses, Reading only realizing now the wall of several dozen men on horseback was mostly made up of horses waiting patiently for their riders.

Reading watched Acton and the Delta Force team swing onto the backs of their steeds with ease. Reading gripped the saddle and struggled to get his foot in the stirrup. The horse's back-end shuffled toward him, almost sending him dangerously under the massive, snorting beast.

"Steady," he heard Acton's calm voice saying to the horse.

"I doubt he understands English, mate," said Reading, at last getting the leverage to push up and swing his leg over the beast's rump and into the saddle. He probed the empty space with his right foot, searching for the other stirrup, with no success. Acton chuckled beside him as Abdullah walked over and grabbed his foot, shoving it into the stirrup, shaking his head.

"Thanks," mumbled Reading. He looked over at BD. "Where'd you learn to ride a horse?"

"The US Army taught me everything I need to know."

"Yeah," said the one he had learned was named Red. "You should see him on a camel."

"Yup, one hump or two, camel, horse, llama, you name it, BD's probably ridden it," said Spock.

"And eaten it," chuckled Niner.

Reading glanced at BD as he leaned forward comfortably in the saddle, wondering what expression was hidden behind the veil covering his face.

I don't doubt it for a second.

Mecca, Saudi Arabia

Cole reached behind him and pulled out his MAC-10 machine pistol, swinging it toward the first group, his finger already squeezing the trigger. As the wide arc of his arm closed in on his targets, they all raised their right arms, aiming at him and the rest of his men as they too prepared to fire. The machine pistol, capable of spurting 1090 rounds per minute, vibrated in his hand as round after round left the chamber, screaming toward its intended targets at over eight-hundred miles per hour.

Just before he squeezed the trigger, he could have sworn he heard a chorus of clicking noises from in front and behind him, and something metallic glinting in the air for a moment as whatever it was raced through the dim light. As the first of their attackers cried out in agony, a searing pain erupted from his shoulder, and he found he too was screaming. He searched for the source of the pain, his finger still firmly pressing the trigger, his arm, now moving automatically, sprayed across the front line of advancing men, mowing them down mercilessly. His eyes rested on a metal dart, or as his brain registered it, a spike, about three inches of which was still visible, an unknown amount buried deep into his arm.

What the hell is that?

All he knew was that it hurt. Gunfire erupted all around him as his men fought back. He reached for the spike, gripped the exposed part, and slowly pulled it out. A sharp pain almost knocked the knees out from under him, his eyes tearing and losing focus, but not before he saw inch upon inch of the spike continue to emerge from his shoulder. Finally, mercifully, it tapered, and with what felt like a pop, it was free, the now open wound oozing blood, but not spurting it, no arteries hit.

He gasped for breath and as the world returned to focus. He saw the crowd of men, now in the dozens, less than ten feet away. He yanked the MAC-10 from his now dead right hand and opened fire

272

again, slowing their advance. He took a moment to glance over his shoulder and saw Brannick firing his TAC-9 wildly as he screamed, several spikes sticking out of him, tears flowing down his face. Pride surged through Cole. Brannick was facing death like a man, not stopping despite the extreme pain he was in. He could have collapsed, but every fiber of his being was telling him to keep firing, to keep killing the bastards, to send as many to Hell as he could before his body gave out.

Another quick look showed only three of his men remained behind him, battling the second group closing from the other end of the alley. It appeared their attackers were armed only with these darts. And their numbers. There was no way they were getting out of this alive.

But at least the weapon can't be deactivated.

As he raised his weapon for one last volley, a door less than three feet away opened, a member of the hotel staff, his back turned to them, ear buds blocking the sound of the gun battle he had backed into, stepped in front of him, pulling a cart of garbage. Cole shoved him and the cart out of the way then darted inside, pulling the door shut behind him. He quickly scanned the hall he was in and found it deserted, this apparently a maintenance corridor of some sort. He stumbled deeper inside, away from the gunfire. As he moved farther in, the gunfire lessened and he heard fewer and fewer separate weapons, until at last one, then none.

The door rattled and he spun around, ready to fire, but it didn't open, it evidently locked from the inside. He breathed a sigh of relief and continued down the hall, then turned a corner, running straight into a burqa-clad woman and her daughter.

Cole raised his weapon and fired.

Mecca, Saudi Arabia

Mitch Fawcett had the window rolled down as he approached the rendezvous point. The last thing he had expected to hear was the sound of gunfire. He cranked the wheel and brought the truck to a stop on the curb, a few hundred feet from the alleyway entrance. To his left were the colossal white walls of the Al-Masjid al-Haram mosque, the largest in the world. Ringing it to his right, the massive hotels that made the vast bulk of their billions in revenues during this week, providing spectacular views to the devotees well-heeled enough to afford the exorbitant fees charged by the Saudis for their visas.

Hotels jam-packed with sleeping worshippers now waking from the noise, light after light turning on.

Fawcett climbed out and opened the secret compartment, letting two of the others out. "We've got trouble."

"What is it?"

A burst of gunfire answered the question. They ran for the alley and their brothers, and as they approached, the gunfire stopped. Fawcett cautiously peered around the corner and his heart skipped a beat as he took in the sight before him. They were all dead. Everyone he had known, all of his friends whom he had lived with, trained with, partied with, fought with, were all dead, lying in heaps on the ground, surrounded by about a dozen men, all dressed in black.

One kicked the body of what appeared to be Brannick. He moaned. The man aimed his arm, unleashing a dart that embedded in Brannick's chest.

Rage flamed through Fawcett, his pulse racing as adrenaline fueled the fire of hate that consumed him. He raised his TEC-9 and fired, pulling its twin from his belt, both hands now spitting death as he strode into the alleyway, mowing down the unprepared men. His two companions joined him, flanking him on either side, their weapons belching lead at those who had murdered their friends. It lasted only seconds, the surprised enemy wiped out without them firing a shot. Fawcett walked among the bodies, piled on top of his friends, the rage slowly waning as sorrow pushed its way through the still glowing embers of hate. His shoulders slumped as he stared at the body of Brannick, several spikes through his chest, his eyes still open in horror, staring up at him as if asking, "Where were you?" Fawcett closed his eyes and said a silent prayer.

The alleyway was abruptly bathed in light, the roar of an engine echoed through the silent alley, the screech of tires punctuating the arrival of a security patrol. Four men leaped out, shouting in Arabic. Fawcett and his companions spun around and opened fire, eliminating the unsuspecting guards, guards who at worst expected to find someone without a permit within the city limits, not a massacre of proportions never before seen in the holy city.

Sirens wailed in the distance.

"We're going to have company," said Fawcett as he ran to the truck carrying the weapon. He no longer cared if he lived. He only cared that he wouldn't be the only one to die.

Outskirts of Mecca, Saudi Arabia

Horseback for less than thirty minutes had put them within the city limits of Mecca, or Makkah as the Saudi's called it. Saudi security was more intent on keeping Christians out and limiting the number of pilgrims to a manageable two million in the five-day period. If a few managed to sneak in through the periphery, they didn't appear to care, their security covering only the roadways leading into the fabled city.

It was the middle of the night, the streets nearly deserted.

No drunks here.

Dawson and his men remained hidden under their burqas, but a dozen six-foot tall women would be conspicuous if any religious police stopped the group. Their Hassassin escort might talk them out of the situation, but they had no time.

Heads down, mouths shut.

Just like good little Muslim women. Dawson mentally kicked himself for that one, although part of him believed it was true. Today he wasn't here to judge someone's culture, he was here to prevent a war.

Was that gunfire?

He wasn't the only one who noticed it—the faint, unmistakable rattle of automatic weapons in the distance. Anywhere else in the Middle East and he might not have thought anything of it. But in Mecca? During the Hajj? Never.

"How far off would you say that is?" asked Red as he came up beside him.

"Hard to tell with this effin' hood over my ears," said Spock.

Dawson removed the hood covering his head and cocked his ear. "Can't be more than a couple of klicks."

Abdullah rushed over, waving his hands at Dawson. "No no no no no," he fired rapidly. "You must keep this in place. If you are found by the religious police, there will be much trouble."

Dawson frowned but pulled the hood back over his head as Abdullah reached in and refastened the veil. He examined Dawson's coverings and gave a satisfied nod. "Much better. Now come, we must find this gunfire."

They set out at a jog. Even the hood which muffled the sounds of the footfalls of two dozen men surrounding him couldn't hide the fact the gunfire was getting louder.

Then it stopped.

And so did they. Their escorts held up their hands for quiet, but it was too quiet. For a city with over a million visitors, it was *way* too quiet.

Talk about piety.

Dawson took the opportunity to examine their surroundings. To his right towered massive white walls of what he assumed was the mosque where this holy rock Acton had spoken of earlier was housed. And to his left, immense hotels with familiar names such as Hilton, Novotel, and Ramada, a capitalist contrast to the solemn view they provided.

A siren cut through the night, sending them all to the white wall nearest them, that, bathed in light, provided no cover whatsoever with their black robes the starkest of all possible contrasts. They ducked and froze as a police jeep, its single blue light spinning as the siren wailed, sped across the road they were on, entering and exiting from a cross street. They heard the screech of tires as it halted, then a burst of gunfire.

Dawson leaped to his feet and bolted in the direction of the shots, his men and the Hassassin entourage, with, he noted, Acton and Reading in the midst, following him. As they rounded the corner they saw the jeep angled into an alleyway, fifty feet away, the four former occupants dead on the ground.

Dawson ran for the alleyway as he yanked the hood off, tossing it aside, and pulled the robe covering his body over his head. He struggled for a moment as it got hung up on his shoulders, but one last yank and it was clear. He flung it to the ground and pulled forward his

MP5K slung over his shoulder and halted at the edge of the alleyway, weapon in hand, ready to fight.

He turned to check his men and noted they all had removed their robes as well. He was about to give instructions when the Hassassin sped past and entered the alleyway. A brief burst of gunfire erupted. Dawson ducked, and with his back against the wall, leaned in and took a look around the corner to see what was happening.

The gunfire had stopped. The Hassassin stood amidst a pile of bodies, a pile too large for them to have just created. And none moved.

Shit!

Dawson stood and entered the alleyway, pointing at the four corners as he did so. His men rushed to set up covering positions at the near and far ends as Dawson, Acton and Reading walked toward their escorts.

Dawson's jaw clenched. "We needed prisoners."

Abdullah motioned at the men they had evidently just shot. "These men would not have talked."

"How can you be sure?" asked Acton. "They might have known where Laura is!"

Dawson glanced at Acton, noting how he held his weapon.

Firmly. Calmly. Easily. Like a pro.

Dawson had found over the past day his animosity toward Acton was fading, and if it wasn't for London last year, he and Acton could be friends. He didn't seem afraid to get dirty, knew how to handle a weapon, and had a brass set that couldn't be denied. Last year, Acton was an adversary he *should* respect. This year, he had a feeling Acton was someone he *could* respect.

"Look at this." Dawson turned to Reading, who was pointing at a nearby delivery truck. There appeared to be a section of it on the ground.

"Is that a ramp?" asked Acton.

Dawson nodded. "Kind of looks like it, doesn't it?" He knelt down in front and pulled a flashlight from his belt. He turned it on and crawled up the ramp, the small light filling the chamber he found

278

himself in. It was empty save half a case of water and a few boxes of ammo.

He backed out and stood, shaking his head. "Nothing in there except some water and ammo."

Red hurried over to Dawson. "We've got an audience, BD." He motioned up with his head. Dawson looked up and saw dozens, if not hundreds, of lights turned on in the hotel rooms, the faces of curious onlookers pressed against the sealed glass windows.

"Shit!" muttered Dawson. Everyone else looked up and saw that not only did they have an audience, apparently it was worldwide. Window upon window was filled with cellphone-toting worshippers, some holding their cameras up recording the proceedings, some on their phones excitedly talking to others. "Okay, we've only got minutes before this place is swimming with Saudi security." He pointed at the second truck. "Check it out."

Red ran to the other truck and climbed up inside. A muffled "holy shit!" sent Dawson rushing over and climbing up inside as well. He found Red sitting on a bench, staring at the opposite wall. Dawson played his light over the area and saw the long, gray cylinder of a missile. His eyes focused on the harsh red LED timer that flashed its countdown to destruction, the square numbers counting off by the second.

01:58:12

"Oh shit!"

Dawson dove down the ramp, hit the ground, and with a quick roll was on his feet, barking orders. "Mickey, check to see if this truck is still running!" He ducked down and shouted up the ramp. "Red, see if you can disarm that thing." He pointed to Abdullah. "We found the weapon. We have less than two hours before it detonates."

"But that's not enough time!" exclaimed Acton. "There's no way we can evacuate that many people!"

Dawson nodded. "We're not going to evacuate the people." He pulled his mike and squawked it several times. "Control, Bravo Zero-One, come in, over."

"Zero-One, Control, go ahead, over."

"Item located and it's armed. Two hours, repeat, two hours on the timer, we need that evac now."

"Roger that, evac on its way. ETA eighteen minutes."

"Confirmed, will light the target at our present coordinates, out." Dawson turned to Abdullah and pointed at an open area that led to a large ramp curving into the Kaaba shrine. "We need to keep that area clear for thirty minutes."

Abdullah nodded. "It shall be so."

He motioned to his men to follow him as he exited the alley.

As if on cue, more sirens sliced through the night.

"What's going on?" asked Acton. "What's happening in eighteen minutes?"

Red poked his head out from the ramp. "No way I'm disarming this thing without setting it off, BD! They've got some sort of failsafe device installed. I uploaded some close-ups to Control and they said there's no way to know if they can disarm it in time."

Mickey popped out from under the hood of the truck, several bullet holed evident. "Rad's cracked. She's not going anywhere."

Dawson cursed then waved at Stucco and Casey who stood guard at the closer end of the alleyway. "Help Red get the weapon out of there." They shouldered their MP5Ks, quickly diving into the bowels of the truck.

Dawson checked his watch.

Acton gripped him by the shirt. "What's happening?"

Dawson stopped and glared at him for a second, Acton staring directly back at him. Dawson eyed the hand gripping his shirt and it was removed, but the stare remained. "The weapon is armed and set to detonate in under two hours. We can't disarm it. I've requested evac."

"Of us?" Reading shook his head. "There's no way I'm leaving all these civilians here to die, not while we can still warn them."

Dawson regarded him. "Did you serve?"

"Falklands."

Dawson's lips pursed in respect. "I had you pegged when we last met." He relaxed his stance slightly. "The evac is for the weapon. We need to hold a landing area and get the device in position."

Acton's eyebrows rose. "Landing area? You're flying it out?"

Dawson nodded. "A Harrier is inbound now."

USS Enterprise, Carrier Strike Group Enterprise
Red Sea

"Control to Carrier Strike Group Enterprise, roll the package, I say again, roll the package."

"Roger that control, rolling package Tango X-Ray." Captain Leland Dexter, the Carrier Strike Group Enterprise CAG, motioned to the carrier's Air Boss.

"Light-House, you are cleared for takeoff."

The distinct sound of the Harrier launching, its engines churning out 23,500 pounds of thrust as it raced for the end of the deck and the dead of space after it, signaled the launch. It had been re-tasked from the Marine assault ship USS Kearsarge for this mission, arriving minutes earlier to refuel and receive its specially briefed pilot.

"Light-House away, Knight-Hawks One and Two, cleared for takeoff."

Dexter turned his attention away from flight control and to the skipper. "Sir, flight operations under deployment for package Tango X-Ray."

Captain Halloway turned to his Executive Officer. "XO, as soon as the last bird is in the air, turn the fleet to course oh-four-five, flank speed."

Dexter watched the flight deck as the last of the dozen Super Hornets launched, followed by six high-speed Seahawk choppers.

The Saudis are going to shit their pants when they see this on their screens.

He walked over to the ATC station and checked the scope. He saw their aircraft steadily progressing toward the Saudi coast, the F/A-18E's quickly opening a large gap on the choppers.

The scope lit with missile lock warnings and several new bogeys appeared.

"Saudi's are scrambling to intercept, sir."

Dexter jacked in his headset. "Put me on their frequency."

The controller hit a few buttons, putting him on the Saudi Air Defense Corps standard frequency.

"This is United States Carrier Strike Group Enterprise to Saudi aircraft moving to intercept. We are on an emergency mission to recover a weapon of mass destruction on your soil. Request you stand down, I repeat, stand down."

Dexter waited for a five count. Nothing.

"I say again. This is Carrier Strike Group Enterprise. We are on an emergency mission to recover a weapon of mass destruction on your soil. Your government has been contacted informing them of the situation"—Dexter looked at the Captain, who shrugged, indicating no new information had come in on whether the State Department had successfully informed the Saudi's yet or not—"you are requested to stand down and to allow us to complete our mission. Please acknowledge, over."

Dexter watched as additional bogeys popped up on the scope. "How many is that?"

"Fourteen so far, sir," said the controller.

Dexter turned to the Captain. "Permission to launch the reserves?"

The Captain nodded. "Granted."

"Launch everything we've got," said Dexter. "I want their scopes lit up like it's the Fourth of July."

As the Air Boss launched the remaining fighters, Dexter switched the comm to the inbound flight. "Tango X-Ray, this is the CAG, over."

"Go ahead, CAG."

"Get a weapons lock on all inbound hostiles, but do not fire, I repeat, do not engage unless fired upon."

"Roger that, CAG, initiating weapons lock, will hold for orders, over."

Dexter switched back to the Saudi frequency, hoping their Air Operations people were monitoring.

"Saudi Air Command, this is United States Carrier Strike Group Enterprise. We have over seventy aircraft at our command, and six ships with over two-hundred cruise missiles. We will meet any force with overwhelming force. You will *not* survive. This mission *will* proceed. Turn around and contact your government for confirmation of our mission. This is your final warning."

The Harrier was now in Saudi airspace, heading directly for its target. Six of the first wave continued with him, the remainder had turned to intercept the Saudi aircraft. They were now only miles apart.

This is going to turn into a shit storm.

Dexter glanced back at his Captain whose squared jaw revealed little of his emotions, but the white knuckles gripping the arms of his seat showed he was as tense as Dexter.

The speakers squawked then a heavily accented voice came over the PA. "US Carrier Strike Group Enterprise, this is Saudi Air Command. We welcome you to Saudi airspace and thank you for your assistance. We are ordering our welcoming party to return to base. Out."

"Look, sir!" said the controller, pointing at his scope.

Dexter watched as the Saudi aircraft turned, rapidly retreating to their base, and away from the wing of Hornets speeding toward them.

The speaker squawked again. "CAG, this is Tango X-Ray flight leader. The *welcoming party* is standing down, say again, the welcoming party is standing down!"

A roar of celebration followed by high-fives and clapping all around filled the bridge for a few moments. Dexter smiled and patted the young controller on the back. "Let's get the reserve back here. I want the decks cleared for when the primary flight returns."

Hurdle number one cleared.

Over Mecca, Saudi Arabia

Major Keith Miller eased back on the throttle as he neared the coordinates he had been given. The massive temple he had only seen in pictures loomed on the horizon. His HUD beeped as it picked up the laser designator from below, indicating his landing zone. He did a slow circle around the area to scope it out and cursed. Thousands of people, if not tens of thousands, spread below him, an undulating carpet of human flesh. A small area, near a massive ramp that led either in or out of the temple, sat cleared.

"CAG, this is Light-House. LZ spotted, I'm going in, over."

He shoved the nozzle selector lever, the four massive vectorable nozzles slowly redirecting toward the ground, and began his vertical descent. As he neared the ground, the crowds became clearer, and they were not happy to see him. Fists raised in the air, they shouted and shoved against a cordon of what appeared to be Saudi security and a group of Bedouins. A group broke free and raced directly toward his left wing. He rolled slightly to the right, giving them a blast from the Rolls-Royce engines, sending them tumbling along the ground and back toward the mob.

His gear hit the ground and he cut the power then threw open his canopy. The roar from the crowd was almost as deafening as the engines. He surveyed his surroundings and saw a group of robed men running toward his bird from an alleyway. He reached for his sidearm when one waved. "Thunder-Heart!"

"Light-House!" he replied, easing somewhat. One revealed his face and Miller breathed a sigh of relief. "Good to see you. For a minute there, I didn't know what to think. I assume you're Sergeant Major Dawson?"

Dawson nodded. "Sorry about the disguise, Major, thought we better look like the locals while waiting for you." He pointed to the alley where several men carried the old, beat up missile. "We've got some cargo for you."

Miller climbed out and opened a storage hold in the fuselage, pulling out a case. He flipped it open, revealing a docking collar for the missile. "The ordnance guys tell me this should fit that thing," yelled Miller over the roaring crowd.

The men arrived with the weapon and went to work, attaching the collar then hoisting the missile, attaching it under the wing as Miller supervised, wanting to make sure the job was done properly. He couldn't risk it tearing off at the speeds he planned on doing.

Gunfire erupted as the Saudi's opened fire over the heads of the crowd, sending thousands running in the opposite direction and thousands more surging toward the small landing zone. "This is messed up, Sergeant Major. I hope you guys can get out of here."

"Don't worry about us, just get that damned thing out of here."

One of the Delta team stepped away from the wing, giving a thumbs up. "We're good."

Miller double-checked everything. "Looks like we're all set."

Dawson nodded. "Okay, Major, but we've got a problem." Overhead six Hornets slowly circled the area, the roar of their engines mixing with that of the crowd.

"What?"

Dawson leaned in and yelled louder. "We can't disarm it and there's about one hundred minutes on the clock."

Miller frowned. "There's not enough time."

"What do you mean?" asked Acton, he and Reading now standing with them.

Miller turned to the professor. "We need to get this thing to a safe zone for detonation. We're clearing one now, but it's almost ninety minutes from here."

"You mean—?"

"It means I've gotta get out of here now." Miller shook the hands of Dawson and Acton. "It's been a pleasure, gentlemen." He climbed into the cockpit and fired up his Auxiliary Power Unit as Dawson helped strap him in. Dawson jumped clear and Miller ignited the engines. More gunfire erupted as the crowd surged toward the plane. As the canopy lowered automatically, Miller turned to the men standing at attention below, all of whom saluted. He returned the salute then shoved forward on the throttle as the canopy sealed him in one last time.

Acton and the Delta team sprinted toward the alley as the Harrier's roaring VTOL engines bathed the entire area with scorching heat. As it gained altitude, Acton watched as the nozzles redirecting the engines' thrust downward, slowly straightened out, their power now angled toward the rear of the plane. Within seconds it was soaring over the temple then banking to the south and out of sight, followed by the circling aircraft.

He gripped Dawson's arm, finally having his real name thanks to the Harrier pilot. "What did he mean, 'it's been a pleasure knowing us'?"

"Think about it, Doc. If that nuke goes off anywhere near here, there's going to be a holy war like no other. He has to get it as far away from holy land as possible."

"Right, and they're clearing an area," said Acton. "He just drops it, and leaves."

"That was a docking collar we put on that thing," explained Dawson. "There's no way for him to drop the weapon—it's strapped on there until someone manually removes it."

"You mean—"

"It's a one-way trip."

The horror of the situation finally dawned on Acton and he felt sick to his stomach. "Oh my God." As he came to grips with this new revelation, helicopter rotors thundered overhead, their rhythmic slicing of the air pounding everything around them.

"Let's go!" yelled Dawson, grabbing a still stunned Acton by the shoulder. "Those people aren't looking too happy!" Acton stumbled toward the chopper as it landed, quickly pulled inside by a Marine and shoved into the rear corner. Acton simply stared at the metal floor, unable to get the image of Miller from his mind.

"What's wrong?"

Acton looked up to see Reading taking a seat beside him.

"It's a one-way trip."

Reading eyebrows narrowed. "What do you mean?"

"The bomb. It can't be dropped the way they attached it."

Acton watched as his friend's face changed, the eyebrows elevating slightly and his jaw dropping, a touch of color leaving his cheeks, the realization of Acton's words sinking in.

"Rest in peace, Major."

Yemeni Air Space

Major Miller eyed his HUD. Over a dozen hostiles now approached him and his escort of six F/A-18E Super Hornets. He heard the CAG over his comm screaming at the Yemenis to disengage, but it didn't sound like it was working this time—no one had thought they would need to cross their territory, so no one had contacted their government.

His threat indicator lit up, an alarm sounding in the cockpit as his aircraft detected a weapons lock. He glanced at the display and saw the lead aircraft launch two missiles. With the aircraft approaching each other at a combined two thousand miles per hour, there were only seconds to respond.

"Get behind us!" yelled his wingman, Captain Scott Hanson.

Miller eased back on the throttle slightly, letting his escort take the lead.

"Knight-Hawk Two engaging!" yelled Hanson as he launched two AIM-9 Sidewinder missiles. His comm lit up with reports of the others launching and a stream of a dozen missiles raced for their targets, their contrails tracing their path of destruction. The Yemeni fighters were within sight now, and he watched as they all scattered in an attempt to evade the state-of-the-art heat seeking missiles. They didn't stand a chance. Within seconds ten aircraft were erased from existence, their planes and pilots merely dark splotches of smoke and falling wreckage on the sky's clear blue canvas, and the two primitive missiles they had managed to launch flew harmlessly past, unable to get a lock, their second generation design requiring a much bigger heat signature than the front of a Super Hornet provided. The remaining aircraft bugged out.

"We've got a SAM site going active!" yelled Hanson. Miller's HUD lit up again, the SAM site broadcasting in their path, not from behind.

"This is Light-House, unable to evade, I repeat, unable to evade, there's not enough time!" Miller pushed forward on the throttle.

There's no going back now.

The accompanying Hornets went full throttle, forming a flying wedge in front of him. One launched a Joint Air to Surface Standoff Missile as his HUD flashed another warning. If the missile eliminated the SAM site, then any launched missile would lose its ability to track, the Yemeni defenses Vietnam-era at best.

"This is Knight-Hawk One, we have four SAM launches from our six, over."

"CAG to Knight-Hawks, protect Light-House at all costs, repeat, protect Light-House at all costs!"

Miller watched Knight-Hawks Three and Four launch JASSMs at the SAM sites as in the distance the first site was destroyed. Miller checked his watch, the timer he had set showing seventeen minutes remaining before detonation. He glanced at his HUD.

Shit!

The Yemeni fighters had regrouped behind them and opened fire. Knight-Hawks Four, Five and Six peeled off to engage, but Miller knew it wouldn't be enough. There were too many and the quarters too tight. He was minutes from the coast and less than ten minutes from international waters and safety. Knight-Hawk Three reversed course to engage while Knight-Hawk Two fell back to the right of Miller's wing.

"Let's get that thing out of here!" yelled Hanson.

"You don't have to tell me twice!" With the plane already at max throttle, Miller could do nothing but wait. He looked at the HUD and saw the Yemeni counterattack falter as three of their birds were splashed, along with their missiles falling to countermeasures. The scope was a fog of confusion as the sky filled with debris. His HUD screamed with a missile lock. Miller's eyes dropped to look and his heart sank. One of the missiles had made it through and reacquired a lock. It was hopelessly ahead of the rest of his escort and Hanson had no time to turn and engage.

"Do you see that?" yelled Hanson.

Miller pushed forward on the stick, sending the Harrier into a steep, rapid dive. "We're still too close!"

"Understood."

Miller glanced over his shoulder and saw Hanson drop back behind him, the missile acquiring his plane as the target.

"Scott, no!"

"Tell my wife and kid I—"

The transmission ended in a burst of static as the missile made contact, Hanson's Hornet exploding in a ball of red hot aviation fuel, the shockwave of exploding ordnance buffeting Miller as he rapidly left behind his friend of over ten years. He punched the console in front of him and blinked the tears from his eyes.

"CAG, this is Light-House, we lost Knight-Hawk Two, over."

"Acknowledged, Light-House, stay on course."

Miller checked his watch. Thirteen minutes. His scope showed the remaining five Hornets behind him, now burning the air to catch up. Within minutes he reached the coast unmolested, the Yemeni's not risking any more of their aircraft.

"CAG, this is Light-House, I am now in international waters, recall the escort, over."

A pause and then the CAG's voice sounded over the comm, slightly more subdued than Miller was used to hearing him. "Knight-Hawk escort, return to base, over."

"CAG, this is Knight-Hawk Three, request permission to continue with escort, over."

Miller activated his comm. "Guys, this is Keith. Go home. Please, go home."

There was a pause as Miller pictured them all in their cockpits, fighting their instinct to follow their comrade, and their training to follow orders.

"Good luck, old friend."

Miller watched as Knight-Hawk Three and the others peeled off, returning to the carrier group. He checked his watch.

Seven minutes.

He reached into his flight suit and tore open the Velcro of one of the many pockets, removing a photo of his wife and daughter as he put the plane into a slow descent. He thought of his family and took some comfort in knowing they would receive the letter he had written them on the carrier. As soon as he had heard about the mission, he knew it was probably a one-way trip, but he went anyway. His life was a small price to pay to protect his family from the bloodbath facing the world.

He kissed the photo and again checked the timer.

Sixty seconds.

He activated his comm. "CAG, this is Light-House, I have less than sixty seconds on the clock, over."

"Light-House, this is CAG, acknowledged." A pause. "Major Miller…Keith…it's been an honor."

Miller smiled as he pushed the stick forward, placing the plane into a steep dive toward the ocean surface. "Jim, tell my wife and daughter I love them, and if they're ever allowed to know about this, tell them I did it for them, and I did it with no regrets."

"Will do, Keith. I promise they'll know this wasn't a training accident."

Miller smiled.

"Ten seconds."

The Harrier was now in a near vertical dive, the ocean floor rapidly filling his entire field of vision.

"Five seconds!"

The Lord's Prayer started in his head as the final seconds ticked down.

"…hallowed be Thy name…"

The Harrier hit the ocean at over one thousand miles per hour, the surface as hard as concrete at this speed. The aircraft's nose cone crumpled into the cockpit as Miller squeezed his eyes shut, the photo of his family clutched against his heart.

Deck of the USS Enterprise
Red Sea

"Look!"

Red pointed at a flash on the horizon. Acton and the others shielded their eyes instinctively, but at this distance they were in no danger. Acton's chest tightened as he realized the implications. Major Miller had succeeded. And now he was dead. Chatter among the carrier crew was that the major was a family man with a daughter he adored, he heading back home on leave next weekend for a piano recital he had promised her he wouldn't miss. Acton thought of the two lives now destroyed, the one life lost, the tens of thousands saved, and the future millions that would surely have died.

It was hard to feel it was worth it.

As if he knew what Acton was thinking, Dawson stepped up beside him.

"His sacrifice saved millions."

Acton nodded. "I know, but..." He trailed off, afraid how it would sound if he said it.

"But was it worth it?"

Acton frowned. "I guess you guys deal with this a lot."

Dawson glanced at his team standing nearby, their attention focused on the horizon where a comrade had just died. "Far too often." Dawson turned to Acton. "It's a cliché to say it's our job. It *is* our job, but it's more than that. Signing up and putting in four years so you get a free university education is not being a soldier. Serving your time then re-upping, sticking to it while men you went through hell with are wounded or killed, that's not a job, that's a calling. Every man in this unit would die for each other, and would die for their country. They wouldn't hesitate. The bond made in combat is something that the average civvie can't understand. They watch CNN and see a few minutes of footage from Iraq or Afghanistan and think they understand what a soldier goes through. They haven't a clue. Sitting nice and cushy on your couch, watching TV, it never would occur to them to sign up and serve their country. And you know what? They don't have to. They don't have to because the generations before them *did* stand up, and *did* fight, and won a way of life that we now take for granted.

"Today we don't need huge numbers to defend our country, but this country will always need a military to protect it. Those few proud men and women that do sign up, who are career soldiers, they're the ones that keep all of this together. If it weren't for them, America's enemies would have long since taken her down. It's men like Major Miller, who made the ultimate sacrifice to save hundreds of thousands of people he has never met, who will never know what he did, and who would just as soon kill him where he stood if they had found him alone on the very streets he saved, it is men like him that make me proud every day to be in the service of my country. *He* is why we fight, because *he* is the best of us, and we need to preserve our country, and our way of life, so more like him can be born to serve future generations." Dawson leaned forward and gripped the railing in front of them. He turned and looked Acton in the eyes. "I'm sorry for what happened in London. You're a good man."

Acton leaned on the railing, staring at the churning water below, then out at the horizon where Major Miller had once been.

"It takes all types to preserve a way of life. Us civilians to take it for granted, and people like you to keep it that way." He sighed. "It's just"—his voice cracked—"I just don't know how you get used to seeing someone you know, die. My students last year, one of them right before my eyes, Major Miller, these people you get to know, sometimes love, and they are snuffed from the face of the earth through no fault of their own, leaving us behind to try and honor their memories." He stared at the deck. "So much pain."

Dawson looked back at the carrier deck now loaded with planes. "You never get used to it. You just learn how to deal with it. You push through the pain and honor them by being a better person, and if you have faith, believe that they're in a better place. But never dishonor them by feeling sorry for yourself because you were left behind when they weren't. That's selfish. Honor them every day by remembering them through your deeds and actions, and the pain will go away, and you'll realize that their sacrifice *did* make a difference, even if only in some small way. Everyone can make a difference, no matter how short a time in this world they have, or how small a perceived contribution they make."

Acton looked at Dawson. "You're quite the philosopher."

Dawson chuckled and slapped Acton on the shoulder.

"I'm glad I didn't kill you, Professor. I think the world's a better place with you in it."

Acton had to smile. "That makes two of us."

Dawson leaned back against the railing and crossed his arms, all joviality wiped from his face.

"Now we need to find that lady of yours."

MS Sea Maiden
Red Sea

Agent Dymovsky leaned against the railing, staring at the RFS Pyotr Velikiy sitting off the port bow. She was an impressive ship, a ship that harkened back to a time when Russians had something to be proud of, regardless of how misguided they may have once been.

Now there is nothing to be proud of. A history of shame, and a future of corruption.

But he wouldn't give up. He'd continue to do his small part, to protect Mother Russia from her enemies, both external and internal, and to clean it up a little bit. Hopefully, in time, others would join him and fight back. Fight back against the corruption, against the gangs, against the politicians who would take them back to a past that failed once, and was doomed to fail again.

It had been a frustrating day. Troops from the Pyotr Velikiy scoured the ship for evidence, Yakovski was interrogated time and again, and calls were placed to the highest sources to find out more information, but for now, they were stuck at a dead end. They knew the weapon was sold, apparently to Americans, but had no idea of the destination.

The entire horizon in front of him flashed, the sky lighting up as if he were staring directly into the sun, then moments later, it was gone.

"What the hell was that?" asked Koslov.

Bile filled Dymovsky's mouth and he leaned over the railing and vomited. He wiped his mouth and turned to Koslov.

"What direction is that?"

"I don't know?" Koslov looked up at the sun. "South."

Dymovsky spun to Chernov and pointed at his radio.

"Find out where that detonation took place!"

Jeddah-Makkah Highway, Saudi Arabia

Cole squeezed the trigger twice, the shots muffled by the seatback the gun was pressed against. The driver groaned and fell forward against the steering wheel, his head hitting the horn. Cole reached forward and pulled him back against the seat, silencing the blare, then climbed out the back door of the Mercedes G55 AMG he had commandeered. Getting out of Mecca was far easier than getting in. Security couldn't care less about those leaving, they were more worried about Christians and other infidels getting in and causing trouble.

Unfortunately for the camel jockey now dead in the front seat, security didn't pay attention to one man driving his burqa-clad wife, dutifully silent in the back seat, leaving Mecca. After liberating the burqa from the woman in the hotel, Cole had stepped out into the street, anonymous among the onlookers racing toward the excitement one block away, and had climbed into the back of the Mercedes, much to the shock of his soon to be chauffeur. Fortunately for Cole, the man spoke English, and they were soon out of Mecca and on the coastal highway, heading back to where some of his men should be waiting for their return.

He had kept an eye on the rear window, praying for the sky to light, for that beautiful mushroom cloud that would signal the beginning of the end of the Islamist tyranny, but it hadn't come. A bright flash too far on the southern horizon to be Mecca, sank his heart.

All of this for nothing.

He thought of his friends dead in the alley, of this once in a lifetime opportunity that had failed. He could think of no other way to trigger the war needed to begin the cleansing of the West. He had lost the chance to destroy Mecca. And Islam had no figure like the Pope he could assassinate to trigger a war.

But what if—

His thought was cut off by a burst of gunfire at his feet.

He dove to the ground, behind a small dune.

"Stop shooting, it's me, Cole!"

Another burst of gunfire and the ground inches in front of him exploded into tiny sand storms, showering him in the grit, but shielding him at least until they repositioned themselves.

"Goddammit, stop shooting, it's me, Cole!"

"Cole, is that you?"

Cole breathed a sigh of relief at the sound of Jack Brown's voice, a trusted friend. Cole waved his hand over the dune. "Yeah, it's me. Hold your fire, I'm coming out!"

Cole pulled the hood of the Arab monstrosity off his head and slowly poked it out above the dune.

Brown waved and dropped his gun to his side. "What the hell are you wearing?"

Cole got to his feet and strode toward Brown. "An oppression suit." Cole pulled it over his shoulders and tossed it to the ground. "Let's get out of here."

Brown looked up the hill Cole had descended.

"Where are the others?"

Cole walked past him, toward the small boat waiting on the shore. "They're all dead."

Brown pushed the boat into the water and climbed in with Cole. "What happened? I didn't see any explosion, just a flash."

"We failed." Cole started the outboard motor and steered them for the yacht offshore. "They knew we were coming, right from the start."

"But how?"

Cole gunned the motor, the boat skipping along the waves now.

"I'm guessing our partners had friends."

"So what do we do now?"

"Plan B."

"We have a Plan B?"

"We do now."

Saint Peter's Square, Vatican City

Acton checked his watch for the umpteenth time.

Thirteen seconds later than the last time you looked!

He stood near a fountain to the side of the obelisk that dominated the center of St. Peter's Square in the Vatican. He held a tourist guide book in one hand, and his other held a video camera he occasionally pretended to film one of the many sites with, but in reality was filming the crowds, the image transmitting to the Vatican security staff, manned as it always was by the Pontifical Swiss Guard, and today a special guest, Interpol Agent Hugh Reading.

Acton knew he wasn't alone out here. Among the crowd were dozens of undercover security officers, all waiting for the appointed time and the hoped for opportunity to fulfill their objective—the safe recovery of the most important thing in his life—Laura Palmer.

It had only taken two days to get the call. 'Only' probably wasn't the right word for it. Those two days were the longest of his life, especially when he had discovered the group responsible was the same group he had rescued Jason from. During the entire events of the past few days, it wasn't until after it had all concluded that a casual mention by one of the Delta Force members of New Slate's headquarters being raided in Knoxville, that he had realized why he and Laura had been pulled into these horrifying events.

It was his fault.

If he hadn't stuck his nose where it didn't belong, if he hadn't played hero and volunteered to rescue Jason, they never would have known who he was, never would have known Laura's connection to him, and never would have been anywhere near her dig site to kidnap her.

But he *had* rescued Jason, and judging by what his captors had tried to do, Jason's life had probably been saved. He couldn't see them leaving the boy alive, knowing what he did.

299

He had done the right thing.

And he knew deep down that he'd do it all over again, even knowing what he knew now.

Because it was the right thing to do.

He just prayed Laura would be safe, because if he lost her, he knew he'd never forgive himself. Not knowing where she was, if she was safe, if she was even alive, had driven him crazy. He had stayed in Europe in case word arrived, and this had proven wise.

The call came direct to his cellphone and lasted ten seconds.

"Bring ten million dollars in bearer bonds to Saint Peter's Square at exactly eleven-fifty-five a.m. Instructions have been emailed to you."

Those instructions had arrived as promised, and he and Reading had managed to get the bonds together with no problem, the accounts and passwords obviously provided by Laura, working perfectly. Acton had known she was rich, though hadn't realized how much so until the moment the bonds were handed over in a secure briefcase, the combination set by him and only known to him and Reading, who he told "just in case".

Acton checked his watch again.

"Bloody hell, if he looks at his watch one more time I'll go out there and throttle him!"

Reading checked his watch.

Two minutes.

In two minutes, the exchange was to happen. Security was tightened but relaxed at the same time. The crowd was flooded with plainclothes agents from the Vatican's security force, as well as Interpol and the local Italian police. The front entrance security was relaxed to ensure Laura Palmer and her captor could successfully enter. The last thing they wanted was an incident at the front gate that might get Laura and other innocents killed. Once inside the gates, they could control the situation better and quickly isolate the area with the rapid response teams placed strategically around the Vatican grounds.

"Sixty seconds."

Reading looked at the display counting down the time to the meeting, then at the Commander of the Swiss Guards, Inspector General Mario Giasson, his shaved head beaded with sweat.

He'd fit right in with these white supremacists.

Giasson glanced at Reading as he ran a handkerchief over his scalp. "Let us hope they are on time."

"Don't count on it," replied Reading, again checking his watch, then the screen. On the display, Acton turned to face a couple of tourists as they approached him.

Acton fought the instinct to run to Laura. The relief at the sight of her was overwhelming. His heart raced and his face flushed with both excitement at knowing she was okay, and anger toward the man gripping her arm. Acton placed the tourist guide and camera down on the statue base he was standing near, not only to free his hands, but as a signal to all those watching that the exchange was about to happen.

"James!"

Laura's cry of his name betrayed her fear.

"Don't worry, babe, this is almost over."

The look in her eyes told him she wasn't convinced.

Did she just shake her head?

Acton scratched his left butt cheek, another signal.

Something is wrong, but wait.

The man holding her was now feet away. "Professor Acton, so good to see you again."

Acton controlled the urge to reach out and tear the man's throat out. "Mr. Cole."

"You have something for me?"

Acton removed the backpack he was carrying and held it out.

Cole shook his head. "Ah ahh, not so fast."

Laura handed a plain black bag to Acton. She looked directly into his eyes then took a darting glance to her right.

"Put the bonds into the bag."

Acton complied, taking a knee to do so, and dropped his head so he could get an angle on where he thought Laura wanted him to look. He saw nothing, just a large crowd of tourists slowly making their way around the square.

He stuffed the last of the bonds into the new bag and looked again.

Wait a minute.

"Now zip it up."

Acton complied, and as he stood, he glanced again. One man was standing, facing them, not moving with the crowd, wearing a long, bulky trench coat. Acton knew they had relaxed security, something he hadn't thought wise, but he wasn't the expert. He just wanted Laura safe.

Could he be a backup?

Acton made a mental note as to where the man was and scanned the crowd for other possible accomplices. As soon as the handover was complete, and Laura was safely free of the man, Cole was to be taken down, but only if Acton gave the signal.

"Hand it over."

Acton handed the bag to Laura's outstretched hand. She passed it to Cole who slung it over his shoulder, momentarily releasing Laura. Acton saw her tense, her stance changing slightly as she fought the urge to bolt. As soon as the bag was positioned, Cole reestablished his iron grip.

"Now what?" asked Acton.

Cole checked his watch, a sickening smile creasing his face. The crowd cheered in unison and faced the west. Acton followed their and Cole's gaze. On the middle balcony of Saint Peter's Basilica, the Bishop of Rome, Vicar of Jesus Christ, Successor of the Prince of the Apostles, Supreme Pontiff of the Universal Church, Patriarch of the West, Primate of Italy, Archbishop and Metropolitan of the Roman Province, Sovereign of the State of the Vatican City, Servant of the Servants of God, or, as known to the cheering throng, the Pope, stepped out and waved. A roar of adulation filled the square as the people surged forward. Cole turned back to face Acton, his face dark, conveying an evil Acton had never before experienced.

"Now we change the world."

Acton's stomach flipped and bile filled his mouth as Cole raised his left arm in the air, revealing some sort of trigger in his hand.

"Allahu akbar!" he screamed.

Laura tore away from him and dove toward Acton. From his left he glanced and saw the man from earlier pull open his jacket, revealing a vest bulging with explosives and dozens of wires. He raised both arms to the heavens and yelled, "Allahu akbar!" Acton distinctly heard two other praises to Allah screamed from other parts of the square as he grabbed Laura and leaped backward toward the fountain feet away.

Cole pressed the button.

And changed the world.

"Take the shot! Take the shot!"

Niner squeezed the trigger. Edison Cole dropped, but too late. Through the scope, he saw three distinct plumes of smoke, fire, and debris tearing through the historic square and merging into one cloud, a thick, black cloak of evil consuming the entire area. The rooftop he and Jimmy occupied shook and a moment later the sound of the triple blast ripped through the innocence, the sound unlike anything heard in Hollywood but all too familiar to the Bravo Team surrounding the square.

"Oh my God!" cried Jimmy. "Do you see him?"

Niner scanned the area with his scope. "No, I can't see a thing, there's too much smoke!"

"Mission aborted, return to rendezvous point Charlie!"

Niner heard in Dawson's voice that he was shaken. No one had expected this. This was to be an easy hostage exchange, maybe a takedown, but not a suicide bombing. Niner glanced at Jimmy. "Keep looking!" Niner quickly packed away his M24A2 SWS Sniper Weapon System while Jimmy scanned St. Peter's Square with his scope. "Anything?"

"No, I can't see—" He paused and adjusted his scope. "I think I see him." Jimmy fell back on his haunches, making the sign of the cross, his face green, eyes closed.

"God help us all," whispered Niner.

Reading raced into the square, the chaos that greeted him bringing him to a halt. Hundreds of bodies littered the ancient cobblestone now covered in blood and other remnants he couldn't bring himself to look at. It was worse than anything he had experienced as a soldier and a police officer. The carnage was on a level his brain couldn't cope with and his vision narrowed, the world becoming dark. Tears welled in his eyes as he saw the bodies of children strewn about like the Devil's playthings, some whole, some missing limbs, some still holding the hands of parents no longer attached to their bodies. He bent over and vomited, collapsing to his knees. The security team that had accompanied him stood nearby, their weapons limp at their sides, their jaws slack as they too reacted. Some turned around and stumbled back inside, others collapsed as he had, others stood, frozen in place.

Jim!

Reading closed his eyes and took a deep breath, immediately regretting it, his mouth filling with the dried taste of death. He opened his eyes and willed himself to his feet. Focusing on the fountain where he had last seen his friends, he walked, careful not to step on any of the poor souls who moments before were in a rapture of religious fervor at the sight of the Holy See.

Oh my God, the Pope!

Reading turned to where the Pope had appeared promptly at noon, despite his security detail pleading with him to wait until the hostage situation was resolved. But he had refused. He would not disappoint his flock. He would leave his life in God's hands. The entire side of the building was scorched, the stonework cracked and pockmarked as if the clawed hand of Satan had reached up from the depths of Hell and tore at the facade.

He resisted the urge to find out what had happened to the man, and instead turned his attention back to his friends. As he stepped through the carnage, the smoke slowly cleared, a stiff breeze sweeping through the square as if the hand of God had waved across them, clearing the cloak of sin stifling the area, and revealing to all the true horror this act of evil had wrought.

Reading's eyes focused on the fountain. His heart leaped as he saw a hand gripping the edge. Then his chest tightened as he realized it wasn't moving. He ran, zigzagging through the mangled bodies and debris, toward what he hoped wouldn't be the final act in this unfathomable tragedy.

As he neared, another hand appeared. Someone was alive. Reading raced to the fountain edge and reached over the side, pulling both hands, praying against all hope the bodies they belonged to were still there, and alive.

Laura's head appeared first, gasping for breath. Reading pulled her over the edge, enough for her to rest, sprawled across the stone and out of the water. He let her go and pulled with both hands, lifting his friend from the water. The soiled liquid ran off his body, mixed with what Reading soon discovered to his dismay was blood, blood oozing from his friend's back.

Reading tore open Acton's shirt, revealing a six-inch sliver of stone, protruding from his back, near his left kidney.

"James!" Laura gasped as she saw the wound.

Acton moaned.

"Stay still mate, I'll get help."

Laura reached for the shard, as if to remove it on instinct.

Reading grabbed her hand. "Don't touch it! It may do more damage on the way out."

Laura stared at him blankly for a moment. Reading gripped her by the shoulders and shook her. "Laura, snap out of it! You're okay. I need to get help! Are you with me?"

Laura stared into his eyes then gasped. "Oh my God!" She looked at Acton then back at Reading. "I'm okay, go get help!"

Reading stood and searched for a medic. He didn't need to look far. Ambulances filled the square, emergency personnel racing toward the worst terrorist attack in Italy's history. Reading ran toward one pair and seized them by their collars. "Follow me!"

Within moments, they were at Acton's side and Reading breathed a sigh of relief as he saw his friend being tended to.

That's when he heard the weeping.

He and Laura turned toward the sounds, toward where the balcony should be and no longer was. Below, in a pile of rubble still being desperately cleared by the survivors, lay a mangled body, trimmed in white and gold, twisted among the wreckage.

Another gust of wind filled the square. The Papal mitre, his ceremonial hat, tumbled toward them and came to rest at Reading's feet. He reached down and picked it up, looking at Laura, then at the horror in front of them. He hugged the stained hat to his chest and closed his eyes in silent prayer.

"Il Papa è morto!" someone yelled. More wails filled the air, and more screams as the word spread.

"Il Papa è morto! The Pope is dead!"

EPILOGUE

"Look!"

Acton, Laura, Reading and the Milton family all sat around the television, watching the live coverage of the Papal Conclave. "Is that white smoke?"

Reading grunted. "Certainly looks white to me."

"CNN is confirming white smoke! The Papal Conclave has decided and a new Pope has been chosen!"

"I guess it's white smoke," said Milton as he stretched his legs out from the couch. Acton glanced over and smiled at his friend and the tremendous progress he had made over the past couple of weeks. He still wasn't walking, but he had movement back, and that was more than they had expected.

"I wonder who they chose?" asked Laura.

Reading shrugged. "No idea, but whoever he is, I don't envy the mess he's going to have to deal with."

Contrary to Edison Cole's hopes, the world hadn't fallen into chaos. There were protests, there were some isolated murders and backlash against the Muslim community, especially in the hours that had followed. But Vatican security was quick to get the news out that it was a white supremacist group behind it, and the footage of Cole squeezing the trigger proved enough to have the protests turn quickly into prayer vigils.

Around the world, political and religious leaders of all stripes had condemned the attacks and pledged to work toward peace. Whether it would succeed was doubtful, but at least the holy war to end all holy wars had been averted. What came out over the coming days had also clarified some of the confusion. The three bombers were indeed Muslim, but had been coerced into wearing the suicide vests, their families kidnapped by New Slate, their detonators controlled by Cole, their cries of "Allahu Akbar" not those of celebration at what was about to happen, but pleas for deliverance from the horror they were about to participate in.

Cole was dead—shot by a sniper, probably Delta. Reading thought Cole had underestimated the force of the blast, one of the bombers, the one Acton had spotted, simply too close for Cole to escape unscathed. It made sense. Acton had little doubt Cole had expected to walk away in the chaos of the bombings. He had wanted the money, probably so he could try again, and men like him rarely died for their cause, they content to have others do it for them.

Coward.

His chest tightened as a news update began.

"In other news, India has claimed responsibility for detonating an underwater nuclear weapon in the Arabian Sea as part of its continued testing program. The President condemned the test, calling on India and Pakistan to return to the negotiating table. The Pakistani Prime Minister, in an uncharacteristically conciliatory tone, condemned the Indian government, however, pledged to not escalate the situation by conducting any tests of their own."

Reading looked at Acton. "I wonder how much that cost the US taxpayer."

Acton frowned, thinking of the brave pilot who had sacrificed his life to save them all. "I'm sure the Treasury had to print a few billion for both sides."

Laura squeezed Acton's hand then pointed at the screen. "Look, there he is!"

On the screen, the new Pope appeared on the hastily rebuilt balcony, still covered in scaffolding. He stepped out in full regalia including the mitre Reading had salvaged, and raised his hands to the heavens, waving at the roaring crowds below. The arms of his robes slipped to his elbows, revealing his bare wrists, the camera zooming in, the image filling the screen.

Acton gasped, grabbing the remote and freezing the picture. "Look!" He winced as he hoisted himself from the couch and pointed at the left wrist of the new representative of God on Earth.

The frozen image revealed a small tattoo. Two thin lines, with a thicker, slightly curved line underneath.

It was the symbol of the Triarii.

ACKNOWLEDGEMENTS

The concept for Brass Monkey germinated during a visit to my parents' home several years ago. An old Air Force comrade of my father's was visiting, and they were talking of old times when the term Brass Monkey was mentioned. The mere sound of these two words conjured up images of James Bond, old Cold War movies, and of course, a sequel to The Protocol. A plausible explanation for a lost American nuclear missile had been found.

But what to do with it?

Obviously, I figured that part out, this book the result. As usual, many were involved in the writing of this book. I would like to take the opportunity to thank these individuals specifically. My wife, Esperanza, of course, my daughter, Niskha (who in real life was just as adorable as her fictional namesake in this novel at that age), my parents, Hugh and Bernice Kennedy, as well as Brent Richards, Ian Kennedy, Jennifer Dunn, Klaus Rößel, Ron Blank, Deborah Wilson, Richard Jenner, Eid Choueiri, and finally my friends for supporting me, and the many thousands of readers who have embraced my novels, proving you don't have to be a household name to be on the best sellers list.

To those who have not already done so, please visit my website at www.jrobertkennedy.com then sign up for the Insider's Club to be notified of new book releases. Your email address will never be shared or sold and you'll only receive the occasional email from me as I don't have time to spam you!

Thank you once again for reading.

ABOUT THE AUTHOR

With over 500,000 books in circulation and over 3000 five-star reviews, USA Today bestselling author J. Robert Kennedy has been ranked by Amazon as the #1 Bestselling Action Adventure novelist based upon combined sales. He is the author of over twenty-five international bestsellers including the smash hit James Acton Thrillers. He lives with his wife and daughter and writes full-time.

Visit Robert's website at www.jrobertkennedy.com for the latest news and contact information, and to join the Insider's Club to be notified when new books are released.

Available James Acton Thrillers

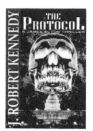

The Protocol (Book #1)

For two thousand years, the Triarii have protected us, influencing history from the crusades to the discovery of America. Descendent from the Roman Empire, they pervade every level of society, and are now in a race with our own government to retrieve an ancient artifact thought to have been lost forever.

Brass Monkey (Book #2)

A nuclear missile, lost during the Cold War, is now in play--the most public spy swap in history, with a gorgeous agent the center of international attention, triggers the end-game of a corrupt Soviet Colonel's twenty five year plan. Pursued across the globe by the Russian authorities, including a brutal Spetsnaz unit, those involved will stop at nothing to deliver their weapon, and ensure their payday, regardless of the terrifying consequences.

Broken Dove (Book #3)

With the Triarii in control of the Roman Catholic Church, an organization founded by Saint Peter himself takes action, murdering one of the new Pope's operatives. Detective Chaney, called in by the Pope to investigate, disappears, and, to the horror of the Papal staff sent to inform His Holiness, they find him missing too, the only clue a secret chest, presented to each new pope on the eve of their election, since the beginning of the Church.

The Templar's Relic (Book #4)

The Vault must be sealed, but a construction accident leads to a miraculous discovery--an ancient tomb containing four Templar Knights, long forgotten, on the grounds of the Vatican. Not knowing who they can trust, the Vatican requests Professors James Acton and Laura Palmer examine the find, but what they discover, a precious Islamic relic, lost during the Crusades, triggers a set of events that shake the entire world, pitting the two greatest religions against each other. At risk is nothing less than the Vatican itself, and the rock upon which it was built.

Flags of Sin (Book #5)

Archaeology Professor James Acton simply wants to get away from everything, and relax. A trip to China seems just the answer, and he and his fiancée, Professor Laura Palmer, are soon on a flight to Beijing. But while boarding, they bump into an old friend, Delta Force Command Sergeant Major Burt Dawson, who surreptitiously delivers a message that they must meet the next day, for Dawson knows something they don't. China is about to erupt into chaos.

The Arab Fall (Book #6)

An accidental find by a friend of Professor James Acton may lead to the greatest archaeological discovery since the tomb of King Tutankhamen, perhaps even greater. And when news of it spreads, it reaches the ears of a group hell-bent on the destruction of all idols and icons, their mere existence considered blasphemous to Islam.

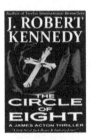

The Circle of Eight (Book #7)

The Bravo Team is targeted by a madman after one of their own intervenes in a rape. Little do they know this internationally well-respected banker is also a senior member of an organization long thought extinct, whose stated goals for a reshaped world are not only terrifying, but with today's globalization, totally achievable.

The Venice Code (Book #8)

A former President's son is kidnapped in a brazen attack on the streets of Potomac by the very ancient organization that murdered his father, convinced he knows the location of an item stolen from them by the late president. A close friend awakes from a coma with a message for archaeology Professor James Acton from the same organization, sending him on a quest to find an object only rumored to exist, while trying desperately to keep one step ahead of a foe hell-bent on possessing it.

Pompeii's Ghosts (Book #9)

Two thousand years ago Roman Emperor Vespasian tries to preserve an empire by hiding a massive treasure in the quiet town of Pompeii should someone challenge his throne. Unbeknownst to him nature is about to unleash its wrath upon the Empire during which the best and worst of Rome's citizens will be revealed during a time when duty and honor were more than words, they were ideals worth dying for.

Amazon Burning (Book #10)

Days from any form of modern civilization, archaeology Professor James Acton awakes to gunshots. Finding his wife missing, taken by a member of one of the uncontacted tribes, he and his friend INTERPOL Special Agent Hugh Reading try desperately to find her in the dark of the jungle, but quickly realize there is no hope without help. And with help three days away, he knows the longer they wait, the farther away she'll be.

The Riddle (Book #11)

Russia accuses the United States of assassinating their Prime Minister in Hanoi, naming Delta Force member Sergeant Carl "Niner" Sung as the assassin. Professors James Acton and Laura Palmer, witnesses to the murder, know the truth, and as the Russians and Vietnamese attempt to use the situation to their advantage on the international stage, the husband and wife duo attempt to find proof that their friend is innocent.

Blood Relics (Book #12)

A DYING MAN. A DESPERATE SON.
ONLY A MIRACLE CAN SAVE THEM BOTH.

Professor Laura Palmer is shot and kidnapped in front of her husband, archaeology Professor James Acton, as they try to prevent the theft of the world's Blood Relics, ancient artifacts thought to contain the blood of Christ, a madman determined to possess them all at any cost.

Sins of the Titanic (Book #13)

THE ASSEMBLY IS ETERNAL. AND THEY'LL STOP AT
NOTHING TO KEEP IT THAT WAY.

When Professor James Acton is contacted about a painting thought to have been lost with the sinking of the Titanic, he is inadvertently drawn into a century old conspiracy an ancient organization known as The Assembly will stop at nothing to keep secret.

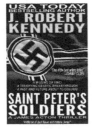

Saint Peter's Soldiers (Book #14)

A MISSING DA VINCI.
A TERRIFYING GENETIC BREAKTHROUGH.
A PAST AND FUTURE ABOUT TO COLLIDE!

In World War Two a fabled da Vinci drawing is hidden from the Nazis, those involved fearing Hitler may attempt to steal it for its purported magical powers. It isn't returned for over fifty years.
And today, archaeology Professor James Acton and his wife are about to be dragged into the terrible truth of what happened so many years ago, for the truth is never what it seems, and the history we thought was fact, is all lies.

The Thirteenth Legion (Book #15)

A TWO-THOUSAND-YEAR-OLD DESTINY IS ABOUT TO
BE FULFILLED!

USA Today bestselling author J. Robert Kennedy delivers another action-packed thriller in The Thirteenth Legion. After Interpol Agent Hugh Reading spots his missing partner in Berlin, it sets off a chain of events that could lead to the death of his best friends, and if the legends are true, life as we know it.

Raging Sun (Book #16)

WILL A SEVENTY-YEAR-OLD MATTER OF HONOR
TRIGGER THE NEXT GREAT WAR?

The Imperial Regalia have been missing since the end of World War Two, and the Japanese government, along with the new—and secretly illegitimate—emperor, have been lying to the people. But the truth isn't out yet, and the Japanese will stop at nothing to secure their secret and retrieve the ancient relics confiscated by a belligerent Russian government. Including war.

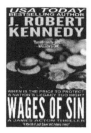

Wages of Sin (Book #17)

WHEN IS THE PRICE TO PROTECT A NATION'S
LEGACY TOO HIGH?

Jim and Laura are on safari in South Africa when a chance encounter leads to a clue that could unlock the greatest mystery remaining of the Boer War over a century ago—the location to over half a billion dollars in gold!

Available Special Agent Dylan Kane Thrillers

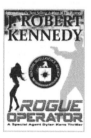

Rogue Operator (Book #1)

Three top secret research scientists are presumed dead in a boating accident, but the kidnapping of their families the same day raises questions the FBI and local police can't answer, leaving them waiting for a ransom demand that will never come. Central Intelligence Agency Analyst Chris Leroux stumbles upon the story, finding a phone conversation that was never supposed to happen, and is told to leave it to the FBI. But he can't let it go. For he knows something the FBI doesn't. One of the scientists is alive.

Containment Failure (Book #2)

New Orleans has been quarantined, an unknown virus sweeping the city, killing one hundred percent of those infected. The Centers for Disease Control, desperate to find a cure, is approached by BioDyne Pharma who reveal a former employee has turned a cutting edge medical treatment capable of targeting specific genetic sequences into a weapon, and released it. The stakes have never been higher as Kane battles to save not only his friends and the country he loves, but all of mankind.

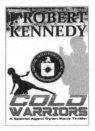

Cold Warriors (Book #3)

While in Chechnya CIA Special Agent Dylan Kane stumbles upon a meeting between a known Chechen drug lord and a retired General once responsible for the entire Soviet nuclear arsenal. Money is exchanged for a data stick and the resulting transmission begins a race across the globe to discover just what was sold, the only clue a reference to a top-secret Soviet weapon called Crimson Rush.

Death to America (Book #4)

America is in crisis. Dozens of terrorist attacks have killed or injured thousands, and worse, every single attack appears to have been committed by an American citizen in the name of Islam.

A stolen experimental F-35 Lightning II is discovered by CIA Special Agent Dylan Kane in China, delivered by an American soldier reported dead years ago in exchange for a chilling promise.

And Chris Leroux is forced to watch as his girlfriend, Sherrie White, is tortured on camera, under orders to not interfere, her continued suffering providing intel too valuable to sacrifice.

Black Widow (Book #5)

USA Today bestselling author J. Robert Kennedy serves up another heart-pounding thriller in Black Widow. After corrupt Russian agents sell deadly radioactive Cesium to Chechen terrorists, CIA Special Agent Dylan Kane is sent to infiltrate the ISIL terror cell suspected of purchasing it. Then all contact is lost.

Available Delta Force Unleashed Thrillers

Payback (Book #1)

The daughter of the Vice President is kidnapped from an Ebola clinic, triggering an all-out effort to retrieve her by America's elite Delta Force just hours after a senior government official from Sierra Leone is assassinated in a horrific terrorist attack while visiting the United States. As she battles impossible odds and struggles to prove her worth to her captors who have promised she will die, she's forced to make unthinkable decisions to not only try to save her own life, but those dying from one of the most vicious diseases known to mankind, all in the hopes an unleashed Delta Force can save her before her captors enact their horrific plan on an unsuspecting United States.

Infidels (Book #2)

When the elite Delta Force's Bravo Team is inserted into Yemen to rescue a kidnapped Saudi prince, they find more than they bargained for—a crate containing the Black Stone, stolen from Mecca the day before. Requesting instructions on how to proceed, they find themselves cut off and disavowed, left to survive with nothing but each other to rely upon.

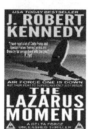

The Lazarus Moment (Book #3)

AIR FORCE ONE IS DOWN.
BUT THEIR FIGHT TO SURVIVE HAS ONLY JUST BEGUN!

When Air Force One crashes in the jungles of Africa, it is up to America's elite Delta Force to save the survivors not only from rebels hell-bent on capturing the President, but Mother Nature herself.

Kill Chain (Book #4)

WILL A DESPERATE PRESIDENT RISK WAR
TO SAVE HIS ONLY CHILD?

In South Korea, the President's daughter disappears aboard an automated bus carrying the spouses of the world's most powerful nations, hacked by an unknown enemy with an unknown agenda. In order to save all that remains of his family, the widower president unleashes America's elite Delta Force to save his daughter, yet the more they learn, the more the mystery deepens, witness upon witness declaring with certainty they never saw any kidnappers—only drones.

Available Detective Shakespeare Mysteries

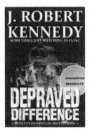

Depraved Difference (Book #1)

SOMETIMES JUST WATCHING IS FATAL

When a young woman is brutally assaulted by two men on the subway, her cries for help fall on the deaf ears of onlookers too terrified to get involved, her misery ended with the crushing stomp of a steel-toed boot. A cellphone video of her vicious murder, callously released on the Internet, its popularity a testament to today's depraved society, serves as a trigger, pulled a year later, for a killer.

Tick Tock (Book #2)

SOMETIMES HELL IS OTHER PEOPLE

Crime Scene tech Frank Brata digs deep and finds the courage to ask his colleague, Sarah, out for coffee after work. Their good time turns into a nightmare when Frank wakes up the next morning covered in blood, with no recollection of what happened, and Sarah's body floating in the tub.

The Redeemer (Book #3)

SOMETIMES LIFE GIVES MURDER A SECOND CHANCE

It was the case that destroyed Detective Justin Shakespeare's career, beginning a downward spiral of self-loathing and self-destruction lasting half a decade. And today things are only going to get worse. The Widow Rapist is free on a technicality, and it is up to Detective Shakespeare and his partner Amber Trace to find the evidence, five years cold, to put him back in prison before he strikes again.

Zander Varga, Vampire Detective

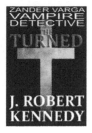

The Turned (Book #1)

Zander has relived his wife's death at the hands of vampires every day for almost three hundred years, his perfect memory a curse of becoming one of The Turned—infecting him their final heinous act after her murder. Nineteen year-old Sydney Winter knows Zander's secret, a secret preserved by the women in her family for four generations. But with her mother in a coma, she's thrust into the frontlines, ahead of her time, to fight side-by-side with Zander.

Made in the USA
Monee, IL
14 February 2022

91243524R00194